Copyright © 2024 Rick Brindle.
All rights reserved worldwide.
No part of this book may be copied, reproduced, stored in or introduced into a retrieval system, or transmitted, in any form or by any means (electronic, mechanical, photocopying, recording or otherwise), or sold without the prior written permission of the copyright owner. No part of this ebook may be used to develop generative Artificial Intelligence (AI) without the prior written permission of the copyright owner.

This novel is a work of fiction. All characters and events in this publication, other than those clearly in the public domain, are fictitious and any resemblance to actual persons or events is entirely coincidental.

The moral rights of the author have been asserted.

For Linda
The best is yet to come

Rick Brindle was born in Dorset, England, to an Army family. He was educated in Germany, then returned to the UK, working mainly in pubs before joining the RAF Regiment for three years. Afterwards, he trained as a nurse. He is currently working on his next novel.

Also by Rick Brindle:

Cold Steel on the Rocks

We Are Cold Steel

Cold Steel and the Underground Boneyard

It's Not For Everyone

Sister Alex

For the residents of Berkshire, England

You may well recognise some of the places, and more of the place names in Sister Alex. I'll be the first to admit that I've taken more than a few liberties with the geography and distances between. I hope you'll forgive me on this point and can still enjoy Alex's adventures as she struggles through Berkshire's post-apocalyptic wilderness.

Prologue

'Signals received,' rapped Wing Commander Strauss. 'Thirty seconds to decrypt, people, and then I want all return messages sent. No sloppy ciphers this time.'

Lines of seemingly unreadable text flew across my computer screen, and I made sense of it. For months now, my training had solidified and I started to know what to do, instinctively almost, and no one was more surprised about that than me.

My fingers flew over the keyboard, typing ninety words to the minute, and I clicked send at exactly the right time.

'Good work.' I sensed Strauss standing behind me. 'Nice timing,' she said. Through my camouflage jacket, I felt her light touch on my shoulder. Even without looking, I knew her uniform would be pristine, her ash-blonde hair scraped back and immaculate, and in my mind at least, the worry-lines around her eyes were erased. 'Everything to the second, Alex. Well done.' She was the only Wing Commander I knew who used first names with her team.

Well, she was actually the *only* Wing Commander I knew.

And that was my life inside the bunker, where everything, *everything* happened the second it was supposed to. And even though I wore a watch, literally, *all* the time, there were so many clocks and sensors around me that I really didn't need to. Deadlines and schedules became obsessively important. What time to be on duty, what time to clock off, when to eat, when to sleep. And my job was even more exact. Signals, messages and communications all had to be received and sent precisely on time, because dead-on punctuality was even more secure than the encryption. Out by less than a heartbeat, and your message was deleted.

'Will they even be alive at the other end?' I asked.

'We'll know in six hours,' replied Strauss. And although she *must* have been feeling the same fear as the rest of us, she was always in control, always assured, always there, and that gave me hope. 'Right now, Alex,' she said. 'Just focus on your job.'

I looked around the Comms Room. So many empty stations, so many vacant chairs. All that remained of us now, myself included, were six operators and the commanding officer. All women.

The bunker had room for forty, but we knew there wouldn't be any replacements coming.

'Listen in,' said Strauss. Straight after the last signal was sent, she stood in front of the Comms Room's main screen, showing a rolling news feed of the mass deaths, the jumbled piles of bodies everywhere. In contrast, she was an image of organisation, of life, and hope. 'Medication has been dropped off,' she said. 'It's experimental, top secret, it's called a selective neuro-cognitive insulator, and you're the guinea pigs.'

'Will it keep us alive?' asked Lucy, sitting at her station three abandoned screens away from me. It was the question we all wanted the answer to.

'Nothing will do that,' said Strauss. She walked among the screens and desks, most of them crammed with equipment but missing the people.

'Then why give it to us?' I asked.

'The Alpha Bug's live or die,' said Strauss. 'We've known that for a long time. If you survive, you won't remember a thing, and we've known that for a long time, too. But according to this,' she read a small-print medication leaflet. 'If you take these tablets, you'll remember your name, your training, your job. It's important, people, and we need this to work.'

'What good will that do?' I asked.

'It's better to come back knowing something instead of nothing,' said Strauss. 'It's about giving the ones who make it through all of this a chance. And right now, Alex, we need all the chances we can get.'

*

At seventeen hundred exactly, my shift ended. I'd swallowed three grey capsules five hours earlier. We all had. I felt no different, and now it was the moment I'd dreaded, wanted, feared.

'Your turn, Alex,' said Strauss.

'Wouldn't I be safer here?' I asked. I looked at my screen and gripped the mouse as though it would somehow keep me in the bunker.

'What, you mean like all the others who puked and then died on station?' replied Strauss. 'Nowhere's safe and you know it.'

'But we haven't lost anyone for over a week.'

'So maybe we're the strong ones,' said Strauss. 'Lucy came back last night, and at least she knew about her family. We've all got to do the same. They need to depend on you, Alex, and you owe it to them to let them know.'

'What if they haven't made it?' My voice shook and I felt tears blurring my vision.

'You'll never know unless you go,' said Strauss, softly. She sat on my desk and I felt the comfort of close contact. 'Now get changed into your civvies and make the trip, Alex. Tell your parents you're fine, tell them they'll be fine, and enjoy a home cooked meal. Then I want you back here for zero six hundred. Can you do that?'

'Yes, Ma'am.'

'Yes, Tanya.' She smiled. 'You're one of us now; remember that.'

Chapter 1

'Wake up!' The shrill scream lanced into my eardrums and I was plucked from unconsciousness.

My eyes flickered open and I saw a burning bright bank of overhead lights. I jerked my head left and right, seeing the white-tiled hospital room. Brown and red matter had splashed onto the floor and walls and been left there to dry. I didn't need to guess what it was; the smell narrowed down the options. But it was the stench of my own vomit soaking my shirt that crimped my nose-hairs.

Still drowsy, my mouth was yanked open and a dry plastic tube was shoved past my teeth and flaccid tongue. A hiss of vacuum air, and then a wet, gurgling noise as the remaining un-chucked puke was sucked free and clear. I struggled to sit up, but a strong hand pushed me back.

'What's your name?' A woman's voice, firm and insistent. Thumping hammer-pain, worse than a tequila hangover bolted through my head. I pushed back a soiled lank of normally well-kept auburn hair and looked right. My bleary vision cleared and I focused on a dark-haired nurse who wore stained scrubs and a look of zombie-like exhaustion. 'Your name!' she demanded.

'Alex,' I stammered. 'It's Alex.'

'What's your age? What's your job?' More questions, fired at me like a machine gun. I lifted my head off the narrow trolley and tried to concentrate, struggling with the questions, obvious questions that demanded an instant, unthinking answer. 'What's your age? What's your job?' she repeated.

'I don't know.' I shook my head and tried to concentrate. I didn't know. But I had to. I *had* to know how old I was. Didn't I?

I fought through the fog of not knowing, not understanding. Shapes and memories solidified in my mind and I knew. I *knew*.

The knowledge scorched into my brain with an intensity that was almost painful.

'I'm nineteen,' I stammered. 'I'm a cyberspace communication specialist, Royal Air Force.'

'You're sure?'

'I'm sure. I'm sure.' I struggled to know more, to remember more, but I couldn't.

'You're the first survivor we've had this week.' Her voice softened. 'And you've been sick like you wouldn't believe. That happens to everyone, and for most of them, it's the last thing they ever do, but you're the only one who's ever come through *and* remembered anything. None of the others have.' She smoothed my hair without the slightest sign of revulsion. I mean, I was covered in my own barf and she didn't even blink. 'Right now,' she said. 'You could fit all of Bracknell's live humans into Bisley and still have room for more. Here.' She thrust an unopened box of tablets into my hands.

I looked at the medication and a vague sense of meaning filtered through my mind, but it wouldn't quite take. 'I wasn't prying,' she said. 'When they brought you in, we had to unbutton your shirt to hook you up to the heart monitor.' She pulled the leads from my chest. 'I saw the augmentation scars. Don't worry, they'll fade and no one will know.' Modesty took over and I buttoned up my shirt with trembling hands. The nurse looked back at me. 'There's no time for that,' she said. 'Not any more. We need you out of here right now if you're alive. There are hundreds still waiting, and no room to spare if you can fend for yourself. Do you know where you're going?'

'No,' I replied. Still shaking, I swung my legs over the side and sat up, clutching the pills to my chest like a hot water bottle. 'How come I remembered?' I asked her.

'You tell me,' she replied, raising an eyebrow. 'Did they give you military types some medication? Something they've been keeping to themselves and haven't said to the rest of us?'

Oh shit! Her words hit me like a sledgehammer and I remembered.

And then I remembered my orders. *Don't tell anyone.*

'What did you forget when you woke up?' I asked her, switching to deflection mode.

A tear formed at the corner of her eye and she swiped it away. 'I haven't caught it yet,' she whispered.

*

What might have been a hospital just weeks, days earlier, was now an over-run panic-destination, where peoples' last hopes ended in projectile vomiting, followed by unconsciousness. I clutched my stash of tablets, still not entirely sure why I needed them, then stumbled out of the operating room, and along a corridor that heaved with bodies. Some of them were moving, some still, while the floor was slick with upchucked carrots and cookies. If I hadn't already lost my last meal at some un-remembered point that day, I would have done right there, all over the stained tile flooring. Managing to keep my footing despite the slippery floor, and thanked by my entire sense of smell, I pushed open the main door and was back outside in the fresh air.

Where was I? I knew my name, my job, and I remembered being told that I was volunteering to try out a new, untested medication. I remembered changing into civilian clothes and going home to my parents, but then?

Nothing.

Some of this made sense, but some of it was terrifyingly unknown.

The nurse said Bracknell and Bisley. Were they places? Was I in one of those towns? My recall clearly wasn't complete. Would it ever return? I staggered outside and looked back at a squat, square, red brick building. A sign above the door said Bracknell Healthspace.

So I still knew how to read.

Next to the hospital building was a car park full of jumbled, haphazardly parked vehicles. It was a scene that perfectly mirrored my own sense of utter confusion. Some cars were dumped and empty, clearly abandoned. Some had crashed to a halt, while others contained twitching or motionless drivers, all of them reeking of regurgitated food gunk. Death flowed around me and mixed with the bitter smell of gastric acid. How many were still alive? I couldn't see many, and those who were didn't look like they would be for long. There was only one thought in my mind: get somewhere safe and try to remember more about my unit, my base, my mission.

I walked over to the nearest four-wheeler, an all-terrain type. I followed my instincts and wondered how far I'd get. The engine was still running, the driver still strapped into the seat, but motionless and slicked with warm vomit-slime. All around me were dead bodies, all of them covered in the reappeared remnants of their last meal. My mind was contracting and exploding at the same time as I tried to make sense of this whole, awful reality.

But I couldn't take it. I just couldn't deal with it. *Get out, get away, survive.* It was all I was thinking. As far as my partially functioning memory was telling me, I'd never seen a dead body before, much less actually touched one, but now I had to do just that, and my supercharged need to leave this place forced my actions. I leaned into the car, unfastened the seatbelt and pulled out the still-warm, freshly dead driver. I forced myself to look away as his face swung around and his unseeing eyes stared at me, then I climbed into the driver's seat and looked at the instruments. The clock said one-thirty and the unbidden thought flashed through my mind that it was four hours to tea-time. Time. I knew straight away that it was important.

I forced myself to focus on getting the vehicle to move. My mind blanked and I felt my throat tighten and my heart rate speed up. I closed my eyes, took a deep breath and my foot instinctively felt for the clutch. I could do this!

Get out of here. Self-preservation kicked into my mind. *Get out of here now!*

I pushed down on the clutch and slammed into first gear. Whatever else I'd forgotten, I still knew how to drive.

Weaving past the vomit-stained bodies, I edged the car onto the road and along a street called Brants Bridge, which meant nothing to me. I had no direction, no destination, just my instincts. I turned left, avoiding the corpses and flipped cars that littered the road. I was driving somewhere safe, and I was going to find some answers, some meaning.

Chapter 2

Fifteen years later

I've always loved the summer time, and I've always hated the rain. But on that early June evening, I had no choice but to live with both, as the persistent raindrops pattered against my back and slowly soaked through my thick-weave camouflage smock. At the same time, the grass I lay on absorbed the rainfall all around me, and my trousers soaked it up like a disruptive patterned sponge. My hair was tied back in a ponytail with a pink band – well, I couldn't go *completely* tac – and my eyebrows dripped raindrops which then trickled onto my eyelashes, making me blink them away before they landed on my binoculars. As soon as the clouds darkened I knew I'd be soaked through to my last stitch of clothing before I could head for home, but I was still on a mission.

Some mission.

Slowly, my core temperature notched downwards, autonomic shivering kicked in and my mind wandered, thinking longingly about the hot bath I'd promised myself.

A bath and a cooked meal that had been delayed from my normally obsessively precise schedule. I looked at my watch, the second hand silently traversing the numbered face beneath the slightly scratched glass. Four-thirty was normally down tools and eat, but right now I was busy.

What was I even doing here, and not for the first time, either? I was lying on a forest ridge, spying on the settlement, a functioning community that had been built up, maintained and permanently inhabited since The Change. I couldn't get any closer and I knew it, but sometimes I lay there and just watched, drawn to their trappings of civilisation, technology, and wishing, dreaming, yearning to be a part of it. Their buildings had lights, they grew crops, they had a partially fenced perimeter, they looked after their own, and they didn't like intruders.

More importantly, this community straddled both sides of the river. And that pissed me off, because the river was the safest way for me to get where I wanted to go.

I even knew what the place was called. Well, what it *used* to be called. Purleyont Hames. Whatever the hell it was called now, I had no idea, but I did know that it wasn't going anywhere, and I couldn't get past it. Well, I mean, I *could* get past it physically, even though I didn't need to. What I *couldn't* get past was the psychological need to go beyond it, and then take myself off on a stupid pilgrimage to the south east.

Seriously, it wasn't going to kill me if I didn't go, but it bloody well might if I did. I'd seen the inhabitants of Purleyont Hames protect their homes from others who came to take a slice of their lives, their luxuries, their knowledge.

It was a suicide-light of shared security that I wasn't even going to try to get any closer to. And that meant I either found a way to get past them on the river, or I took a huge detour into very unknown territory, against very unknown threats, and spent more nights out in the open than was either safe or sane.

But really, did I have to? I had everything I needed, and it was only my own stupid obsession that kept me coming back, looking for just one way to get around an immovable obstacle that I wouldn't ever be able to get around.

It was going to get me into trouble one day.

And it suddenly did.

A massive dead-weight slammed into me and I felt a microsecond of panic. My face was pressed into the ground and I couldn't breathe. I felt the unmistakable feel of a hostile human body and questing hands groping my breasts. Even as I lifted my mouth clear and breathed once more, I could have predicted that last move.

'Hold still, bitch,' he hissed in my ear, because strangely enough, I *was* struggling. I instinctively reach for my Glock, but he read my moves and pinned my right wrist. I lashed back with my left elbow and got in a glancing blow that did no damage. 'Like to fight, do you?' he chuckled. 'Why were *you* spying on them? Aren't you one of them yourself? What do you think, Brig?'

'Ask her later, Marlo.' Another male voice behind me added to the joys of life I was feeling right then. 'This is as close as we need to get, and she's coming with us. We'll get all the answers we need from her.' Marlo's hands gripped my collar and I was yanked to my feet. 'What's that she's wearing?' and I just *knew* he was looking at the last thing I wanted him to: my watch. Marlo spun me around and I faced Brig, who stood before me, a dirt-stained giant wearing desert camo.

It was all the break I needed. I brought my leg up and my foot flew forward and slammed into Brig's groin. Even before he groaned and pitched forward, clutching his nether regions, I yanked my right hand forward as hard as I could, and helped by the rain, I slipped free of Marlo's grip and shot my elbow backwards into his ribs, properly this time. He staggered away from me. I jumped clear and saw a quickly recovered Brig coming towards me, his unwashed face a grimace of anger. I pulled back a fist and punched his nose, feeling the welcome crunch of fractured nasal cartilage. His eyes rolled back and he dropped face-down to the rain-soaked grass. Strapped to his back was a rusty MP5, held there by a frayed sling.

No time to think. I spun around and kicked Marlo hard in the guts. He folded and fell, and just before he instinctively contracted his legs, I stamped on his balls, gifting him with universal, instant pain, and enough time for me to get away.

There was a time when basic self-defence used to be the three D's: Distract, Disable, Disappear. Since The Change, it was distract, disable, *disarm,* and then disappear.

Just kill them, I thought, *they'd have killed you.*

My right hand flew towards my holstered Glock.

Why didn't I? That's a good question, and the only answer I've got is that I'm not a killer. I was live-armed with an automatic and I knew how to use it, but now I had the chance to run, I wasn't cornered, and I didn't actually *have* to kill anyone. It was flawed logic and potentially stupid, but none of us are perfect. So instead, I made sure my watch was still secure, grabbed my binoculars, then snatched at Brig's MP5. The sling snapped and it was mine. It wasn't that I wanted it, and the chances were that it didn't even work. I just didn't want him to have it. He was still writhing in agony, so I grabbed his spare mags and even better than that, two bars of chocolate. Chocolate! Where the hell did they get that from? My eyes gaped as I saw it, even tasted it in my mind. I hadn't seen chocolate since I didn't know when. No time for niceties. I shoved both bars down the front of my combat smock and hoped my body heat didn't melt them by the time I got home. The day's warmth was going but not gone, and by the time I'd got out of this mess I'd be sweating like Maria Sharapova on Centre Court, whoever the hell *she* was.

And then I just couldn't resist it. I pulled out a signal flare.

'You fuckers want to talk to a woman?' I said, my voice deep and shaky with the adrenaline. 'I'll call some for you.'

I fired the flare and then tracked backwards as fast as I could go. My nerves jangled and my moves were sloppy, but they'd do. Hopefully the inhabitants of Purleyont Hames would find my two suitors, they'd welcome them both as only they could, they'd think my tracks were Brig's and Marlo's, and that would be that. Brig groaned and got to his knees. I ran back and kicked his nads once more, then gave Marlo the same. They needed to be there just a bit longer. Leaving them both on the floor and in pain, I disappeared into the undergrowth.

The newly-grown vegetation quickly enveloped me. After a hundred metres I turned and ran for the stream, then splashed through it for a quarter mile before climbing out on the other side, close to what used to be a low road bridge, its concrete now overgrown and the girders rusting and paint-chipped. I grabbed the metal and pulled myself up, lying on the pot-holed tarmac next to a rusting Ford cadaver as I got my breath back.

Thankfully, most of the bodies had long since gone, which was kind of a relief. It's much easier to bump into a long-dead car than a mossed over and ragged bone-pile.

No time to stay still, though, not with a Purleyont Hames hunting patrol and two pissed off Alphas out there and nearby. It was time to get up and get home, in a roundabout way of course, just in case I was followed.

*

So, what had I learned since that first insane drive out of Bracknell fifteen years earlier?

Some things, but not all. Never all. Tanya Strauss had been absolutely right about that.

First, the essentials. The men who survived became the Alphas, solitary or small group hunters and scavengers, while the Strauss were women, and at Purleyont Hames, if nowhere else, they'd got it together and created a working society.

Strauss? Well, what else was I going to call them?

Anyway, the men and women, Alphas and Strauss, they're two completely separate tribes, breeds, civilisations, whatever you want to call it, and they both hate each other's guts. The Alphas *want* the whole group thing, the technology, the progress, but the only way they know how to get anything is to take.

And the Strauss aren't giving.

Of course, it might all be different over the next hill, or across the next river. Around here, though, that's how it is.

But enough about geopolitics, I *really* had to get home.

The rotting road led into a reclaimed woodland. I ran for half a mile between adolescent oak trees, jinking and twisting, losing my way but desperate to make sure I wasn't followed. Heading south, I crossed the pitted, overgrown remains of a motorway, which still hosted a chaotic jumble of decomposing, one-time vehicles.

Focus, Alex!

Keeping your home location secret is one of the many golden rules to survival out here. Not that the Strauss would bother me, simply because I lived a long way from Purleyont Hames. But the Alphas weren't as organised; they just ran in ones and occasionally twos, went wherever, and took whatever came across their path.

So it was very important I wasn't tailed.

The trees cloaked me in shadows and I dropped to the ground, again, and got soaking wet, again. I gave Brig's MP5 a once over, making sure he'd at least kept the damn thing, if not clean, at least serviceable. It had more range than my trusty Glock, and out here, more range always gave you an edge. My hands shook slightly as I settled into a fire position, sighting back down the way I'd just run. I lay there, prone, concealed and unseen. If Brig or Marlo came this way, I'd be ready for them.

But here's the thing. It doesn't matter what I absolutely remembered being trained to do, I've never shot anyone. Not for real. Sure, I'd sent a few rounds their way and likely missed. I'd done that loads of times. Haven't we all? But I've never actually, really, killed anyone.

And I still wasn't sure I could do it for real. Kill someone, that is. Which, in this world, is a definite weakness.

Time trickled past. Time, time, always time. My own, self-imposed and insanely, obsessively followed schedule was now slipping, which meant my supper would be late tonight. Really late. I considered reaching for the chocolate bars stuffed down the front of my smock, which were probably already turning into a foil-wrapped fondue in my cleavage. Time for the sugar-rush later, I had to make sure they weren't following me. I glanced at my watch, glad beyond words that it was still with me. It was an old aviator, hand wound, rugged, and accurate enough for the short work I'd expected that day. Give it half an hour, I thought, plenty of time for things on the crest to settle down, one way or the other.

The rain wasn't stopping. Heavy drops pattered against the leaves all around me and drowned out the sound of any approaching footsteps. My camo was soaked through to my base layer, cooling the beads of sweat from my exertions and making me shiver. Hot, cold, wet, dry, and sometimes all at once. It was typical British weather, and venturing outside in it was rarely comfortable.

Thirty climate-soaked minutes crept by and the only constant was my own stillness and the perpetual rain. *So much for this summer.* I slid backwards, and then knelt, still looking back the way I'd come, waiting to gut an unwary pursuer.

No one came. Five minutes more and I crouched and moved backwards a bit further, staying in cover, still surveying the path. Still no movement. I stood up, next to a tree trunk, unseen and enveloped by shadow and leaves and branches.

I sighted along the MP5, straining my ears for the sound of approaching danger. Nothing. My heart rate subsided and I began to believe that Brig and Marlo weren't coming this way, and that the Strauss hadn't even realised I was there. I sighed and relaxed, lowered the MP5, and turned around.

Then fell to the forest floor from a solid kick in my ribs.

I was winded for a second, but adrenaline and fear got me moving. I spun onto my back, brought up the MP5 and saw Brig standing over me, bleeding from what looked like a serious head wound.

'Takes more than a woman to stop me, you bitch.'

'And it takes more than a stupid, stinking Alpha to stop me,' I replied. But I wasn't as sure as I sounded. 'Don't move.' Covered by the MP5, I stood up and faced him, less than two paces away. My wet clothes clung to my skin. 'Where's your buddy?' I asked. Not that I was concerned for him, you understand. The Alpha stopped and smiled.

'How do you think I got away?' he said. Blood seeped through his teeth and trickled over his lips. 'Marlo screamed a good death and while they were on him, I shifted.' He glanced at the MP5. 'You got that from me, right?'

'What if I did?'

He chuckled. 'Pull the trigger.'

'Don't make me,' I hissed.

This time he laughed. 'Go ahead,' he said. He took a step towards me. 'Do it. Shoot me. You'd better, if you want to live.'

I stepped back, but I knew if I reached for the Glock he'd be on me before it cleared the holster. I flicked the MP5's safety to single shot. 'I'll fire.'

'You think you will.'

I looked down at the weapon for that one fatal, stupid second, and it was all he needed. He sprang forward, ripped it from my hands and it was his once more. I sobbed in frustration, didn't even try for a retaliation, just turned and bolted into the woods.

Why did I rely on an untested weapon? I had the Glock, I knew it worked, and I went for the trophy instead. Stupid, stupid bitch. But that wasn't going to help me now. What I needed right then was a fast pair of legs, which thankfully I had.

And that was just as well, because I then quickly found out the MP5 worked fine, and I automatically bent double as the bullets flacked into the leafy undergrowth. Then I heard the unmistakable sound of boots crashing through foliage in pursuit. I swerved, weaved, and just plain ran.

I crashed through the wet undergrowth between the tree trunks and a gut-swooping hillside yawned away to my right. I veered along a narrow erosion path, and suddenly, there was only one direction, one choice to run. Behind me, I heard the sounds of approaching danger.

Brig didn't look fit, or fast, but he was, and he was gaining on me. I tried to speed up but I was reaching my limits. Didn't that bastard ever get tired? From out of nowhere I felt a rough hand grab my shoulder, spin me around and slam me face-first into a nearby tree trunk. I gasped, my breath whooshing out of me. I reached for the Glock but he snatched my wrists together and held them above my head. Heavy breathing in my ears, I felt his free hand roam over my body and I closed my eyes as the unjustified self-shame churned my insides. Danger screamed at my senses. I struggled in his grip like a fish on a hook but it was no good. His hand groped my breasts, then slid down between my legs.

'Hey!' Shock. Massive shock and surprise. 'You've got—'

I yanked my hands free, elbowed him in the ribs and ran once more. He roared vengeance and bulldozed after me. I opened up some distance, but he gained on me, then shouted a brutal challenge and jumped.

At the same time my foot caught in a tree root and I went down, sprawling on the slippery, rain-soaked floor.

He flew straight over me and plummeted down the hillside. His cries of pain were punctuated by solid thunks as he hit stubbornly growing tree trunks and rocky outcrops, none of which seemed to stop him. The sounds of his descent got quieter and further away. Almost sobbing with relief, I stood up on shaking legs, made sure my Glock was still safe in its holster, and then pulled out my compass. *Where am I?* Stuck in the woods with no real reference point, I needed a bearing to get back home.

A sudden prickling at the back of my neck made me turn around, and a loud conscience-voice in my head screamed at me to keep away from the Glock. Ten metres from me stood two Strauss, who I guessed were the chasers sent to investigate the flare I'd sent up. Barely visible in the rain-gloom forest, they wore black and dark green leggings and base-layer tops. Both of them carried sports bows with sights and pulleys designed to send arrows almost as far as a bullet. Athletic curves and toned arms told me they were every bit as capable and dangerous as the Alpha I'd inadvertently sent down the hill. I stood there and marvelled at their clear skin, high cheekbones and clean, ponytailed hair. Their eyes gleamed with health and energy. Even soaked by the rain, they looked amazing, and left me wishing I looked even a fraction as good as them.

'You're not from the settlement?' one of them said, her voice soft and magical in my ears. I shook my head, not daring to risk my voice.

'What are you doing out here alone?' the other Strauss asked. 'You don't need to be.'

I shook my head again at the impossible dream she was offering me, and she didn't even know it. There was no way either of them would have said it if they knew, if they *really* knew.

'We're always stronger together,' she said.

'Maybe one day.' I risked a whispered reply.

'That's always your choice,' said the first one. 'But know this, we'll never turn a sister away. Did you send up the signal?'

'I had a problem,' I said, and distant grunts of pain told them what it was.

'You won't have to worry about the other one,' said the second Strauss. 'And whoever it was you sent down the hill, they won't last long out here. But there's always a home for you with us, whenever you want it.'

They spun around and disappeared within seconds, leaving me reeling at the day's events. I looked back at my compass, checked the time, then picked up the bearing and jogged home.

Live for the day, get supplies for tomorrow, but don't think about the future. Never think about the future.

Because in this new world it's one side or the other, and no in between. The Alphas are all men, the Strauss are all women, and all I am is trans, hopelessly and forever lost somewhere in the middle.

And I'm a target for them all.

Chapter 3

Now, you probably think that's weird, and I wouldn't blame you, because even *I* think it's weird. Back in the real world, the normal world, although I'm sure it was never normal for me, I imagine I used to look at myself in the mirror, and like the song said, I was just eighteen and in between a lady and a man. Not that I'm eighteen anymore, and I've spent years trying to find an answer, but you know what? There isn't one. Isn't, wasn't? You tell me, but just like you and just like everyone else, we are what we are, it's as simple as that. And ever since The Change, who the hell did I have to prove anything to, anyway?

But even before the world changed, I'd changed. Small breasts and thighs had replaced pecs and snake hips, thanks in part to the augmentation surgery, and also helped by the stash of hormone tablets I'd been given by the nurse who'd saved my life all those years ago. I wondered what happened to her. Had she survived? Was she a Strauss right now, or part of some other group?

Anyway, the hormones. God, I felt sick every time I took one, but it was so worth it, along with the frantic and sometimes horrifically hazardous search for more of the same to complete the transition as far as it would take me. It was even worth being chased to exhaustion by a pissed off mother capybara twelve years ago, as I exited a half-pillaged pharmacy in the remains of Bagshot. It definitely wasn't my most elegant moment, and I didn't have time to wonder if she used to be a pet, or a zoo escapee, but I made damn sure I didn't get too close another one when they had young nearby. As I threw myself over a conveniently placed wall that was too high for her to jump over, I really did ask myself if there was some other way I could secure some meds. Because a usually cute, but still super-protective capybara one day could very easily be a bear with a migraine, or even a rattled snake the next.

But hey, I got away, and more importantly, I got another stash of oestrogen tablets.

And eventually, I got the result.

Woman-ish figure? Good enough. Body hair, what was that? Well, mostly. And while it would have taken more than pills to get rid of that damn pecker, the days of morning glory were long gone. Which, actually, was fine by me. I might not have made that part of the reassignment surgery, but it was the only step I'd missed.

My hair, always auburn, was still auburn and no grey. Wrinkles? Never, although a few more lines at the corners of my mouth and under my eyes than I had ten years ago were always going to happen. But that's better than not being around to see it, though, right?

Anyway, I looked female enough to have fooled a pair of Alphas, *and* the chasers who'd come after them.

So that's me.

What about The Change? Well, having been one of the lucky few who lived through it, I can tell you that it's a very polite term for the almost total extinction of humanity, all caused by the Alpha Bug.

How did it happen? I don't know, but that's people for you, only too keen to ditch the masks, go out on the piss, burn some more fossils and make another million, because that's what's important, right?

Signs? They're just for ignoring, and I think you know what I mean.

Anyway, the irony of all that was the term that was given to the surviving males, because it was the alpha males who went first. And when I say went, I mean died. And it really was gender-specific. Absolutely the first to go were the men, the hard men, the shouting in the street, I-hate-everyone-who's-not-just-like-me men. The antagonistic, tailgating, beer-brawling, football hooligan, Walford men. And while society was still functioning at the start of this, and all sorts of theories flew around, no one really knew why it was happening. No one. It was colloquially called the Alpha Bug because they were the ones who were dying, and then everyone else died before it could be called anything else.

Six months after I puked, lost most of my memory and survived, I'd say that ninety-nine per cent of the world's human population had dropped dead.

Looking back, it seems incredible to me now just how many ideas were talked about, considered, tried. I still have trembling memories of reading the increasingly panic-struck signals that were sent back and forth to increasingly high levels of command, those that were still alive. Food sources were mentioned and then rationed, quarantined, discarded. Air quality, ambient temperature, virus, bacteria, vaccines, placebos, exposure, isolation. It all got talked about, all got tried, and none of it worked.

None of it.

Covid? Not even a dress-rehearsal. That was nothing.

People just died. That's all anyone knew. And if you did come through to the other side, unless you'd taken the grey pills, you didn't remember much from before.

The numbers went even further south once those still alive bumped into each other. Two groups meet, one group survives, and even now, that's how it goes. No one trusts anyone, no one wants to catch anything from anyone, so the few of us that made it this far tend to avoid the hell out of everyone else.

Which, taken as a whole, was fine by me.

Because now, I could finally be this weird, messed up, outcast trans woman, with absolutely no one around to judge me. And before you say it, the fact that the only reason I wasn't being judged was *because* there was no one around wasn't lost on me, either.

Although now, being judged was mild compared to the reality I faced. The Alphas would have killed me as soon as they realised what I was, and it wouldn't have been pretty. As for the Strauss? Well, for someone like me, it was best that I avoided them as well.

Chapter 4

Seven years ago

It wasn't my fault. I mean, all I wanted was a piss, and the rain didn't help. Still, when you're alone in the woods and the urge comes upon you, you just face the nearest tree trunk and away you go. Trouble was, when you're standing up and taking a waz in the woods, peripheral awareness kind of goes out of the window.

Which was why two Strauss got the drop on me in the first place. I mean, I didn't even smell them coming. And it's not as though they stank like the Alphas, all stale sweat and unwashed arses. No, the Strauss smelled a whole lot better, like long hair after light rainfall, a warm body, gentle perspiration, and soap. All of which tells you they had water and they knew how to use it.

Well, actually, so did I, but it still didn't put me in their top forty.

I'd barely finished and tucked back in when I felt their hands clamp onto my arms and yank me away from the tree trunk. I got a brief glimpse of the grey clouds above the treetops, then felt a solid impact, like my shoulders had been driven two inches into the ground. One of them straddled my chest and pinned my wrists to the forest floor.

'What have we got here?' she asked. 'An Alpha up to no good?'

'I'm not an Alpha,' I said, helpless in her steel-wire grip.

'Care to prove that?' grinned the Strauss. 'Pissing when you're standing up isn't really a woman thing.' I looked up at a thin, drawn face with a deep scar down her left cheek and sandy brown hair tied into a tight ponytail. Her arms were whip-thin, but damn she was strong.

'This isn't why we're here, Collar,' said the second Strauss, I couldn't see her, but at least she sounded friendly. 'And stop doubting people. This one looks like a woman to me, and it is actually possible to piss standing up.'

'The traitor we're chasing is a woman,' snarled Collar. 'And we were bloody right to doubt her. What's your point, Addison?'

'She's not the one we're after,' said Addison.

'That's right,' I said, through gritted teeth. 'I'm not the one you're looking for, so let me go.'

'Really?' chuckled Collar, and leant her whole body weight onto my wrists. 'You going to make me?'

'We can't take her with us,' said Addison. 'She's out here alone, she's a survivor sister, we're supposed—'

'I know the rules,' snapped Collar. 'But not this time. The trail led us here, and look what we found. We've been lied to and cheated by one of our own, so until that's been sorted, I'm sure as hell not taking a stranger on face value.'

'No, Collar,' said Addison. 'She's a sister; we should offer her sanctuary.'

'Not if we suspect her.' Collar pinned both of my wrists with one hand, then pulled a knife from her belt and my eyes bulged wide.

'Stop!' Said Addison.

'Look away if you want to,' growled Collar. 'We can't take a chance that she'll get away and warn others.'

'You'll have to kill me as well,' said Addison.

'What?'

I heard the sound of another knife sliding free of its sheath. 'If you harm a survivor sister,' said Addison. 'I'll harm you. If you kill her, I'll kill you. And I know I don't stand a chance, but I'll still try. So make a choice, Collar. Either kill both of us, or neither of us.'

I still couldn't see Addison, but I sure liked the sound of her. Looking up at Collar, I saw her clenching her jaw and felt her squeeze my wrists. She screwed up her face and thrust her knife back into its sheath.

'Well, Addison?' said Collar. 'Let's hear your suggestion.'

Fighting them all the way, and giving them bruises and scratches to remember me by, they left me spread-eagled and staked out on the forest floor as the rain softly pattered down.

'Don't go away,' sniggered Collar. She stood over me in mud-stained leggings, a testament to my struggles, and a last memory of me that would soon be washed away. 'We'll be back once our job's *done.' She said. 'If you're still here, then maybe we'll see what kind of survivor sister you really are. There. Are you happy now, Addison?'*

'I still think—'

'It's the best you're going to get,' said Collar. 'Now let's go.'

And then they were gone, while I lay on the ground and struggled like hell. The rain soaked through my clothes as I fought to get free, because as much as Addison didn't want to kill me, this was actually a lot worse.

After The Change, the dogs that everyone had as pets were now the top predators, and running in packs. They were big, aggressive, wild and seriously un-tameable. It wouldn't take them long to pick up my scent, and if they did and I was lying here helpless, I'd have no chance.

I yanked and tugged at the stakes. The forest floor's thick clay expanded with the rain and sucked the wooden poles in place. I felt waves of panic and struggled to keep my focus as the rain really started hammering down. I pulled and pulled and felt the mud squelch and smear underneath me. Then with a barely audible creak, I felt one of the stakes give. Slowly, slowly, painfully slowly, it started to work free, and if anything, I got even more scared, dreading a disaster just as I glimpsed an escape.

I pulled again, my vision starred and I felt my chest tighten with the effort, and then suddenly, my left arm schlooped free, droplets of mud splattered over my face, and the crudely cut stake thudded against my chest. Without stopping for anything, I scratched at the improvised twine holding my right wrist in place, and after five minutes of frantic clawing, cursing, and a fair degree of sobbing, I had both arms free and it was then relatively easy to pull at the stakes that were tied to my ankles. I stood up, windmilled my arms and fished through my pockets for my compass. Bearing set, I ran like hell to get back home, racing the gathering dusk all the way. I also didn't need the growing hunger pangs to tell me that along with the dogs who'd just lost their meal, my supper would also be late.

And ever since then, when I have to pee outside, it's back against a tree trunk, squat down and keep your eyes open.

And, just so that you know I'm not completely uncivilised, my aim had never been that good, and even before my *change, I'd always sat down for a number one if there was ever a real toilet around.*

Chapter 5

Now

Whatever it was about the Alphas that kept them living in caves and shitting in abandoned buildings, the Strauss got over it. Maybe women are just more sociable than men. Make your own mind up on that one, but the Strauss came together and they're the only viable Post-Change group out there. Well, the only one I'd found.

And, as far as I knew, that was it. A few Alphas here and there, the Strauss, and me.

Me, who was now thoroughly spooked by the day's events and desperate to get back home. The weirdest thing of all was the actual conversations. It had been years since I'd heard anyone's voice apart from my own, years since I'd had any contact. And the Strauss actually *thought* they *liked* me. Until they saw what I really was, and then it would be one less trans woman in the world. After that, they'd probably back-track and steal my wardrobe as well. Talk about judging by appearances. I identified as a woman, *was* a woman, but being accepted as one? That was a whole different plane, and one I'd never reach.

Or at least, that was how I remembered things being before The Change. My memories beyond the Comms Room weren't as good, damn those grey pills. I knew all about my job, my training, like Tanya Strauss said I would, and just like she said I would, not much else. I'd filled some gaps, a few, but not very many, with scavenged books. It was patchwork and incomplete, mostly food and medical. What I did remember was confused, contradictory, and uncertain.

I remembered, though, that she had no doubts about me. Right alongside my memories of the communication drills, encryption code and all the rest, I had a vivid recollection of standing to attention in her office, and hearing her words, watching her say them as she looked straight at me.

'I don't care a damn if you're a man, woman or anything in between,' she said. 'As long as you do your job and you follow orders, I've got your back with everything else. If you want to transition while you're in service, that's fine by me, because you're excellent at your job and I don't want to lose you. Consider the paperwork done.'

So she'd known about me, she'd accepted me, but would anyone else? *Did* anyone else? And for all of their 'survivor sister' mentality, I really didn't think the Strauss were a hundred per cent with even partially female strangers, especially after I'd met Collar.

And you couldn't really blame them. Pretty much all of the outsiders who came looking for the Strauss didn't want to be friends. They just wanted to take.

Crazy thoughts of actually being accepted filled my head and I struggled to focus. I got my bearings, literally, thanks to my compass, and inclined upwards to get a clear view and a landmark.

I reached the top of the hill and looked around. I needed eyes on the river and the church spire. Old stone buildings survived the best, and they were placed on maps for that very reason. I relied on steeples and spires a whole lot more than the Christians who'd built them.

I got the fix: spire, river, steep hill. It was enough.

And then the terrain started to get familiar. A group of trees, one set of stones, even the change in gradient as I crested the hill and began splashing downwards through puddles. There, hidden by the new-growth silver birch trees, and vision-subdued by its one-time grey exterior that was camouflaged even further by patches of moss and lichens, was where I lived.

My house, the place I called home, was the bunker where I'd once served, and it had taken me a year to work out from my partial memories exactly where it was. It lay squat and alone in the wilderness, practically indestructible, and once I'd made it habitable, it was exactly what I wanted, although it wasn't particularly welcoming when I found it. The crew-cut lawns that once surrounded it had been lost and reclaimed by the encroaching forest, and the bunker's paintwork was faded and peeling. Small, wire-reinforced windows were sunk deep into the concrete walls, and even when they had just been installed, I knew they'd never reflected the sunlight, but they worked, they provided illumination, and they were utterly secure.

On that first day of reunion, once-forgotten memories had flooded my mind. I shed unashamed tears as I pulled five bodies out from inside, all camouflage-clad, and some with their name-tapes still visible above their chest pockets. And the last one I saw made me scream loud enough to bring out all of the survivors for miles around, but I didn't care.

Wing Commander Strauss.

She was dead. Proof beyond question as I looked at her lifeless husk. Her remaining blonde hair was all that marked her out as anything other than just another dead body, a dried remnant of a vital, caring, believing person. Scraps of skin still clung to exposed bones, and eyeless sockets stared accusingly at a cruel world that had abandoned a whole species.

Tanya Strauss, my commanding officer, mentor, role model, protector and life-coach. She had been everything. She'd believed in me, encouraged me, even told me that one day I might make officer. Me, an officer? She thought so, and she said so with no judgments.

I don't know that I should have expected anything other than what I found, but no way was I living anywhere else, even when I saw how a year with no power had ravaged the place. I squelched through puddles along the bunker's spartan corridors, and shivered inside the damp interior that was no longer kept well-lit and ambient. And the legion of clocks that I'd looked at, lived for, and worked for. None of them worked anymore.

There was lots to do, but I had plenty of time.

It was all I had.

And having made the place mine over the years, I made damn sure no one else laid a claim on it. As I did every time I came home, I went to ground next to the three stone markers I'd put down when I left, and then watched.

My nerves were still jangling after everything that had happened. I just wanted to get inside and lock the door behind me, but I knew the danger of not being ultra-cautious. The rain kept up with no sign of stopping, the puddles got deeper and I could feel my purloined bars of chocolate cooling against my skin.

My teeth chattered and every layer I wore was soaking wet. If my hair hadn't been tied back it would have been straggled around my head like an auburn coloured mop.

I checked my watch. It was time to move and way past time to eat. I squelched to my feet and jogged quickly around the immediate perimeter, then headed to the front door. Well, the only door: an utterly uninviting slab of bulletproof steel plate with a fucking big keyhole. I unlocked, stepped inside and clanged the door shut behind me.

Chapter 6

It's hard to describe the intense feeling of safety from being inside your own four walls and behind a locked door, and there aren't many places safer and more secure than a bunker. It didn't sound homely, but for me, it was personal as well as safe.

   I pulled the blackout curtains across thickened glass windows, then flicked a switch and the lights came on. Most of my power came from the sun and I checked the solar panels every day. Some of them, I'd bolted to the flat roof, and some were staked to a small clearing I used as a vegetable garden, and then fed back along a buried cable. Believe me, digging twenty metres of powerflex into the ground to keep it safe and unseen was a labour of love, I can tell you. Along with the wind pump as my backup, they were the engine of everything. Weeks of stripping the nearest IKEAs bare of DIY solar panels and home batteries, then learning how to install them at breakneck speed was the best thing I ever did. And I made damn sure I had plenty of spares and replacements.

   Routine checks first. I went to the store rooms and made sure the random damp and puddles hadn't reached the shelves where I stashed my supplies. After that, I checked the med room, as yet unused and crammed with plundered med packs on top of a re-purposed canvas bed. I shuddered as I always did when I peered inside. *I hope I never need to use this stuff.* Then I walked into the kitchen and switched on the water pump. My system of underground tank and carefully hoarded rainfall gave me enough hot water for a bath, which I'd then use to wash my clothes.

   I unbuckled my webbing belt and my kit dropped to the floor. I peeled off my soaked camo and looked at my reward for the day's events, two bars of chocolate. Still sealed, no nuts, and joy of joys, made with milk. I put my cold and wet clothing into the laundry sink that was in a small utility room next to the kitchen, and headed barefoot into the bathroom.

Steam rose as I slowly sank into the hot bathwater and gave in to the warmth and relaxation. I thought about the day and what I'd do next.

For the past two months, all of my plans had been the same.

Get to Greenwich.

Because for me, my obsession is time. And that was because of this bunker, because of Wing Commander Strauss, because of what I was, what I did, and what I remembered. My entire role was about communicating, sending signals, receiving them, decoding them, and it was all done by the clock.

Religiously.

I had to be at work on time, sending messages on time, receiving them within certain timescales. I had a certain amount of time to decrypt and then re-encrypt, compositions had to be done to the letter, and then sent to the second. And don't even get me started on meal times and bed times, because all of that was as per regulations as well.

While I'd served inside this bunker, time had absolutely ruled my life. And now that I'd survived the Alpha Bug, it still did. I didn't know, or remember living any other way, so to have even tried to disassociate myself with timekeeping was like telling me to stop washing and turn into an Alpha.

Not going to happen.

So, more than anything else, I guarded and cherished my religiously collected watches and clocks, backed up by an intermittent and unreliable electricity supply.

And, of course, a crappy old candybar phone that I somehow managed to keep charged up. Just.

But that somehow was starting to run out.

Well, the cable was, to be more precise. Because it doesn't matter how careful you are, we all make mistakes, and we all trip over things.

And I'd tripped over the charging cable, which was now broken. Not completely, but enough of the wires had come loose to make charging a sometime thing instead of an all-time thing. So unless I could find some other way to have a dead-on, balls-accurate and reliable way to keep time, I'd lose my reference point.

A small thing, you might say, and you might be right, but supposing I missed a day at the end of a thirty day month, or what if I missed the leap year?

Just thinking about it sent a deluge of anxiety hosing through my body.

Which brought me back to the Strauss.

Because they'd set up shop at Purleyont Hames, right between me and Greenwich.

Or, at least, where Greenwich *used* to be.

Greenwich.

Shit knows if it was even still there, but I had to find out. I had to. Greenwich was where the observatory was, and that's where my incomplete reading had told me about the most amazing collection of massively, totally accurate, centuries-old clocks and a whole load of other weird timepieces, all of which were designed to be atomically precise, without being hooked up to mains electric, or the internet.

Once my charging cable went, and eventually it would, one of those babies was the only thing I could think of to replace what the phone could do.

And apart from doubling the size of my wardrobe and keeping it dry, that was what I craved. Having now set myself up as securely as I could hope, getting my manicured hands on a sustainable, accurate timepiece that didn't need to be plugged in had become my main mission in life.

Which was why I'd been spying out Purleyont Hames. I had to get past it to get to Greenwich, hopefully without risking my skin to do it.

The most direct route was along the river. I *could* go across country, but it would take crackerjack navigation and loads more nights outside than I wanted. I'd never survive it.

The only trouble was that the Strauss camp straddled the river, and I had no idea just how far into the dead estates of Reading their reach stretched. They even had a damn bridge across the flowing waterway, which meant they had both sides covered. I'd been trying to find a way around their camp without being seen and all I'd achieved so far was getting chased out of there by a pair of Alphas.

Greenwich. I didn't *need* to go there. Not really. Well, not at all, actually. But the pull of the observatory, the relics, what *might* be there, and my obsession with time, with *the* time, was irresistible. Slowly, the bath water cooled and my thoughts kept me warm. If I couldn't get past Purleyont Hames, which was my initial plan, then maybe I'd have to go around them. I shouldn't, if I was sensible I wouldn't, and maybe I couldn't, but I had to try.

I suppose you could call it a hobby, but what the hell else was I going to do apart from survive? I emptied the bath and towelled myself dry as the water noisily gurgled over the fine-filter and into the washing vat. The wind-warmer, a small cup-shaped turbine on the roof, would keep the laundry water tepid and the first hard job would be to scrub my clothes clean. But that was for later, and I allowed myself an hour before starting my chores.

As well as the secure home, in a world where you're one of very few survivors, where everyone's hostile, it's amazing what comfort a warm, fluffy dressing gown and slippers can be. I curled up on the flatpack sofa I'd built from the box and poured a hot fruit drink. I had a slowly dwindling stash of regular tea bags, and they were only for really special occasions. Maybe once I got back from Greenwich I'd have a cuppa. But until then...

So I really had to plan my trip. I munched a handful of dried fruit and considered the options. And much like that cyborg which I think was called the Dalek, I imagined my brain as some kind of neuro-net learning processor, constantly working out ingenious ways to survive.

Ideas coalesced in my mind. I finished my drink and changed into leggings and a gym top.

First job, scrub my day clothes and hang them in the conservatory. Well, it wasn't *actually* a conservatory; it used to be the observation room at the bunker's centre, with a huge square of super-toughened glass where the slightly raised roof was, but even in midwinter it turned into a fantastic greenhouse and dried things almost as quickly as an airing cupboard.

Then it was a trip to the garden before it got dark and pick out this month's crop of potatoes, beans and cauliflower. I'd long known that tinned food was a great stopgap, but even with serious rationing, scavenging, and half of the bunker full of it, it probably wouldn't last as long as me, so it was a case of learn to be a gardener or starve.

Which, let me tell you, does wonders for your waistline and complexion.

Chapter 7

For as long as it was still working, I slept with my phone on trickle charge, and on the morning of my planned trip to Greenwich, its alarm went off at six. I stretched my body into wakefulness, grumbled at the early hour and fixed some breakfast and a hot drink.

I set my maps out on the table, got my bearing and set my compass on the first landmark, a hilltop with step sides on the north. Forget about the forest boundaries on the map, most of the roads had also disappeared and the fields were now either gone or going as the trees took over, slowly cleaning the air and pulling out the carbon dioxide.

My route skirted the Strauss camp. By staying on the other side of the hills there was a big, huge, forested barrier between me and them. Lost in that expanse of creeping woodland that was chock full of returned-with-a-vengeance animals, no one would even know I was there. At least I hoped not. And if it did all go south and I had to start shooting, I'd be long gone before any curious humans of whatever gender turned up.

My kit was laced tight, my weapons, Glock and shotgun, were cleaned and oiled. The whole thing was nuts, really nuts, but I was ready.

Time to go to Greenwich.

The morning was perfect, light cloud and summer weather. The rain from my last trip out had gone, although the morning dew still dampened the grass as I lay flat and watched the bunker. The moisture slowly seeped through my camo but I knew that as long as the sunshine stayed, the heat of the day would dry me within an hour.

Satisfied that I was alone, I got to my feet, slung the shotgun over my shoulder and jogged through the woods. Jog, walk, jog, walk. It was my preferred method of foot travel for the first hour, then down to walking with regular stops to check bearings and catch my breath. With a mid-heavy pack and a long distance ahead of me, it was always a marathon, never a sprint.

My boots were soft on the yielding forest floor of last autumn's leaves. Low-lying ferns brushed against my legs and I wondered if I'd ever feel safe enough to simply enjoy it for more than just a moment, to hear the birds singing and watch the butterflies fluttering through the greenery, to smell the gentle layers of the living woodland.

Then I saw the bear tracks and froze. Literally froze. Holy shit, bear tracks! Wide and deeply planted into the mud, and the claw marks, Jesus Christ, how big were those bloody claws? I'd rather face a whole herd of dogs than just one bear, because I knew that I'd never outrun one, I'd never be friends with one, and I'd never ever be seen by a bear as anything other than lunch.

There was nothing to think about, just move. Move like shit in the exact opposite direction and don't stop until you're damn certain you're absolutely and utterly nowhere near that half-tonne of furry, sharp-toothed, human-eating, ursine bastard sonofabitch.

And when I say move, I mean run.

I pointed myself away from the bear tracks and ran, elbows pumping, boots thudding on the soft forest floor and somehow sensing the trip hazards of tree roots and tanglethorn. After the first mile, I was still so batshit terrified that I didn't even feel tired. After two, it was starting to hurt and I slowed, then sank to the ground until my breathing gradually normalised and I knelt up and looked around me for bear tracks. I couldn't see any, and I couldn't hear any bear noises, although I didn't actually know what sounds a bear made.

I also had no idea where I'd run to. I reached for my map and then suddenly stopped as I heard the sound of rushing footsteps to my left. I lay flat and held my breath, spread my limbs randomly, and tried to squeeze myself into the ground. The steps got louder, and as far as I could tell, they sounded two-legged. They were quickly approaching, and the jumble of noise made it sound like more than one person. Race or a chase, it was none of my concern, and dangerous to even make it so. As long as they went past without seeing me and carried on, everyone was happy.

Unless it was a chase and someone got caught.

Not my concern.

Over the pounding footsteps I heard the breathing, fast and deep, the rustle of clothing as arms and legs pumped for extra speed. Then came a thud, a grunt and a crash as bodies fell to the ground. Groans and curses followed.

And sobs.

'Hold her still.'

'She's mine.'

'No. Please, no!' a woman stammered.

'*Hold* her, Ritt!' said one of them.

'Easy for you to say, Teg,' grunted Ritt. 'Try helping me.'

'Right,' cackled Teg. 'That's probably how she stiffed Marlo and Brig.'

Shit! Marlo and Brig. The ambushing Alphas from a few days ago, and now these two knew them?

Two days ago, that had been me, alone and overpowered with absolutely no backup.

And that's what flicked the switch in my mind.

Never again.

No way were those two toxic, testosterone twins doing that to anyone else. Not on my watch, and not *by* my watch.

I silently rose to my knees like a camouflaged ghost come to life. Ritt straddled the lone girl and fumbled with his clothes. He pulled down his trousers and a dirt-stained, hairy arse winked into view. Teg held her arms and tried to subdue her struggles, unaware of my rushing footsteps.

And then my boot hit his face.

He grunted and flopped backwards. With her hands now free, the girl screamed molten fury. Even in the wilderness, women had fingernails, and along with her high-pitched vocal attack, she gouged at Ritt's face.

I grabbed Ritt and threw him across the small forest clearing. He thumped onto the ground face first. I pulled back and kicked him as hard as I could in the ribs.

'Bastard!' I screamed. I kicked him again and heard a satisfying moan of pain. He wasn't going anywhere, and I checked that Teg was still down. Then I stopped for a second. How do you work through the four D's when there's a casualty?

A casualty. Christ, this wasn't a first-aid exercise, this wasn't book learning, this was for real. I scrambled over to the girl and looked closer. She wore green leggings and a black base layer top, just like the ones I saw on the two Strauss a few days before, only this time they were filthy and bloodstained. Practically ignoring me, she pulled out a knife, rolled over on top of Teg and shank-stabbed him, again, again, and again. Her arm rose and fell like a human sewing machine and the blood flew all around her like horror-flick shreds of red candyfloss. Teg groaned once. His body jerked as the girl, transformed from a grubby victim into a vengeful wildcat, turned his dermal layer into a claret-coloured teabag. I looked at the scene in sudden shock. This wasn't death like it happened during The Change, where people just got ill and keeled over into a copious pool of puke. This was violent and primal. I shook myself free of inaction and looked at Ritt.

He was slowly recovering and getting to his knees.

'Kill him,' said the girl. I looked back at her; lines of dirt and blood streaked her face and strands of straight blonde hair escaped her ponytail. Her cheeks were flushed from exertion, fear, exultation, and ... revenge? I didn't really know.

'What?' I gasped.

'Kill him,' she spluttered. 'What's wrong with you?' She yanked her knife free and wiped the blood on Teg's clothes, then re-sheathed it and ran her hands through the dried leaves. Ritt groaned, shook his head, then looked at us. His eyes bulged wide open, and he pulled up his trousers, jumped to his feet and took off the way he came, fast. I watched him run away, still feeling numb from the visceral jolt of watching Teg die.

I heard an exasperated gasp behind me, followed by a twang and a sudden rush of wind in my ear, and then a crossbow bolt magically appeared in Ritt's back. He spun around in a circle, bent his arm behind him, tried and failed to pull out the bolt. He gurgled, choked up some blood, then fell face down on the forest floor.

Two deaths inside two minutes and my mind reeled at the speed of it. In the distance, Ritt's arrow-shot body twitched, then lay still.

'Thank you, Sister.'

I spun back around and looked at the Alphas' victim. She was sitting on the floor, covered in blood like a slaughterhouse, with a rickety metal-frame crossbow across her lap. Duct tape held it together but there was no doubting her aim. Another bolt was already in her hand and a lock of blonde hair played across her dirt-smudged face.

'What did you call me?' I asked. Jesus, I was actually talking to her.

'Sister.' She shrugged. 'What else would you be?'

'I…I'm…that is…' I stammered.

Then I saw the blood oozing from her thigh. 'Pressure,' I snapped.

'What?'

'Pressure.' I dropped to the ground next to her and pressed my palm hard into her inner thigh. She groaned in sudden pain and I looked into her ice-blue eyes. 'Direct pressure,' I said. 'We need to stop the bleeding.' Instinct had taken me this far, then I realised what I was actually doing. I grabbed her left hand and guided it to the wound. 'Press here,' I said. 'Hard.'

'How hard?' she asked. She was curious, this one.

'Until it hurts,' I replied. 'I'll be right back.'

'What?'

'Got to get my kit.' I said. 'You need help. Right now.'

'But…?'

I didn't stay to talk, just blundered through the undergrowth, grabbed my pack, then dumped it on the forest floor next to her.

'You're a Rescue Sister,' she said. 'That's why you couldn't kill them, right?'

'Keep pressing on that wound,' I said, as I zipped open a side pouch and yanked out the first aid kit. I looked back at her and she smiled at me. She smiled. At me.

'Sorry,' she said. 'I didn't mean to dis on you just now. Killing's not your special, right?' She shrugged. 'I never realised you came out to check on us so soon, but I'm glad you did. Strange clothes.' She looked closer at me. 'When did we ever dress like that, and what's with all that stuff you're carrying?'

'Dress like what?' I looked at my camo, then back at her leggings and top. Both sets of clothing were entirely practical, both completely different. I was dressed for prolonged periods outside, my clothing designed to be hidden from view, and I was carrying lots of kit. She was dressed for the chase, always close to home, moving fast and deadly.

I looked at her legs. Well, her leggings really. They were slicked with blood. My gaze shifted back to her face.

'It doesn't hurt anymore.' She looked at me, and I could see just how pale she was.

Pale.

She'd lost blood.

A lot.

'It doesn't have to hurt to be serious,' I replied. Surgical scissors made short work of her leggings. Whatever Ritt had done to her, she'd been cut hard and deep into her thigh, and the combination of a six inch gash and bright red blood told me the one thing I didn't want to know.

Artery.

After the first aid training, after years of reading and looking at pictures, I knew where everything was. At least, I sure as hell hoped so. I ripped open an out of date field dressing, balled it up and held it in front of her eyes. 'On three, this replaces your hand, right?'

'Right,' she said.

'One ... two ... three!'

She rolled her hand to one side and I pushed the dressing firmly into place. Another strained gasp and she dug her nails into my arm. Even through the camo I felt it.

'Ahhh,' she moaned. 'Aren't you going to give me herbs?'

'Herbs?' I snapped. 'Herbs? You'll need a fuck ton more than bloody herbs to help you now.'

'What do you mean?' Her voice quivered, and I looked at her. She had fine lines of pain at the corners of her mouth, and firm, toned limbs. But even out here, even though no one actually knows how old they are anymore, a woman's age was still a loaded question, and one I'd never dream of asking. Without saying it, I guessed she was somewhere in her early twenties, which would have made her a child when The Change happened. Jesus, even if she *could* remember, this shit would be all she knew.

'That wound needs to be stitched,' I said. 'You've got a severed artery, you'll need fluids to get your pressure back up, and then,' I looked hard at her, 'you'll have to learn to walk again.'

Maybe that wasn't the right thing to say.

'I...' she stammered.

'Look,' I said. 'Just know that you're hurt, but you're alive.' I backpedalled. 'We need to find a way to get you home that doesn't risk my neck from any of your trigger happy sisters.'

She looked at me more closely. *'Now* what do you mean?'

'You still think I'm one of you?' I was looking at the wound, but I could feel her eyes drilling into me. 'Look, I'm not killing you, I'm not doing anything else bad to you, so you figure it out.'

'You're *not* one of them?'

'Do I *look* like an Alpha?' I asked. I jerked my head towards Teg, motionless, cooling and already attracting a thin cloud of flies. She looked at him, and then back at me, her brow furrowed in concentration. 'No, I'm not one of them,' I said, knowing that the hormones hadn't made my voice any less deep. 'But I'm not one of you, either.' *Oh God,* I thought, not daring to look at her, *what is she thinking?*

'You sure as hell don't act like an Alpha,' she murmured. 'That's for sure. Patching me up like this.' *Good enough,* I thought, *I'll take that.* 'And you *really* don't look like one.' *I'll definitely take that!* I pushed down on the field dressing and bound it tightly into place with a compression bandage. 'So what happens now?' she asked. 'I've heard about the nomads out here. I thought they'd all been killed, but two of our Stalkers saw one a few days ago.'

'That was me.' I tried to focus on what I was doing, but I couldn't escape the enormity that I was actually talking to a Strauss, as well as wondering what a Stalker did, although *that* was probably pretty obvious.

'For real?' she asked.

'You don't believe me?'

'I don't know,' she said. 'I've only just met you.' She was direct, and now that she realised I wasn't going to kill her, she was friendly.

'The bleeding's stopped for now,' I said. 'But you need to get back to your own.'

'So they can do all that fluid and artery stuff to me?'

'Can't do it out here,' I said. 'And maybe your people have got more than herbs.' *I fucking well hope so,* I thought, *for your sake.* 'How far away are you?'

'I don't know,' she replied. 'I lost my bearings when I was being chased.'

'And just what the hell were you doing out here on your own?' I asked, trying to sound wise and ignoring the fact that I was doing the exact same thing.

'I want to be a Stalker,' she said. 'They always need new ones.'

'I'm not surprised if they keep coming out here.' I looked at her fragile crossbow. 'And it would help if they gave you better kit. The other Stalkers I saw both had lux bows.'

'You've got to earn one of those,' she said. 'And I'm still not a real Stalker. Not yet. I'm an Outcast.'

'An Outcast?'

She shrugged. 'Some of us don't fit in, don't show the right thinking, so we're put together until the other sisters decide what to do with us.' She gasped as I tightened the bandage.

'I know that feeling,' I said. 'So what did you do that was so wrong?'

She shrugged. 'They said I wasn't a team player, spent too much time on my own, I wouldn't talk about my problems, and not enough friends. Isn't that what it's like out here?'

'No,' I said. 'Out here you've got *no* friends.'

'Then why are you helping me?' she asked.

'Call it the courtesy of strangers,' I said. 'So tell me, what do you have to do to be a Stalker?'

'I've got to survive out here for a day and a night.'

'That's a quick way to get yourself killed.' Kneeling next to her, I checked the bandage and packed away the first aid kit, then pulled out the map and tried to figure out where we were. Purleyont Hames lurked, unseen but somewhere beyond the trees to the north.

If I was going north, *if* I took her back. Which would mean taking a hell of a chance on being used for archery practice, or worse. I really didn't fancy being staked out again. No one who lives out here gets lucky twice.

'What's your name?' I asked her.

'What's yours?'

She was starting to wind me up. 'Alex,' I said.

'I'm called Juno,' she replied.

'What's that?' I said. 'After the place?'

'Is there somewhere called Juno?'

'A place and a beach,' I replied. Well, there *used* to be a place called Juno. But like everything else... I stowed the map and looked back at her. For someone who'd just killed two Alphas, been wounded in the wilderness and was now alone with a stranger, she was amazingly calm. I suppose she could just as easily kill me as well. Maybe I should have taken the knife off her. I looked at the blade in its sheath and she flinched away, closing her fingers tightly on the hilt.

No getting the knife.

I worked out the times and distances in my head. Get Juno close enough to the Strauss to be safely picked up, but far enough away for me not to be. I looked at her leg. Christ, she'd need to be left at the bloody gates in broad daylight to be safe from the predators out here. The forest seemed empty once more, but it wasn't, and the Alphas were the *least* dangerous things to contend with. If I took her back, by the time I left her I'd be off my path, in the dark, and likely as not, being chased.

None of which sounded good.

What other choice did I have?

One, and I didn't like it.

'You can't stay out here overnight.' I glanced at my watch. 'Not like this.'

'What do you mean?' she asked, like she *really* didn't know.

'What?' I said. 'You think you'll cope out here with just your knife and that fancy bow of yours?'

'I did for those two.'

'Sure you did,' I replied. 'After I chinned one of them and pulled the other off you.'

'And then I killed them.' She looked straight at me and I felt a little sick. 'Why didn't *you?*'

'I didn't have to,' I deflected.

'Oh.' She smiled again. 'Maybe you'll be a World Sister one day.'

'What is it with all this sister shit?' I snapped. 'Bloody hell, if I *was* a sister, I'd be a sister who could walk.'

'I can walk.' Her jaw set and I saw the determination once more.

'Sure you can,' I said.

'You're damn right I can,' she replied. 'Watch me.'

I knew what would happen. Keeping her injured right leg in front of her, she bent her left knee, and with her arms straight, she got to her feet with her weight on her left leg.

'See.' She swayed slightly, both arms outstretched to balance her pendulum movements. She stepped forward, shifted onto her right, swayed, spread her arms wide, then crashed to the floor in a less than tidy heap. Straight away, she sat up, repositioned the crossbow on her back, and tried again.

And again, and again, and again.

In the end, she was less than ten feet from where she started. 'No more,' I said, kneeling beside her and checking the dressing. 'Keep this up and you'll bleed to death.'

'What am I *supposed* to do?' she whimpered. 'If I stay out here I'll be dead by nightfall.'

Finally, she was talking some sense.

'Then we need to get you somewhere safe,' I said.

'Where?'

Chapter 8

This was a *really* bad idea.

I kept telling myself that, but I wasn't listening.

And it wasn't like I had a choice. I mean, really, what could I do, let the poor bitch die a horrible death out there, or get myself killed just for taking her back? Neither plan was a winner. It was just that the solution was even worse.

The key to survival, the absolute golden rule, was to avoid everyone.

Everyone. And that included a wounded Strauss who now depended on me to stay alive.

Welcome back to the world of living with other people and having all your plans thrown to shit because no one else's life is as organised, or as planned, as yours.

All of which completely ignored the fact that sometimes, shit just happens.

Like it was *really* her fault she'd been out there in the first place. She'd probably been brainwashed into having to do something, into having to be some kind, any kind, of sister. And she'd settled on the danger and the romance and the excitement of being a Stalker. I'd quickly learned how stubborn she was, and I'd pretty much clicked that if it was something she decided on, then wild horses – which now survived as *very* wild horses – couldn't have stopped her from leaving the safety of Purleyont Hames for her dumbass vocational initiation.

And like it was *really* her fault she'd been chased by the Alphas. Although actually, it might have been, if she'd done anything other than go in the exact opposite direction once she clocked them.

Not for the first time, I realised I'd never been a people person, and even though I knew there was no choice, and that it was the right thing to do, it didn't stop my doubts.

It was a slow, slow walk back to the bunker and Juno limped all the way, leaning against any nearby tree trunk for stability, or my shoulder when there were no trees within swaying reach.

One thing about her though, she asked a *lot* of questions.

'What's that you keep looking at?'

'My watch,' I replied. 'It lets me know what time it is.'

'Why?'

'Why?' I spluttered, looking at her in disbelief. 'What do you mean, why? Why does anyone need to know what the time is? How can you *not* want to know what the time is?'

'Well, what time is it?'

'It's ten o'clock,' I said. 'Which is a long time since breakfast, two hours 'til lunchtime, and we *really* need to speed up to get under a roof before eight o'clock tonight.'

'Okay,' said Juno. 'I didn't understand any of that.'

'Then stop asking me questions,' I muttered.

Advice that she duly ignored.

'Do you dress like one of us?' she asked. 'Even though you're not.'

'You think the Alpha clothes would look better on me?' I grinned.

'They might do,' she said. 'If you, like, washed them and stuff.' She wrinkled her nose. 'You *definitely* smell better than them.'

'Nothing about them is like me,' I said. 'And I'm nothing like them. I never was.'

'Have you got a thing?' she asked. 'I mean, if you're not a sister, you've got a thing, right?'

'A what?'

'You know.' Juno pointed to my crotch. 'Down there.'

'Yes,' I snapped. 'I've got one. Jesus Christ, I was born with it, so there wasn't much I could do about that, but it still doesn't make me an Alpha.'

'That's not what everyone else in the world thinks,' she replied.

'I'm not everyone else,' I said. 'I'm just me, just like you're you, and the rest of your Outcast friends are themselves. You're what *you* say you are, not what other people tell you. Right?'

'I guess.'

'You guess?' I said, scanning the undergrowth. 'More than that, surely. Especially if you don't fit in. You know, you Outcasts sound alright, always questioning things, not going along with the rules.'

'It's not easy,' said Juno. I had my arm around her waist and she leant into me, like a human walking stick. 'Everyone else says we're selfish, that we need to get over ourselves.'

'Don't listen to them,' I said. 'I never did.' Then I thought about it. 'At least, I don't think I did.'

'Me neither,' she replied. 'Can I see it?'

'See what?'

'Your thing.'

'No you can't, for fuck's sake. Bloody hell, Juno, I thought *my* social skills were bad.'

'It's just that I've never seen one before,' she said.

'I guess not,' I replied. 'Living in a camp full of women. Tell you what, the next hopefully dead Alpha we come across, you can look at his thing all you like.'

'What does fuck mean?' she asked.

'What?' I gasped. Her questions hit me like an intellectual cricket bat, while my returning enquiries were like a kind of repetitive, spluttering defence mechanism.

'You've said it already,' said Juno. 'And all the Stalkers say it.' She chuckled. 'Fuck this, fuck that, fuck off, fuck me, fuck you.' She stopped walking in mid-stride and looked at me, and I nearly tripped over at the sudden change in pace. I returned her stare and those pale blue eyes went right through me. 'Does your thing grow and explode when you get mad for it?'

It dawned on me that she'd be recovering for at least a few days, and she'd probably be asking questions the entire time. 'If I fix your leg,' I said, 'do you promise to *please* stop asking me these damn questions?' We started walking again, and a few seconds later I just couldn't help myself. 'Mad for what?'

'*Now* who's asking the questions?' She laughed. 'I'm not sure what mad for it means, either. No one will tell me and I thought maybe you could. Were those two Alphas mad for it?'

'Oh yes,' I said.

'And were their things ready to grow and explode?' she asked, wide-eyed and sounding far younger than I reckoned she was. 'It doesn't sound too good.'

'You don't have to worry about that with me,' I said. 'None of that's me. I might have been born a man, but I was never one for real. Not really.'

Outside of my job, my training, my memories were, at best, a blur. I could really only remember fragments of how I felt before, and nothing about my experiences. But since The Change I'd read books about sexuality and gender equality, or inequality.

Can't blame me for being interested.

'The sisters call it social conditioning,' said Juno, as we brushed into a thick fern belt.

'What do you think?' I asked.

'Maybe they're right,' said Juno. 'But maybe I needed to see things for myself, just to be sure.'

'Questioning the leaders.' I chuckled. 'No wonder they made you an Outcast. Some things *don't* change.'

'And what about…?'

'Quiet,' I interrupted her and looked anxiously ahead, pulling the shotgun off my shoulder at the same time. My ears pricked at the sound of a low-pitched, threatening growl.

Dogs.

I flicked off the shotgun's safety catch and sighted along the barrel, aiming for the sound. All I could see to my front were waist high ferns, dense and green and easy to walk through, but ideal for concealment.

Two disembodied, furry ears poked over the fern cover, telling me that the growling dog in front of us was at least waist high. Slowly, the ears moved to our right and I kept the shotgun slaved to the movement. The danger levels had just gone off the scale, because where there was one dog attached to those ears, there were now sure to be others all around us.

We had just seconds before they attacked.

At times like this, the shotgun became the perfect weapon. All I could see were the ears, but there was a much bigger, hidden target that I absolutely had to hit. One single bullet would likely miss, trigger a charge, and that would be that, two dead women in the backwoods, chewed down to pieces and left to fertilise the forest.

I heard a second growl in the undergrowth to my front. I shifted my aim and fired. The metal butt kicked into my shoulder and the sound of gunfire made my ears ring. A thin cloud of white smoke quickly dissipated in the morning breeze and I heard the agonised whine of a wounded dog. I pumped another round of twelve-bore into the breech and spun a slow circle, taking great care to raise the barrel as I traversed around Juno.

But the wounded dog-whine told its own story. In another world, I'd have been on my knees and in tears at the sound, but out here it was exactly what I wanted. Anonymous and barking clouded out from the undergrowth. I didn't see the dogs, but I saw the ferns moving, hidden pathways all vectoring like a torpedo trail towards the one I'd wounded. Snarls and agonised whimpers were followed by the sickening sound of living flesh being ripped away from a dog's body as the remaining healthy members of the pack turned on their wounded counterpart for some instantly available food.

I took Juno's arm and we slipped away.

Chapter 9

Twenty minutes after I'd fired the shotgun, my senses slowly subsided to half-alert and thinking that maybe, hopefully, we'd got clear.

And all the while we'd been walking, Juno stole curious looks at the Glock and shotgun.

'Don't you have guns?' I asked.

'What do you mean?'

'I mean you use your crossbow and your knife like a natural,' I said. 'And you haven't stopped staring at this.' I patted the Glock in its holster and then unslung the shotgun.

'Do those things kill Alphas?'

'Yes,' I said. 'It's what they were designed for.'

'So how come you didn't use them to help me?' she asked.

'They're a last resort,' I said. 'And they're loud.' I looked at her. 'You heard it back there. One shot at those dogs and everyone who heard it had a fix on us. You fire one of these things and you have to keep moving. A boot in his face was a lot quieter.' I looked at her. 'Just like that bow of yours.'

'Well,' she said. 'However you helped me, I'm glad you did. I'd have helped you, too.'

'Not everyone would,' I replied. 'Including your lot.'

'A sister always would! We—'

'Sure you do,' I interrupted her. 'I was out here a few years ago and two Strauss grabbed me and left me for dead.'

'Strauss?' she asked.

'Oh, that's just my name for you.' I thought about Tanya Strauss, my role model and mentor when I knew her, and in the years since, she'd been elevated in my mind to the ideal woman. I hoped she'd appreciate me calling the inhabitants of Purleyont Hames the Strauss, because if anyone personified that tribe of women, with their unapologetic, fierce sense of purpose, surely it was her. 'Believe me, Juno,' I said. 'They didn't do me any more favours than you showed to those Alphas back there.'

'Were they Stalkers?' she asked.

'Hey,' I said. 'You tell me. All I know is that I ended up staked out on the ground as food for the first furry bastard to find me.'

'But that's not what they do,' said Juno. 'The Alphas, fine, I believe you. Out here, if anyone tries to harm you, then they're the enemy. But you *helped* me, and we're all taught about the Survivor Sisters. If we find them, we bring them in. You're—'

'I'm not a Survivor Sister,' I snapped. 'If that's what it means to be a lone woman out here. I have to stay out here, Juno. It's where I'll always be. I'm not a Sister and I can't ever be a Strauss. I just can't.' I thought back through the years. 'Collar and Addison.'

'What?' asked Juno.

'Collar and Addison,' I said. 'That's what they were called.'

'Really?' she looked at me, wide eyed, and I swear she was shocked. 'Collar and Addison, stalking together?'

I shrugged. 'They made it work. They crept up on me and I didn't even notice.'

'No,' said Juno. 'You don't understand. Collar and Addison working together as a team. That's impossible.'

'Believe it,' I said. 'I didn't actually *see* Addison, I just heard her name mentioned. Collar was the one in my face.'

'But they're both so different,' said Juno. 'Collar, I can believe, but not Addison. She's an Outcast now, just like me. I know her. She's taught me so many things, and she cares so much about everything. She never wanted to be Stalker, even when they told her she had to be.'

'What about Collar?' I asked. 'I reckon she was born to be out here.'

'Collar's a real fighter,' said Juno. 'She's the Stalkers' main girl, and she told me herself that I could be one as well, that I could be just like her if I can survive out here.'

'Well, I don't want meet her again,' I said. 'I don't think I'd be so lucky a second time.'

The conversation dwindled, and after another two hours of tree-leaning and stumbling, we reached the gentle rise that cradled my home. My mind was filled with problems I never knew I'd have, like how to get Juno better, and then how to get her safely the hell away from me without her knowing how to find me again.

'You live in *there?*' She looked at the bunker for the first time.

'Yes,' I whispered. 'And I'd like to live there a bit longer. So let's keep it quiet and make sure no one's waiting for us.'

Lying there in the midsummer warmth, and unseen amongst the undergrowth, it was almost a pleasure to watch that empty heap of concrete. Well, it would have been if Juno wasn't fidgeting next to me, and if I wasn't worrying about her wound. I took a chance and didn't check the stone marker, which wasn't a bad thing as it would have been like giving away my secrets. I might have saved Juno's life, we might have been talking, but really, we'd only just met and that didn't make us friends.

Although we weren't enemies, either.

Juno leaned against me on the walk across the stony undergrowth to the bunker and I felt her strength flaking away. Not bothering with the walk round, I unlocked the door and, once inside, Juno collapsed, slowly pulsing blood over the impersonal cement floor, and I knew I had to take her where I didn't want to go.

I half-dragged, half-carried Juno into the med room, cleared away the piles of boxes and flopped her down on the narrow stretch-canvas camp bed. I grabbed a pair of surgical scissors and cut off her bloodstained and already shredded leggings. Dark blood oozed through the dressings and I knew she was draining close to empty. Her skin was pale and clammy and her eyes were closed. This shit was getting really scary, really quickly, and I didn't need my watch to tell me I had to move fast.

I ripped open a well out of date cannula pack and straightened her arm. Within seconds I realised that veins were a lot easier to find on the practice dummy I'd found, three years ago in the crumbling remains of Basingstoke's corpse-littered hospital. My hands shook as I tightened the tourniquet and looked, felt, *prayed* for a vein to spike, for real this time. She didn't have much juice left inside her, and this was my first hypovolaemic shock.

Hopefully my last as well.

Got it! Hitting the pasta-like firmness which the dusty, faded manual told me I'd find, I gently pushed the needle against the vein's bendy resistance. It slipped in and I felt the first rush of euphoria. I might actually save her.

I sure as hell didn't want to bury her.

I secured the cannula and grabbed a bag of fluid. I don't know what impulse made me go for two whole boxes of the stuff, but I was weak-kneed glad that I had. I primed the giving set and, with still-shaking hands, connected it to the cannula and turned the tap on full.

With replacement fluids going in, I looked at the ripped leg and worked on plugging the gap. Gloves on, I gently prised out the field dressing. There was a hole in Juno's right leg the size of a ripe courgette, and as I pulled out the blood-soaked wadding, the hole gradually filled up with her remaining red stuff. But not before I'd eyeballed the artery. Or, more accurately, two severed artery ends. I yanked open the pristine, but equally out of date, trauma kit and snipped the artery ends shut with clamps. It was warm, red, slippery, and tricky, and if Juno wasn't unconscious by this point, I reckon it would have really hurt.

With the ends clamped shut I slowed down and gave myself time to think. The leak was plugged and she was slowly filling up again. The next step was to make sure that everything held, healed, and didn't get infected.

So as well as treating for shock, this was also my debut at vascular surgery. I peeled off my gloves, dropped my camo jacket to the floor, exposing my arms and t-shirt base layer, then washed up and tried to calm down. I still trembled as I put on a fresh pair of gloves, but I had to do this. The clamps wouldn't hold for ever, and Juno's disconnected arteries had to be stitched back together.

Alongside the fluids, a slow drip of sedative and pain killer rain-dropped into Juno's veins. I found three suture kits in the trauma pack and I had no idea which one was the best. Weren't they all good? Surely they wouldn't have put something in here that couldn't be used, so I guessed it was down to the preference of the surgeon, who in this case was me.

Apparently, arteries could be stitched together and then they'd heal on their own. At least, that was the very simplified summary I'd read, but the books didn't say how sticky the blood got, how slimy and slippery the ends of the arteries were, and how utterly and fiddly-difficult the whole damn process was, especially for someone who wasn't a doctor and had never done it before.

Reality check: she'd bleed to death otherwise, so I really didn't have a choice.

I suppose if you were a really good surgeon, you could have stitched Juno's artery together with Bernina standard embroidery, while at the same time discussing what you'd got up to the previous week end. Not me. It took twenty minutes just to get the needle into one of the split ends. I was dripping sweat-tension by the time I managed it, and felt weak with relief. With the thread safely in place I paused, changed my gloves again and put up another bag of fluid. Juno was relaxed, and her cheeks had coloured up slightly, hopefully because her blood pressure was slowly climbing, and not because I'd introduced an infection.

While I was thrashing around trying to get the first stitch in, I'd learned a lot about the process. The text books and perfect reality would have given me a whole team which I didn't have, so I was left having to do more improvising than an actor with no script. There wasn't anyone to hold the artery still while I stitched, and I quickly discovered it was impossible to hold it with one hand and sew with the other. It was too slippery and I was way too much not trained at doing this. But as rubbery as the artery walls were, the needles were sharp, really sharp, and as if by accident, my first stitch had gone in almost by itself. The trick for me was to leave the artery end alone and simply poke the needle in. It wasn't pretty, and if I *had* been a surgeon doing that for real, I'd probably have been struck off.

But if it worked once, it would work again, so I stuck with the plan and this time the needle slid though vessel walls after just ten minutes. A thin line of suture now joined both artery ends. I gently pulled them together and tied an untidy knot. Then I looked at the needle. It was straight.

The realisation was like pulling open a blackout curtain on a bright sunny day, and I dived back into the trauma kit. *That* was what the curved needles were for. I was almost drunk with the insight flashing through me. With the join now fixed, a curved needle would be almost too easy to make extra stitches and keep the two ends really secure together.

Actually, it wasn't easy at all, it was just less difficult. An hour after starting, Juno's artery was stitched back together, by which point I was sweating buckets.

I stepped back and thought quickly about what to do next. The hole in her leg still had a stagnant puddle of blood in it, but at least it was no longer constantly filling up like a peat bog in the rain. It was time to clear out the wound and get it closed before it really did get infected.

I mopped up the remaining blood pool with the last of the trauma pack's swabs, placed a drain where I thought it should go, and then stitched the hole closed. Christ, she was going to have a scar, and I was making it. Well, the Alphas were really responsible for it, but I was confirming its legacy.

Were scars still a thing for women? I didn't know, and I tried to keep the stitches small and close together. It might have been a long time since short skirts and bikinis, but I reckoned these things still mattered. *I* wouldn't have wanted a scar, and I absolutely did my best to minimise the Alpha's infliction on Juno's leg.

The last stitch went in and was tied off, and by this time my hands were shaking like I was a withdrawing alcoholic. It was done, and now all I had to worry about were the post-trauma complications, with infection and re-bleed up there as worst case scenarios. Sure, I had antibiotics, but they were well past the sell-by date, and what the hell were the best ones to use? By the time I'd delved into my medical books and tried to work it out, Juno would have been carried away by the ghost of sepsis past.

Book learning helped, but it had its limitations.

I looked around the med room in a post-action, adrenaline daze, and I couldn't believe the blood that was everywhere. The place looked like a cannibal's dinner table.

I scooped up the sharps as carefully as I could and placed them on a tray. In my world, safely getting rid of them was called burying it, and one of my OCD, micro-managed routines was to always have a disposal hole dug out the back. After sifting through the needles – scissors were definitely *not* single use – I then put up Juno's third bag of fluid, stopping the sedative at the same time. She seemed asleep as opposed to knocked out. Her breathing was deeper, more regular, and she was moving around slightly, like you did when you slept, as opposed to slab-like immobile when medically zonked. *I wonder what she's dreaming about,* I thought, then shook my head vigorously and got back to work.

Despite my wash-and-reuse existence, some stuff was beyond saving, like Juno's leggings. They were ripped and shredded and bloodstained to hell, but I kind of thought I had a spare pair I'd never taken out of the packaging that would fit her much better than me, so no dramas there. I stepped outside and dumped the rubbish in the current disposal pit and shovelled a layer of earth over it.

While Juno slept, I scrubbed the med room, then cleaned the dried blood off her. Fourth bag of fluid up and I risked a blood pressure check. I'd read the parameters for normotensive, and she was it, just. One hundred over sixty was low but liveable, and after what she'd been through, those numbers were actually a fucking miracle. I felt a warm surge of achievement flow through me. She was going to survive.

Chapter 10

'So you just *wanted* to be a woman?'

Juno was definitely on the mend. After a week-long post-op nightmare where I thought she might die, she was finally out of bed, and if she was awake and not eating, she was asking questions.

'Are you always this curious?' My returning enquiries were less incisive, even though I already knew the answer.

'What?' She sat in a chair that I'd propped up in the small, untidily arranged vegetable garden next to the bunker's east wall, and she watched me strip and clean the Glock. 'You mean normally,' she said. 'When I'm back with the sisters and not being held in a mysterious wilderness hideaway where everything is new? Of course I'm bloody curious, who the hell wouldn't be?'

Sitting opposite her, I realised that the new pair of leggings she was wearing *did* fit her much better than me. 'I guess,' I said, looking back at the Glock. Its receiver was in bits, very small bits, and if Juno hadn't been constantly badgering me about getting some fresh air I'd have definitely done this inside. Lose a firing pin spring out here and you're back to knives and sharp sticks.

And probably a lot of screaming as well.

'You guess, what?' she asked, not letting it go. She *never* let it go.

'I guess I'd be curious too,' I said. 'But when it comes to being a woman, it was more of a feeling, *knowing* that I wasn't supposed to be a man, that I was trapped inside my body. It wasn't what I was meant to be.' I reassembled the Glock's slide. 'And this place.' I swung my arm in a random gesture at the bunker. 'This place was my home, my work, my life, and my boss.'

'Ah,' said Juno. 'The famous Wing Commander Strauss. Her again.'

'Her again,' I said. 'She was okay with me being trans. She supported it; she let me start the process.'

'I think that's okay,' said Juno. 'You're just trying to find out who you are. It's the same with the outcasts.'

'Maybe,' I replied. 'And I'd have been just as much an outcast back in the day as you are now.'

'And you can remember things?'

'Some things,' I replied. 'They gave us these tablets which partially protected our memories, the things that were most important to us. That way, *if* we survived, we'd have something to offer the world, a chance to rebuild.' I shrugged. 'Something like that, anyway.'

'And you remembered that you wanted to be a woman.'

'Partly,' I said. 'But I also remembered my job, this place, weapons, and the rest I picked up from books and practice.'

'You remembered everything straight away?' asked Juno.

'No,' I replied. 'I remembered my name on my own. It's what they asked me after I came round.'

'Who asked you?'

'A nurse. At least, I think she was a nurse.'

'What's a nurse?' she asked. See what I mean, always with the questions.

'Like one of your Healing Sisters,' I replied, then grinned. 'Like what I've been doing for you since you fell onto that Alpha's knife.'

'I didn't fall, you bitch,' she laughed. 'So, a nurse looks after sick people?'

'Doctors did the curing,' I said. 'And the nurses did the caring, or so my medical books said. I don't suppose nurses were ever armed, though.' I snapped a magazine into the Glock and then slipped the loaded weapon back into the holster. 'Time you got up and walked some.'

'Again?' she moaned. 'Come on, Alex. I walked out here, didn't I? And what's with *all* of this time stuff as well? Is that whole thing really worth the one-way trip you were going on?'

'Time gives us structure,' I said. 'And when it's measured, it tells us when things need to be done.' I was explaining it badly, so I did what I normally did and changed the subject. 'And you didn't walk, you hobbled out here with me as your walking stick.'

'You said I did well.'

'You did,' I replied. 'But it's a long way from normal.'

'Give me a break,' she said. 'It's only my first day on my feet.'

'That's right,' I replied. 'And now that you've got your legs back, use them or lose them. Let's see you stand.'

I stood next to Juno. She planted a hand on each chair arm and pushed upwards. She kept her right leg straight outwards and put all of her body weight on her left. Until the stitches really took and that wound healed, it was the best way. Once she was upright, though, walking with both legs was exactly what she had to do.

As her arms took her weight, I could see her shaking with the effort. Sweat beaded on her forehead, and she slowly rose, shaking, swaying. Balanced on one leg, she wobbled and nearly fell. Then she let go of the chair and lunged for my arm.

'This is fucking stupid,' she snapped. 'Before this I was running.'

'And since then you've had a huge injury, massive blood loss, and surgery,' I said. I put my arm around her waist and held her steady. 'Start using your right leg.' Slowly, she brought her right leg down and rested her foot on the ground. 'You nearly died out there, Juno, and it was touch and go even back here. It's going to take a while, and that's all there is to it.' She put her foot flat on the grass. 'Stand naturally,' I said. 'Get used to it again, make your leg work. How does the wound site feel?'

'Sore,' she said. 'Bruised and tight and aching, all at once.'

'Take a step,' I said. 'Good leg straight, right foot forward.'

It was the smallest step and the biggest step, both at the same time. I held her safe with my right arm, she gripped my left hand tight, squeezing my bones almost to the point of fracture. Steady step left foot, then a quick, faint step right foot, body weight back to the left, and start all over again.

'How far?' she asked.

'Ten steps,' I said. Physiotherapist, I wasn't, and this was all being seriously made up as I went along. 'Then turn around and back inside.'

Thirty steps in all, with a sit down break in between. 'This is going to take forever,' sobbed Juno.

'Then it will,' I replied. 'What else were you going to do?'

'You're right about one thing,' she said as we turned towards the door.

'What's that?'

'There's nothing to be curious about back at the settlement.' Her face creased with pain and effort as she took each faltering step. 'Not for me. I might as well stay out here with you.'

That was worrying. That wasn't the plan.

'When I'm back there,' said Juno. 'It's all the same. Get up, do whatever you get told, go wherever they send you, farm the fields, prepare the crops, store the food, fix the houses, repair the clothes.'

'That can't work for everyone,' I said. 'Hasn't anyone left?'

'No,' she replied. The south-facing door got closer, and just inside was another chair, bathed in summer sunlight. 'That's what the Outcasts are for,' said Juno. 'A safe place to stay while you sort your life out. Leaving's a big thing, Alex, only one person has ever done it, maybe, I think. It was just a rumour.'

A half-forgotten comment from Collar seven years earlier floated through my mind. 'They said they had a traitor to find.'

'What?'

'Collar and Addison,' I said. 'When they found me, they said they were looking for a traitor. Was she this mystery person who left your settlement?'

'Maybe,' she stammered. 'I don't know, it's not something I was ever told.'

'Well,' I said. 'Even if it was, she probably didn't make it. I've never seen her, anyway.'

'But out here,' said Juno. 'You're free. You can do whatever you want.'

'That's because I'm on my own,' I said. 'And what I *want* to do out here is pretty limited to what I *have* to do to stay alive.'

'But *you're* the one deciding,' said Juno. 'No one tells you what to do.' She limped through the doorway and fell into the waiting chair. Thirty steps was her absolute limit.

'If you're looking for meaning,' I said. 'Couldn't you have been one of those other sisters instead? It would be a lot safer.'

Juno shrugged. 'I wanted to see what was out here for real, to see if it was as dangerous as they said, if the Alphas were every bit as bad as the sisters said they were.'

'And?'

'They're fast and they're strong,' she said. 'They're not stupid, and they know the land.' She looked at me and smiled. 'I'd also heard about the Survivor Sisters.'

'Like me, you mean?'

'Sort of.'

'Sure,' I said. 'Sort of something, but not really anything. And I don't think anyone would ever welcome me as one of their own.'

'They might.' This subject was becoming a regular, repeated conversation.

'They won't,' I replied. 'Not when they find out about my plumbing.'

'You could explain…'

'Explain what?' I asked. 'I can't even explain it to myself. However much I might know I'm a woman, I'll never be one in the way that matters to the Strauss. Anyway, let's see how all that walking has affected my needlework.'

When she'd been unconscious and in the med room, I'd had to remove most of Juno's clothes, but now that I had to check on her healing wound, it felt awkward, although that in itself had an aspect of normality. It meant there were boundaries and respect. I'd given her a razor from the trauma pack and told her what she needed to do every couple of days, then left her to it. According to my half-memories and the books I'd read, I was sure it was something she'd know all about and was already doing, already used to.

'That's in the past,' she said. 'We only did it back then because we were expected to, because men wanted it. The Sisters tell us this every day. And even if *we* wanted to, where the hell are we going to get enough razors for everyone?'

Surprised? Bloody right I was. 'Well,' I replied. 'You need to do it right now to let that dressing stick to your skin.' Suddenly I wondered about my own carefully hoarded blades and tweezers, and the accumulated hours and days I'd spent over the years removing what the hormones hadn't, all because I thought that's what real women wanted to do, never once realising that they *had* to. And what about the clothes I'd stashed and hoarded? Were they expressions of femininity, or a locked-in identity that society had forced on us?

Us? Well, them, really. Women, I mean, not me.

Not exactly me.

Whatever.

I shook my head to clear my reflections and focussed on Juno's wound dressing. I looked away as she pulled her leggings down to her knees and straightened the waistband on her knickers. I didn't need to see anymore. 'How's it looking, doc?' she asked.

The gauze dressing remained taped into place. The skin around it, normally pale, was still bruised, although the dark blue and purple shading had turned yellow, making her skin look dirty and unwashed, but to me it said she was healing. 'Looking good,' I said.

'Looking good, as in I'm getting better?'

'Much better.' I blushed and looked away once more as she pulled up her leggings. 'You're healing well, the dressing's in place, no strikethrough, no swelling. Keep it clean and keep active, and I promise this bad time will be just a memory.'

'If you say so.' She smiled.

She'd always have a scar, though. Underneath the dressing it was there on her right thigh, high up, from midline to inside. *Were* visible scars still a thing? I'd thought it was, but now I didn't know. Either way, she was still alive, and no infection. Or at least, no infection anymore. What the hell, never mind no infection, she still had her leg.

All of those possible complications had robbed me of sleep in the days after I'd patched her up.

Straight after her operation, the wound had swelled and gone all shades of red and dark blue, threatening to burst the stitches until I'd learned to clear the drain. As soon as I did, a mass of sickly looking green pus seeped along the clear plastic tubing and out of the wound. The stitches held, and according to the leaflets in the trauma pack, eventually they'd dissolve as Juno's skin and muscle knitted together naturally. During that time, I'd decided she was worth at least a few tins of corned beef and a protein shake every other day to build her up. I didn't know about Outcast or Stalker, but she was definitely a regular carnivore sister.

'I don't feel like I'm getting better,' she said.

'You're getting stronger every day,' I replied.

'So you say, with everything decided by the clock, but I feel as weak as a baby.'

The truth was somewhere in the middle. The high-ish protein diet was building her up and helping her wound to heal. She was also young and healthy, but the week she'd spent in bed had weakened her more than I'd have thought, and the short walk around the garden had left her exhausted. She'd need to be a lot fitter before I took her back.

'One day at a time,' I said. 'A few more steps each day. Keep eating, keep everything clean, and you'll get better.'

'Promise?'

I looked into her pale blue eyes, each with a dark blue, almost back limbal ring. 'No lies,' I said. 'You'll get better.' I smiled. 'You'll be in your party frock and heels before you know it.'

'What?'

'Going out clothes,' I said. 'Dress up and makeup.'

'Makeup?'

'Seriously?' I asked.

'I mean, I *really* don't know what you're saying,' said Juno. She smiled at me. 'Sometimes you're so wise and I just full-on get you, and sometimes, like right now, you're like a whole new world of wonder.'

'Maybe I'll show you my wardrobe one day,' I said. 'And you can decide for yourself.'

'How about teaching me to use that instead?' Her eyes shifted to the Glock, and that was dangerous territory.

'Will you show me how to use the crossbow?' I asked her.

'Why not?' She smiled. 'We're friends, right?'

Right.

Chapter 11

'Both arms out straight.' Juno held the Glock as I talked. We stood at the garden's edge and looked across the semi-cleared ground. 'Sight along the barrel and point it at your target.'

'What's the range?' she asked, quickly getting into the terminology, and now able to walk around the house and garden area unaided.

'Target or weapon?' I replied, standing next to her. I no longer had to check on her wound, which was now a jagged but well-healing scar. Juno described it to me each morning, and while my tinned food stocks depleted, she filled out and looked healthy once more.

'Both,' she said.

'Twenty metres if you want a hit, but if he's further away than that, a few rounds in his direction might keep him there.'

She lowered the Glock and looked at me. 'And what the hell is twenty metres?'

I smiled. 'Good question.' With a roughly fifty centimetre stride I walked forty paces, then turned and faced her. 'Twenty metres, okay?'

'What if I miss?' she asked.

'If he's running away,' I said. 'Fire once more. If you're lucky, you'll hit him, but even if you don't, he won't be coming back,'

'And what if he *is* still coming my way?'

'Wait 'til he gets closer,' I said, walking back to her as I spoke. 'Make damn sure you're not empty, and shoot him again when you know you won't miss.'

'They're noisy and they need supplies,' said Juno. 'Why do you even bother?'

'Because they really help when you're facing more than one.' I looked back at her and studied her face, the sharp features and smile lines around her mouth. 'Maybe your crossbow worked when they were loners, but they're running in pairs now, maybe more. And if they're coming straight at you, you'll get one with an arrow, but both, or all of them?' I shook my head. 'The pistol keeps them further away, and some of the Alphas use them as well.'

'What about the shotgun?' she asked.

'It worked for the dogs,' I replied, then shrugged. 'We used to like the animals before, but those days are gone.'

'Everything changes out here,' said Juno. 'And everyone. The world changes us. All of us, including you.'

'Oh, not this again, Juno.'

'Yes, Alex,' she said. 'This again. You don't want to be an Alpha, and you weren't born a physical woman. I get that. Yet here you are, looking like a woman, acting like a woman.'

'Your lot would never accept me,' I replied.

'*I* do, Alex.'

'And what about the others?' I asked. 'People like Collar? You said it yourself, Juno, you're an Outcast. And as much as I believe you, I don't think you're speaking for all of them back there.'

'So what are you going to do with me?' She stopped and looked at me, her cold blue eyes driving into my soul. 'You saved my life,' she said. 'We're friends.'

I smiled even as I looked away. 'That's something I haven't been for a while. But sooner or later, when you're walking and running again, you'll have to go back.'

'Do I, Alex? Do I have to?'

'Do you want to stay?' I asked, and having said it, I really wasn't sure *how* I wanted her to answer.

'What do *you* want me to do?'

'I don't know,' I replied. 'And it's not up to me, anyway. We all do what we want to, or at least, we try to. *You* definitely want to, otherwise you wouldn't be an Outcast. But if you want to belong, if you want to do something that defines you, then you have to go back.'

'If I do have to go back,' she said, 'why don't you come with me?'

Some decisions were just too big to talk about. 'I don't know, Juno,' I said. 'Truly I don't.'

Chapter 12

Juno didn't like the water.

And she liked it even less at night when she was sitting in a boat, all for the first time in her life. But it was part of the plan we'd agreed to. How could she bring the Strauss to me, even if she didn't want to, if she didn't know how to get to me? This way there was no pull on her loyalties and everyone was happy.

Well, Juno wasn't entirely happy, and didn't I know it. Two weeks of talking, arguing, screaming and crying over what to do. We'd gone through the options again and again. Juno stayed with me, I went back with Juno, or she went back and I stayed where I was. But really, what had changed? Sure, we'd bumped into each other in the wilderness, I'd helped her walk again and we'd got to know each other and we'd bonded, but had the rest of the world moved on?

No, it hadn't, and that meant that if I'd gone back with Juno I'd have been mistrusted, unwelcome, and highly likely to be stabbed in my sleep within a week of arriving there. It was a risk I didn't want to take.

And if Juno stayed…?

Neither of us knew.

All we knew was that we were friends and we'd never hurt each other. There was trust and a connection, even though neither of us could put a name to it. The looks we shared and a similar sense of humour, laughing at the same stupid things, finishing sentences for each other. But it didn't fix everything. She was still a Strauss and she had to go back, and that was somewhere I knew I could never go.

My life, my home, my world, it wasn't right for her. It was nothing that she was used to, and one day she'd miss something about her past life. Even if she was an Outcast, she'd always had people around her. She also had rules, a safe home, and a community she belonged to.

Part of me, a big part of me, wanted her to stay, but I was also terrified that something would go wrong. And if things went off-track out here, it could get really bad, really quickly.

I guess I had commitment issues.

Didn't mean I wouldn't miss her, though.

As soon as it got dark, and with the main goal to disrupt Juno's sense of direction and make it impossible for her to ever find me again, we headed northwest, even though the Strauss camp was east. I deliberately took a roundabout route as well, leaving the tracks and paths at regular intervals, and hurrying through empty, crumbling hamlets.

A couple of years earlier, I'd discovered an old fibreglass rowing boat moored up on the river. I had absolutely no use for it at the time, but hoarding was rewarding, so I moved it half a mile from where I found it and then never used it, although it remained there, just in case.

The boat was secured downstream of the most complicated water feature I'd ever seen, near a place that used to be called White Church, or something like that. Not that I'd ever seen a white church, there or anywhere else. A small island sat in the river, still connected, but only just, by a decaying road bridge, while the waterways on both sides of the island had locks that had been closed ever since The Change. The locks' once grey stonework had long since been coated with a smooth green layer of blanket weed, and over the years, the river's naturally changing levels had overflowed the man-made barrier.

Upstream, the waterway remained a whole lot higher, with a permanent trickle running over the lock's green-stained concrete lip. How the hell I'd ever have managed to get around such a monstrous obstacle in a rowing boat, I had no idea. Thankfully I hadn't had to, and it served its only purpose for me, which was a point to navigate to and find my stashed boat, which remained exactly where I'd left it, nestled against a gently sloping bank and tied securely to the rusty metal peg I'd driven into the ground. I grabbed the boat's frayed mooring rope and pulled it close to the river bank.

Juno's nervousness built. She held tightly onto her crossbow, looked sideways at the boat, and stepped away from the river's muddy edge.

'You'll need to get closer,' I said. 'Unless you're real good at the long jump.'

'I don't know,' she quavered. 'Can't we just walk back?'

'We spoke about this.' I tried to calm her. 'Look.' I stepped aboard and sat on the rowing bench. The boat settled an inch lower and pulled back against the two ropes. 'It's fine.' I pulled out a life vest from the small locker at the front. 'Put this on.'

'What's that?' she asked.

'A life vest,' I said. 'If you *do* end up in the water, it'll keep you afloat.'

'*You* said that wouldn't happen,' she hissed.

'It won't,' I said. 'What did I teach you about belts?'

'They're no good without braces,' she replied.

I smiled. 'That's right. So the boat is the belt, and that vest is the braces.'

Juno squeezed into the vest and looked at me with a deep frown.

'Do you think *I'd* be out here on this thing if I thought it wasn't safe?' I asked her. 'Do you think I patched you up just to lose you now?'

'You'll be losing me forever when you take me back,' she said. 'So what do you care if you lose me in the water?' It was dark, but I could hear her getting misty.

'I *do* care,' I said. 'You know I do. But what choice do either of us have? The wilderness is no future for you.' She looked at me in the dark, and I could just about make out her pale eyes piercing my soul as though she'd shot me with my own Glock. 'There's no future for me with the Strauss,' I said. 'We both know that.'

'There might be,' she said. 'If I told them you helped me.'

'And that would be me taking the chances, not you.'

'Will you think about it?' she asked.

'I won't have much choice once we get going.' I smiled. 'It's all you're going to talk about from here on in.'

She stepped hesitantly towards the boat, climbed aboard and sat at the stern. I untied the ropes and we drifted out into the river. It hadn't rained for a few days and the current was slow as it took us downstream. Juno gripped the boat's scuffed sides and I dug the oars into the water and we slid along quietly. The only noises were the small splashes made by the oars. 'How long do we have to stay in this thing?' she asked.

'I don't know,' I replied.

'You don't *know?*' she said. 'I thought you had a timescale for everything.'

'I wish.' I pulled on the oars and we glided along the dark river, illuminated by the occasional moonsweep emerging from behind the light cloud. Shadowed against the treescape on either side of us, the sky had become unspoiled. Light pollution had gone since The Change, and if I wasn't putting myself in harm's way to get Juno back home, and if I'd been back at the bunker, I could quite easily have enjoyed just laying back and looking up at the immense, pristine infinity of the sky, the stars, and nothing else.

But I wasn't. I was rowing a Strauss back to her own, a Strauss that I'd got to know, and also grown to like.

'What are you thinking?' asked Juno. 'Tell me,' she said. 'Tell me anything, just take my mind off the river and the fact that I'm in the middle of it.'

'If you want the truth,' I replied, 'I'm thinking how close I can get you to your friends so that we can both get away and see the morning.'

'You've decided, then?'

'There's nothing to decide.' I carried on rowing. 'I'm not a Strauss,' I said. 'However much I look like a woman, I'm different, and I'll always be doubted. If I went back with you, Juno, too many people would see me as an outsider. Collar, for one.'

'She's only one person,' said Juno. 'And as selfish as it sounds, I'll miss you. We're friends. I care about you, and I know you feel something for me.'

'That's a dangerous thing out here,' I replied. 'And what does being a friend mean, anyway?'

'You saved my life, Alex, *that* has to mean something.'

It *did* mean something. It meant a lot. It meant everything, but I couldn't say it. 'Maybe you'll do the same for me one day,' I said.

'I'll probably never see you again,' she replied. 'Tell me you don't miss the company of a friend just a little bit.'

'When you're not constantly interrogating me, you mean?' I smiled as I said it. 'What will they do with you when you get back?'

She sighed. 'Oh, the usual, ask me about everything I saw, what I did. The Senior Sisters will probably tell me how weak I was that I didn't kill two Alphas without any help, and how back in the day they'd have wasted four just by looking at them. And believe me, Alex, they'll want to know *everything* about you.'

'You did well,' I replied, deliberately ignoring what she said about me. 'You were on your own against two. What were you expected to do?'

'I'd have been dead, and worse, if you hadn't helped me.'

'But you're alive,' I said. 'And that's not just down to me. I might have stopped the bleeding, but a wound like that? Your strength got you through it, never forget that.'

She threw a random stone into the river. 'None of the sisters will say that to me, ever.'

'What about your mates?'

'Mates?'

'Friends.'

'It's not like that,' said Juno. 'You and me, Alex, we're friends, but the sisters, they're like, well, they're just the sisters.'

'If you'd been out here with one of them,' I said, 'with a Stalker, they'd have helped you, right?'

'Sure,' said Juno. 'And like I said, all they'd have done afterwards is tell me about the mistakes I'd made.'

'You didn't make any mistakes with your knife,' I said. 'Or that crossbow.'

My arms started to ache with the rowing, and I let us drift downstream, only using the oars to correct our course. I looked at my watch and the luminous dial came back at me, two forty-five.

'Time to put you ashore,' I said. I pulled hard on the right oar and we swung towards the river bank. I looked over my shoulder for a good spot to bump up against, but the moon had gone, it was still dark, and I couldn't see a damn thing. I had a torch, but lights in the dark were emergency only, otherwise you'd *have* an emergency.

The boat scraped through reeds and bumped against a shallow bank. I picked up the mooring hook and slammed it into the earth, then pulled on the rope and tied off the slack. The current pulled the stern into the bank, and I secured the second hook into dry-ish land, then scrambled ashore and held the boat steady as Juno followed me onto the riverbank. She stood next to me, both of us uncertain at saying goodbye. Seconds stretched out in uncomfortable silence, the wind rustled gently through the leaves, and the river flowed slowly along, timeless and ignorant to the ways of man. Or woman. Or…never mind.

'You know how to get back from here?' I asked.

'Keep the river on my left,' she said, 'and I can't go wrong.'

'But what if you *do* get lost?'

'Emergency flare, then wait for the Stalkers to investigate.' She pulled the small cylinder free of her pouch. I'd turned her around to carrying more kit. She was a long way from webbing and pack, but a few pouches fixed to a belt was my parting gift for her.

The silence racked out in the darkness. It would have been worse if we'd had eye contact. 'I'm glad I was there to help you,' I murmured.

'You mean you're glad you saved my life?' She laughed.

'Well, if you're going to get all dramatic on me, I thought it was just a paper cut myself.' I smiled, and despite everything, I felt the warmth between us. It was good, strange, scary, and welcoming, all at the same time. And then it was heartbreaking.

'Please come back with me, Alex,' she said, her voice soft now, barely audible, but her words slammed through me like a fire hose at three paces.

'I can't,' I said. 'You know I can't.' I thought I was being strong, but *no one* needed to tell me how much my voice was shaking as I spoke.

'I thought you'd say that,' she whispered. 'But I had to ask. Take care of yourself, Alex.'

'You too, Juno.'

'You'll always be a sister to me.' She kissed me gently on my cheek. I pretended not to sense her approach in the darkness, and I felt my chest tighten, even though I didn't want it to. The night-time hid an unseen tear and I blinked it back, ashamed of my weakness.

'You watch where you step, out here in the dark,' I said, in as deep a voice as I could muster, before turning back to the boat.

And after that, I don't know…

Chapter 13

Well, I do know, or at least I did once I woke up to daylight, clearly remembering a fucking hard blow to the back of my head, and now finding myself suspended by my feet and looking upside down at a nightmare congregation of a dozen Strauss, who looked right back at me with stares ranging from curiosity to pure hate. Mixed in among them and looking very small in comparison was Juno, red-eyed, still crying, and trembling.

I swung my head around and saw an uneven laminate floor that had bowed and split, maybe over time, or more likely due to heavy rainfall through a leaking roof.

So this was what Purleyont Hames looked like.

First impressions weren't favourable. I swayed around inside a big, open room with patched up walls. Back in the day, it might have been a village hall or a school assembly room. Now it seemed to be the place for the hanging meat to wait in hopeless misery while their fate was being debated by others.

Which was exactly what they were doing with me.

I looked from my captors to the floor beneath my eyes. My camo lay in a jumbled pile, my hair dangled, and I felt naked in my base layer of leggings and sports bra.

They'd even taken my watch away.

'Why are we still talking about this, Silver?' asked one of them. The one who spoke had sandy hair tied back in a stringy ponytail, which showed streaks of grey that weren't there seven years earlier. The harsh lines around her eyes and lips gave a cold authority to her voice, and an ugly scar ran down the left side of her face.

Collar.

'She's a woman,' said a second Strauss, the one called Silver. 'And more than that, she saved one of our own.' Like the others, she wore a thin green top, but with the addition of a battered, tan leather gilet. Her black leggings matched her skin, which rippled with athletically toned muscles that were strangely at odds with her own hair. Long, once clearly black and lustrous, it was now shot through with even more grey than Collar's. But there was nothing old about her long, toned limbs or her full lips. She was majestic, edging into mature, but she sure held it well. 'We all thought Juno was dead,' she said. 'And if it hadn't been for the stranger here, she would have been. *That's* why we're talking about this.'

'I don't trust her,' said Collar. She walked around me, her limbs moving with athletic fluidity, her steel-wire arms flexing with a ruthless strength.

'You don't trust anyone,' said Silver. 'But she deserves to be heard. She's a Survivor Sister.'

'Oh please,' spat Collar. 'There *aren't* any Survivor Sisters, and there never will be.'

'Hey, Collar,' I said. 'Aren't you that same sick bitch who left me for dead all those years ago?'

Collar froze and her eyes snapped round to look at me.

'Fu-king-hell!' She spat. 'You!' She quivered like a race-hound about to be unleashed. 'You? We left you staked out for dog food. What the hell, you're still alive?'

'I love you, too,' I muttered.

'Weren't you that weird bitch who pissed against a tree, standing up?'

'*That's* what you remember about me?' I asked.

'Yes,' she replied. 'That's what I remember about you. I thought it was weird back then, and now that I'm looking at you once more.' She stared past my face and at my leggings. I felt her eyesight lashing me as though I was naked, and I knew she'd seen through the skin-tight fabric. Her look of triumph and revulsion told me everything.

'A woman, Silver?' she sneered. 'Take a closer look. This one's pipework's a little unusual. I knew there's something about her, him, whatever, that just didn't add up. I *knew* I should have done the job properly.'

'Why's that?' I asked. 'Didn't you find the traitor you were looking for?' I don't know what I was expecting, or what had made me say what I did, but the sudden silence was a surprise.

'What do you know about that?' asked Silver. She looked at me with her large, honey-brown, almond-shaped eyes, and seemed more concerned about what I'd said than my sudden gender revelation.

'I know what you were looking for seven years ago,' I said. 'But only because Collar told me. After that, I had other things on my mind.'

'And I won't spare you a second time.' Collar strode forward and yanked a handful of my hair. 'Tell me how you got away.' I couldn't stop a grimace of pain, but no way was I giving her the satisfaction of crying.

'It was raining,' I grunted. 'The ground got muddy and I worked the stakes loose.' Collar snorted in disgust, with me or the rain, I wasn't sure, but probably not at herself. She twisted my hair once more, then let me go, and I dangled freely. 'I guess Mother Nature was on *my* side that day,' I muttered. 'Nice change of subject, by the way.'

Collar stomped back to me and slapped me hard across the face. 'Who's going to help you now?'

'That's enough,' said Silver.

'No, it's not,' growled Collar. She grabbed my hair again and I gritted my teeth and kept quiet. 'Sure,' she said. 'We found this one when we were trailing Logan.' She pulled my face close to hers and glared at me, her lips pulled back over tightly clenched teeth. 'All that time ago, and now you're here. What are you really doing here?'

'Ask Juno.' I strained my voice, trying not to let her know how much it was hurting. 'It's not like I planned any of this,' I said. 'All I wanted to do was drop her off and go, after I'd got her walking again, after I'd saved her life.'

'So *she* says,' sorted Collar.

'Don't you believe her?' I asked. 'She's got a surgical scar, inner right thigh. Doesn't sound like a spy's work to me.'

'Sounds like an ideal way in,' said Collar. 'So we don't suspect you. That way you can save one life and kill hundreds of others.'

'I've never killed anyone,' I said. 'Didn't Juno tell you that?'

'You know I did.' I heard her voice, and I knew she'd be ignored.

She was. No one believed her. I could see it in their upside down faces, and Collar still wanted to kill me. She let go of my hair and marched over to my camo and kit, which lay in an untidy heap on the floor. 'And why did you come here with *this?*' She brandished my watch at me.

'Give me that.' I made a feeble attempt to reach for it and ended up spinning in an upside-down circle and nearly being sick.

'Sure,' crowed Collar. 'We all know why you want this. We're not fucking stupid, you know. Put one of these on and you learn all about your surroundings. Why else were they called smart watches?'

'It's not—'

'Shut up!' She turned to Silver. 'The stranger's a spy, trying to look like one of us, and he's brainwashed Juno. At best, he's trying to be something he's definitely not.' She stepped back, arms down and hands open. 'It's up to you, Silver, but you know what I think we should do.'

'I'll think about it,' said Silver. And now *she* was staring at me. Not with a killing gleam in her eye like Collar had, but more thoughtful, like she was trying to work me out, or, if I was being optimistic, thinking of a reason *not* to kill me. 'What do you think, Beck?' asked Silver.

A curvy Strauss with smooth, golden skin and scraped-back jet hair shoulder-barged Collar out of the way. Collar growled but stepped back, then glared at me as though it was my fault she'd been pushed aside.

'Juno *has* got a new scar on her right leg,' said Beck, speaking in a deep voice and precise tones. 'It fits with her story.'

'But?' asked Silver.

'But if it happened as Juno said, and if it had been down to us to heal her, we wouldn't have got her back.' Beck took a step closer towards me. 'The stranger has skills similar to mine.' She paused, then looked at me curiously. 'And maybe…*she* did get lucky with her healing. I don't know, I wasn't there, but one way or another, this…*person* you've got here saved Juno's life, and she did a better job than any of my healers, including me. According to Juno, she's got a bitching medical set-up and a whole stash of meds.' She looked at Silver. 'Shit,' she said. 'We've been down to using herbs for bloody months. It might be worth a trip out there just to see if she *is* for real. Apparently she's got a shedload of spare clothes as well.'

'For fuck's sake,' said Collar. 'Get real, Beck. This is bloody serious and you're pissing around talking about clothes.'

'That's because some of us have got this thing called a life,' sniped Beck. She turned to Silver. 'You want my opinion? He, she, or whatever the hell we've got here, saved Juno's life out there. So, for once, Silver, stop hanging on to Collar's every word, because maybe we're *not* looking at an Alpha.'

'I'm not an Alpha,' I muttered. My back and forth swings had slowly reduced to nothing, but my cheek stung and my scalp still throbbed from Collar's attempt to epilate my head.

'What did you say?' asked Silver.

'I'm not an Alpha,' I repeated.

'You're sure as shit not one of us,' spat Collar.

'Hang on, Collar.'

'Bollocks.' Collar pulled her knife free and strode towards me. 'Who's with me?' Raised voices spurred her on and I desperately waved my arms in front of me.

'Hold!' snapped Silver. Collar looked back at Silver, her eyes gleaming with hostility. 'Do you want to fight me for it, Collar?' Silver put herself between Collar and me. 'You might even win. All the gods that we follow know you're our best killer, but it's not always the answer.'

'It is with this freak,' hissed Collar. 'He's an insult to everything that's normal. We'd be doing him a mercy.'

'You had that choice once before,' I muttered.

'What?'

'What if I can help you?' I said. I guess anyone who was facing death like I was would have said the same, and I really didn't have anything to lose. But Collar wasn't listening. She shoved Silver out of the way, strode towards me, her face a silent snarl, her lips pulled back over chipped teeth and a sub-zero gleam in her eyes. She spun me around and pulled back on my hair, exposing my neck for the killing stroke. All I could see was the worn out floor, a lost and wasted last view of the world. I sensed Collar pulling back her arm, ready to drive the blade deep into my carotid artery and end it all in a hose-out of bright red life-blood. I clamped my mouth shut and willed myself not to cry or show myself weak, determined to die well.

I had nothing else to aim for.

'Collar, stop!'

A gunshot reverberated around the hall. Collar released her death-grip on my hair and a mixture of gasps and screams followed the shot. But it wasn't Silver who'd spoken.

It was Juno.

Thankfully, she'd held the pistol over her head and fired up at the ceiling. And really, what was one more nine millimetre hole in an already leaky roof? Much better than a dead Strauss, which would probably have been my fault as well.

'What the fuck was that?' screamed Collar. She spun around and looked at Juno.

'It's hers.' Juno pointed at me. 'And she knows how to use it. These things are powerful, Silver. They can kill people. They can kill Alphas.'

'We can kill them well enough,' sneered Collar. She grabbed my hair once more. 'And we kill them like this.'

'Stop!' This time it was Silver, and this time she was bossing it.

Collar still had hold of my hair and all I could do was hang upside down and stare at the floor as my life was decided.

'Stop for what?' asked Collar. 'It's not like you to be squeamish, Silver. What about those three you skewered last week?'

'They were taken in the field,' said Silver. 'They killed one of ours and they were about to rape another. They deserved no less.'

'This one deserves the same.' Collar pulled back on my hair, exposing my throat.

'For saving Juno's life?' asked Silver. 'I think not. And...*she* has knowledge, she has skills and abilities.'

'*She?*' spat Collar. I felt her body move and I knew she was drawing back her blade. 'He's *not* a woman.'

Maybe not. I kept my mouth clamped shut. *But I'll die like one.* There was nothing else I could do except face my own death with a still, icy courage that I always wished I had, but until that moment, never really knew.

'Stand back,' said Silver, her voice as hard and sharp as the knife Collar wanted to gouge my throat open with. The grip on my hair released and I heard Collar step away from me. I swung freely once more, still hanging upside down, but washed through with relief. I really thought I was about to die, and suddenly I felt the warm rush of life being handed back to me.

'You,' said Silver. 'Stranger. What's your name?'

'Ask Juno,' I muttered.

'I'm asking *you!*'

'My name's Alex,' I said. 'Do you always ask someone their name before you kill them?'

I heard a knife slide free of its sheath and then the sound of a tightly pulled rope being cut through. No longer suspended, I fell to the floor, landing head first in a painful, uncomfortable, but still very relieved heap.

'You know how to use those weapons?' asked Silver. She jerked her head towards Juno.

'Yes,' I said, slowly climbing to my feet and rubbing my head. 'So does Juno.'

'You taught me well,' said Juno. I saw her peering at me through a wall of hostile Strauss.

'Good job you didn't point it at anyone.' I smiled back at her, glad for a friendly face. Then I checked myself. A friend, a real friend. *That* was unexpected. Friends with the Strauss was almost a dream come true, but seconds away from having my throat sliced open by one of them, it wasn't quite the dream I'd imagined. I held out my hand for the Glock before Silver pushed me back so hard I fell flat on my arse.

'Hey,' I said.

'You know how to use them,' said Silver. 'Means you know how to kill with them. You'd use them to kill us? And what about this?' She held my watch lightly in one hand.

'It's a watch,' I said. 'It tells the time, and nothing else.' Silver raised her eyebrows. 'Ask Juno if you don't believe me. Bloody hell, if it made me that clever, how come she got the drop on me?' I stood up. 'But I do know how to use firearms, and isn't that a knowledge you could use?'

'We've killed well enough without them so far,' growled Collar.

'Sure you have,' I replied. 'And the Alphas kill you as well, yes?' I looked at Silver when I said it. 'They even kill the people you love, right?' She turned her back to me and I saw her shoulders tense.

'They do,' she whispered, shakily. I didn't push her for details.

'Some things never change,' I said. 'But some things do. A few weeks ago I sent up a flare and your Stalkers dealt with two Alphas.'

'We deal with a lot of Alphas,' said Collar.

'And two days after that,' I said, 'another pair chased down Juno, and she killed them.'

'So she should have done,' said Collar. 'What's your point?'

'All four Alphas knew each other,' I said. 'Four Alphas working as a team. When has that ever happened?'

A silent response gave me the answer I didn't want to hear. Collar and Silver looked at each other. They were holding back on me. They knew something, probably plenty, and they weren't about to tell.

'Look,' I said. 'It's taken them long enough, but the Alphas are starting to get it together, and you can sit here and wait for them to come to you, or you can get out there and find out just what the hell they're up to.' I pointed to the Glock that Juno was still holding. 'They use those when they find them,' I said. 'But as far as I know, they don't have any stockpiles, no methods of maintenance, and also as far as I know, they haven't got a ready supply of ammunition. But it's only a matter of time until they do.'

I could see that they weren't completely up on the concepts, but if it was something the Alphas didn't have, yet, and if I could get it for the Strauss, then it was a definite advantage.

'You have all these things?' asked Silver.

'Well.' I fidgeted under her piercing stare. 'Sort of.'

Chapter 14

The hall where I'd been held upside down and stripped to my basics was exactly that, a multi-use Strauss hall, where the people in charge met and discussed the running of the camp. It was where all momentous decisions were shared with everyone else, as well as some kind of communal eating place for those who liked to socialise. And at night time, they actually used it to party.

More about that later.

Anyway, it seemed to have value to them, because behind the drama of deciding whether to kill me or not, they were busy repairing the roof and sealing the windows. It was one of the first things I noticed after I stood up and got dressed. Trying to avoid the hostile glares of Collar and four similarly unfriendly Strauss standing behind her, I clocked the crews working on the hall. It was your typical high maintenance, late eighties brick and plasterboard community centre, like ones that must have peppered thousands of housing estates back in the day. And although this one was probably doing better than most of the others, it was never really designed to survive the DIY attentions of a bunch of sisters who had to re-learn everything as they went along.

I made a move to pick up my gear.

'Leave that,' snapped Silver, before turning to Juno and relieving her of my Glock. 'She's your responsibility, Juno. This one has possibilities, and while we're discussing them, you'll introduce her to our ways.'

'Me?' stammered Juno. 'But I'm an—'

'We all know what you are,' said Silver. 'And maybe in this, you can learn about collective values.'

'I already know—'

'Then perhaps it will teach you a certain respect,' smiled Silver. 'The gods alone know, nothing else has.' She turned to me.

'You've come to know Juno, and we're grateful to you for bringing her back. Look at our settlement, our community. Consider what is of value to you. Juno has her view of the world, as I'm sure you do, as we all do. I'll trust you to make up your own mind about us, good or bad.' She threw my watch at me with a slight, almost unseen underhand flick. I caught it one handed and quickly checked it before putting it on.

'Ten-thirty,' I said.

'Which means what?' asked Silver.

'Means I've missed breakfast.'

'Awesome wisdom.' She smiled. 'Be back here tonight for the festival.'

'Festival?' I gawped. It was the last word I expected to hear.

'We'll be here.' Juno grabbed my arm and pulled me towards the slightly skewed doorway. 'Come on, Alex.'

*

Weird simply didn't describe the surge of emotions I felt as Juno dragged me outside. 'Thank you,' I whispered, as I stumbled along a once-paved path that was slowly grassing over.

'For what?' she asked.

'For saving my life,' I said. 'I thought Collar was going to shank me for sure.'

'Normally she would have,' said Juno. 'That was close.'

'You're telling me,' I replied.

'You save me, I save you,' smiled Juno. 'Did you really meet her out there?'

'I told you I did, didn't I? And you heard what she said.'

'Yes,' she said. 'It's just that…'

'No one's ever got away from her before?' I asked, as we put distance between us and the hall. Juno nodded. 'So *she* says.' I chuckled. 'She's all image. And whoever the hell Logan is, or was, I guess she got away too.'

'Did you see the scar on Collar's face?'

'That wasn't me,' I said.

'I know,' said Juno. 'When she came back with it freshly made, she also came back with the Alpha who did it, and he was literally in pieces. What was left of him was slung over her shoulder in a sack.' Juno shuddered. 'And that was the first time *I* saw her.'

'Jesus,' I muttered. 'Talk about creating a first impression.'

'She's the hardest of the hardliners,' said Juno. 'No one hates the Alphas more than her. Convince Collar that you're not a man, or at least that you're on our side, and you'll be one of us, I promise.'

'Beck may have helped,' I said. 'What's the story with her?'

'She leads the Healing Sisters,' said Juno. 'She says she remembers doing it before, and her skills bear that out. She teaches others what she knows, and she knows a lot.'

'She remembered?' I said. 'Like me?'

'She remembered,' said Juno. 'And she's the only one of us who has.'

'What was she?' I asked. 'A doctor? A nurse?'

'Something like that,' replied Juno. 'She's always using funny words about her healing craft, and sometimes she's bitter about her past.'

'What do you mean?'

'I don't know for sure,' said Juno. 'She says stuff about her bosses never trusting her, that they brought things on themselves.'

'Things like the Alpha Bug?'

'Ask her,' said Juno with a smile. 'It would be a great way to get to know her.'

'Hasn't anyone else?'

'Yes,' said Juno. 'And she always gives different answers. But she was big enough to admit that you did a better job than her. You saved me, Alex, and she couldn't have, and she said it. That takes a special kind of strength. Do you think Collar would ever say that?'

'Not in Beck's company,' I said. 'I don't think they like each other very much.'

'Two leaders of two very different teams,' said Juno. 'What do *you* think?'

'So what's this festival all about?' I asked.

'That's not until tonight,' said Juno. 'And Silver said I've got to show you how we live here.'

'Here' being 'there,' *right* there in Purleyont Hames, and after coming closer than I ever wanted to having my throat sliced open, I was actually being shown around. My head spun like a pinwheel at the change and unbelievability of everything. I should have been back at the bunker, planning another trip to Greenwich, and probably thinking about Juno and what had happened to her, but here I was, quite literally in another world. I didn't realise at the time, although actually, yes I did; nothing was ever going to be the same again.

'Come on,' said Juno. 'We need to meet the rest of the Outcasts. I haven't seen them for weeks and they probably think I'm dead. There's no telling what the Sisters have told them about me.'

I'd never been closer than a mile to Purleyont Hames' mixed, intermittent, but always imposing boundary, and after my own home and nothing else for I don't know how many years, the place seemed huge. Where the tarmac roads would once have been clearly marked out and full of vehicles, they were now being smothered by the encroaching grass, taking on the appearance of farm tracks, although they were kept from complete overgrowth by hundreds, maybe thousands of feet. Juno stayed close to my side, but no one else did. Passing Strauss, wearing worn but functional clothing, stared at me from a distance. It felt strange, really strange, to get all this silent attention.

'Everyone's looking at me,' I said.

'No, they're not,' replied Juno. 'They're looking at me.'

'And why would they do that?' I asked. 'Everyone knows you, right?'

'They haven't seen me for ages,' said Juno.

'No one's seen me at all,' I said. 'Won't that make them just a little bit curious?'

'Not a bit of it.'

'Who's your new friend, Juno?' asked a Strauss in olive green overalls, pushing a rickety wheelbarrow that was loaded up with firewood.

'See what I mean?' I whispered, keeping my eyes on the ground and trying to think small.

'She's a Survivor Sister,' said Juno. 'Just in from the wilderness.'

'No, I'm not,' I hissed, and Juno elbowed me in the ribs.

'Welcome, sister,' said the Strauss, then carried on with her day.

'See what I mean,' grinned Juno. 'She called you sister because what she sees is a woman. How does *that* feel?'

Even if it was only fleeting, it felt good, I have to say.

'We're all blind!' a voice suddenly called out. I looked left and saw a lone Strauss standing in the middle of a small grassed area. Long-limbed and gangly, with an untidy shock of curly ginger hair, she threw her arms out in front of her, as she implored the few Strauss who were near her to heed her words. 'I was born with poor eyesight,' she said. 'But you don't need perfect vision to see that we're not alone out here, and we need to make new friends.'

'That's Arc,' said Juno. 'And she's an—'

'Outcast?' I asked.

'Not too hard to work out,' smiled Juno. 'You don't want disturb her once she's started. You'll see her later.'

'She's talking sense,' I said.

'Until she starts going on about making friends with the Alphas,' said Juno.

'It might come to that,' I replied. 'And if you want to last more than one generation, it'll *have* to come to that.'

'I know,' said Juno. 'We all know, but we don't have the answers, and that's what makes Arc a problem for the Senior Sisters. Most of the things she says makes the Sisters look weak because they don't know what to do.'

'Maybe they should listen to her,' I said.

'Would you?' asked Juno. 'She says she met an Alpha and they *did* become friends.'

'Holy shit,' I said. 'How did *that* happen?'

'She's pretty sketchy on the details.'

'Of course she is.'

'That doesn't mean she's lying,' snapped Juno. 'Who would have believed me if *you* weren't standing here right now?'

*

Back in the day, Purleyont Hames had been a prosperous suburban estate on the edge of Reading, with bungalows and houses surrounded by pleasant valley gardens that were never too close to each other, but never that far away, either. Now though, some of the homes had missing roof tiles and windows, while others had been patched up with rudimentary repairs from uneven planking and dry stones.

There were also open areas of grass that were slowly turning to meadow, with groups of ten or more Strauss sitting together, talking, laughing. As we walked past, the conversations stopped; they stared at us, and my nervousness built.

'They're looking at *me*,' said Juno.

'They're bloody well not,' I replied.

'They're just curious, that's all.'

'They'll be more than curious once they find out.'

'My lips are sealed,' smiled Juno. 'How many times do I have to say it, Alex, you don't look like an Alpha. But even if everyone around here does figure it out, and sooner or later they will, it's not a problem.'

'Are you sure about that?' I asked her. 'Christ, Juno, I feel like I'm walking around here naked.'

'Now *that* would get you some attention,' giggled Juno. 'But, really, believe me on this, Silver's word is the law. Anyone who harms you will answer to her, and that's a line no one, not even Collar, would cross.'

'Really?' I asked. 'Silver's that powerful?'

'I promise,' she replied. 'You've been an outcast in the wilderness since forever, but now you're an Outcast in here, and in here it's more than just a name.'

We walked along pathways that gradually became less populated, into an area that was slowly surrendering to a slow growth of urban trees, and then on to what was once a close of six houses. Three were deserted and derelict, showing collapsing roofs and gaped open doorways and windows, with no attempts made at repairs. The other three were partially covered by a patchwork of yellow and blue tarpaulins, and they seemed secure and waterproof at the doors and windows.

'Welcome to my home,' said Juno, sweeping her arm towards the house in front of her. 'It's a bit different to yours.'

A plywood panel front door with fading paint was flung open and a raggedly dressed group of Strauss boiled out and swarmed around us. I was utterly ignored as they surrounded Juno and crowded her with questions. They ranged from mid-twenties upwards, all heights and looks, with hair and skin colour as varied as their entirely reclaimed clothing.

'Girl, are you okay?'

'It's been weeks, Juno, the bloody Secret Sisters have already allocated someone else.'

'I heard you were dead.'

'I heard you'd been kidnapped by the Alphas.'

'I heard you'd set up a whole new tribe.'

'Juno, what happened? What happened to you?'

No one was looking at me. For all I knew, they just saw me as another Strauss escorting Juno back home, and that was fine by me. I needed the anonymity. There were just too many thoughts and emotions rushing around inside me, too many huge, massive changes to my life and my world. I needed not to be stared at and questioned, just for a while.

But I knew *that* wouldn't last.

'Let's take this inside,' said Juno. 'I need to introduce you to Alex.'

I followed the Outcasts into their collective home. It would have been a standard family house before The Change. The open plan lounge diner was cosy and accommodating. *Really* cosy for sixteen.

Sixteen, including me.

Having taken social distancing to the absolute extreme with my solitary lifestyle, the whole shoulder to shoulder thing took a lot of getting used to. I was ushered towards a wooden kitchen chair and I sat down, while the one sofa and additional mismatched furniture was quickly occupied, along with the bottom two stairs. A well-placed wood burner sat in the room's corner, along with a ready supply of firewood. I took in the well-fitted and functional windows, threadbare carpeting, but also an air of general cleanliness. No dust or grime, not even any muddy footprints on the floor. They were living together and they were making it work.

The Outcasts, still ignoring me, and I didn't mind that, wore a mixture of distressed, often repaired clothes: shift dresses, leggings like Juno's, threadbare leisure suits. None of it was new, but it was all comfortable and practical. Whatever the resources were for everyone else, no one seemed to allocate too much to the Outcasts.

And I think they kind of liked it that way.

'What happened to you, Juno?' asked a short, dark-haired Strauss. Beneath an untidy fringe, her brown eyes stared out at the world and flickered between me and Juno.

'Two Alphas chased me down,' said Juno. 'I took a bad injury, and I'd have died out there if it wasn't for Alex here.'

Like a Wimbledon audience following the ball, or was it an argument, fifteen sets of eyes then fixed straight over to me. The stares were friendly, but the unexpected and sudden attention made me shift uncomfortably. I opened my mouth to speak, to say something, although what, I didn't know.

Juno was way ahead of me.

'This is Alex,' she said. 'She's got a cock, but she's okay. She saved my life, she got me better, and she brought me back.'

So much for Juno's lips being sealed, and it wasn't how I'd have gone about getting a stunned silence, but it sure as hell worked. And like she said, it was going to come out anyway, figuratively, at least. Better to rip that sticking plaster off right now.

Twenty seconds later, without even *looking* at my watch, and, 'A cock, you say,' said an Outcast. She looked at me directly and the first thing I noticed about her was a thick growth of black hair in two long ponytails that snaked over each shoulder, framing her heart-shaped face. A frayed and tasselled buckskin dress stopped at her knees and I looked straight back at a handsome and very well groomed thirty-something woman. I fidgeted slightly under her unswerving gaze. Her lightly tanned face didn't have the fullness of youth, but her skin was smooth and unlined, her large brown eyes knowing but still tender and forgiving, and despite her words, I sensed more curiosity than hostility as she studied me. She might have been the same age as me, but she absolutely looked a whole lot better. Her fingers were clasped together and resting on her knees, and she leaned forward as she spoke. 'That would make you a man?' Her voice was deep, like mine, but not like mine, hers flowed like a slow-moving river in summer. 'That explains why you're such a tall sister,' she said.

'You're right,' I replied. 'I *was* born a man, and biologically at least, I guess I still am.' I looked jealously at her buckskin outfit. She wore it *really* well. 'Nice dress, by the way.'

'Thank you.' She smiled at me and I relaxed ever so slightly. 'I wish I had another one. We don't have too many spare clothes to go around.'

'Alex has got loads,' said Juno. 'Well, she says she has, but she's shy about showing me.'

'I'm a bit of a hoarder,' I murmured.

'Aren't we all,' said Ponytail, looking at me intently. 'So, tell me, how can you *possibly* be a man when you absolutely don't look like one?'

'This is the real me,' I said. 'This is what I am. I've always known I was a woman, but before, I'd look at myself in a mirror and see something different, and it broke my heart.' I shrugged. 'That's probably really lame, but I stopped looking for answers years ago. I just am what I am.'

'So, you simply *changed?*' asked Ponytail.

'One operation a long time ago,' I said. 'And then hormone pills and motivation,' I felt in a weird way like I was at some kind of job interview. 'It took a long time.'

'It must have done,' she smiled at me, showing white, even and very well kept teeth. 'But you can't be all bad, though, if you've got a thing for keeping hold of clothes. All you need to do now is wear them a bit more often.'

'Don't bother,' said Juno. 'I've been trying for weeks.'

'Really?' said Ponytail. 'So then, Alex, you've truly, actually, still got a flagpole?'

Christ, but they were curious, and more blunt than Collar's opinions.

'I've got one,' I replied. 'But it doesn't fly at full mast anymore.'

'Does that mean you've stopped spewing your glue?' asked the dark-haired Strauss with the untidy fringe.

Gasps and embarrassed laughter fluttered around the crowded room.

'And what would you know, Varia?' asked Juno. She looked back at me. 'What would any of us know?'

'It's the easiest time to kill them,' said Varia. 'When their minds are stuck between their legs. I've seen it loads of times.'

'You haven't seen it at all,' laughed Juno.

'If it answers your question,' I said. 'None of that works anymore. Not for me. The hormones did their job well, it's shrunk down to an eelskin, and all it's good for now is peeing.'

'So you're no good for breeding?' persisted Varia. 'That'll piss the Seniors off.'

'I'm as barren as they come,' I replied. 'And I can't say I'm unhappy about it. But even if it didn't fall off, and even though it *is* still a part of me, I'm not the enemy. I'm not a spy.' I looked at Juno. 'I didn't even want to come here.'

'You think you didn't.' She blushed.

'Born a man,' said Ponytail. 'But now, let's face it, you're a woman.'

I'll never know if she realised it, but saying the absolute right thing at the right time didn't come any better than that. If I could have climbed onto the house roof right then I would have, and I'd have sung with happiness. Instead, I sat where I was, smiled, *really* smiled, and turned back to Ponytail.

'Your turn first,' I said.

'My turn to do what?' she asked.

'My name's Alex,' I said. 'What's yours?'

'Addison.' She smiled and flicked her ponytails over shoulders.

'Addison?' I stopped thinking about clothes and being happy. Addison! I never saw the second Strauss with that name when her and Collar staked me out, I just heard a disembodied voice. Somehow this long-limbed and beautiful person wasn't the reluctant killer I had in my mind, but if the dress fits. 'I've heard that name before,' I said. 'Were you ever a Stalker?'

As though an unseen button had been pushed, the room suddenly felt ten degrees colder.

'A long time ago.' Addison shifted her gaze.

'Seven years ago?' I asked.

'We don't measure time in that way.'

'*I* do.'

'Addison didn't fit in as a Stalker,' Juno said quickly, before looking at me.

'No, I didn't,' said Addison. 'I ended up being paired with Collar, and she's a bit of a psycho.' She clenched her fists and her gaze flickered around the packed room.

'I know,' I replied. 'I've met her twice. Once in here, and once out there. That was a long time ago as well. Collar and another Stalker left me staked out for the dogs to find, and it was only the rain that saved me. The other Stalker was called Addison.' I looked at her as I spoke. 'Was that you?'

I felt everyone's eyes on me, but this time my hair prickled at the back of my neck, and danger signals tingled up and down my spine. My heart rate doubled and I felt my guts sliding south.

'I knew it was you,' said Addison. 'As soon as I saw you. But it's not an easy thing to say. My days as a Stalker aren't something I like to talk about. I hoped that maybe you wouldn't recognise me.'

'I didn't,' I said. 'I didn't even see you the last time, I just heard your voice. I heard it, and I remembered it.'

'We didn't kill you,' said Addison.

'Collar sure as hell wanted to,' I said.

'But not me,' said Addison. No smiles anymore, no light humour. She trembled slightly as she looked at me, her fingers twined together with bone-snapping force. She was visibly nervous but her eyes still met mine. 'Look at me.' She sat up straight and spread her arms wide. 'I'm not a Stalker anymore. Not that I ever was, not really, and now I'm an Outcast, just like you. I couldn't kill you any more than I could kill anyone. Collar was right about me, I'd never have made a Stalker, even without her example to live up to. You were my last chance.'

'Your last chance?' I asked.

'Yes.' Addison nodded slowly. 'I had to come back from that mission with a kill. If I was going to be a Stalker, someone had to die.' She looked at me and this time it was my turn to fidget. '*You* had to die,' said Addison. 'And if I hadn't been there, you would have.'

'Should I thank you for that?' I asked.

She smiled. 'Maybe I should say I'm sorry. And I am. Maybe the rain did you more favours than I did.' Addison shrugged and looked at the outcast house. 'It got me kicked out of the Stalkers and sent back here for the third time, and I think even the Senior Sisters gave up on me after that. And now, here you are as well.'

'Here I am,' I repeated, softly. 'So what happened to Logan?'

'That's not a name that's been said for a long time,' said Addison. 'A lot of people haven't heard about her at all.'

'Collar said it an hour ago,' I replied. 'Was she the traitor you were after when you found me? Did she get away? Did she get away because you were too busy debating my future?'

'She got away,' said Addison.

'That's two people who didn't die on your watch,' I said. 'I'm starting to like you, Addison.'

She smiled once more, and my opinion of her softened. 'Logan stood against everything we believed in,' said Addison. 'She didn't even find her calling among the Stalkers. She made Collar seem positively mild, and if she *is* still alive, then the wilderness is probably the best place for her.'

'Do *you* think she's alive?' I asked.

'She was a Stalker for a time,' said Addison.

'Like you?'

'*Nothing* like me,' said Addison. 'She couldn't see our strengths, our togetherness. She was wayward and solitary.' Addison looked at me. 'And she was dangerous. Logan spoke of dark energy, of power, of ruling over others and taking by force. She wanted to tear it all down because she wanted to control everything and everyone. She was charismatic, addictive, even.' Addison looked deep into my eyes as she spoke, and I could tell that whatever Logan had done, whatever she'd said, Addison couldn't quite bring herself to hate her. 'She was a natural leader,' said Addison. 'She was a *good* leader. She made people want to be with her, want to be on her side. She was exciting and promised adventure and glory, and also the power to know what was over the next hill.'

'No chance of her becoming the leader here, then,' I said.

Astonished gasps whooshed around the whole room.

'Oh, she wanted it,' said Addison. 'She wanted it all. She had the desire, she had the passion and the vision.'

'And people agreed with her?' I asked.

'She told everyone what they wanted to hear,' said Addison. 'She made it sound possible. But if she'd ever become leader, she'd have stood no opposition. She wanted people to see it her way, and she'd make everyone think she supported them, but she didn't. She used other peoples' support for her to gain power over them, even though she realised it would never happen here, not in the society we've built, so she left. She was the only Sister who ever took that decision, and she killed two Stalkers who tried to stop her.' Stunned silence echoed around the packed living room. 'And until now,' said Addison, 'until you came here to talk about it, Alex, no one else ever has. But I'll tell you this, if anyone could survive out there, it's her.' Addison looked at me, her wide eyes dewy with restrained tears. 'Maybe it's best if she didn't.'

'And that's enough heavy talk until after the festival,' said Juno. 'Right now, we've got a new girl in the Outcasts, and we have to show her around.'

Chapter 15

One thing the Outcasts had in common was their independent thought. In some way or another, they were seen by Silver and the rest of the Senior Sisters as a glitch, a disagreement, a challenge.

Which meant they all had kind of an attitude problem.

And that meant I kind of liked them. Even Addison. I mean, all she wanted was to belong, to be accepted, just like me, and when she was a Stalker, she'd just been in the wrong place at the wrong time, like me.

Another rebel, another misfit.

Another Outcast.

So yes, I liked Addison, which was a whole lot easier to say because I hadn't died out there, which *was* thanks to her. When all was said and done, maybe I *did* owe her. And she seemed to like me too.

Annoyingly, Juno picked up on it straight away.

'You like her,' she said, sitting next to me in the Outcasts' crowded living room and talking loudly enough for everyone to hear.

'I like everyone,' I replied, evasively.

'Even Collar?' She smiled.

'Okay,' I said. 'So maybe I just like the Outcasts.'

'Sure,' she chuckled. 'Some more than others.'

Time to change the subject.

Paradoxically, the Outcasts were actually tolerated for their individuality, and whether that was since, because of, or in spite of, Logan, I wasn't sure. But in a world where togetherness was everything, the Outcasts were still a part of the equation. They weren't banished or kicked out of Purleyont Hames, and really, it would have been a death sentence if they had been. They were simply put to one side until they came around to the group way of thinking.

Although it didn't seem to have worked too well for Addison, and because Addison was looking out for Juno, I wasn't holding out much hope for her, either.

But it was still Juno who showed me around, although only after I'd checked my watch at twelve, fidgeted, and felt a sudden urge to make lunch.

'Are you hungry?' She laughed.

'That's not important,' I replied. 'It's—'

'I know.' She smiled and passed me a handful desiccated fruit. 'Pit stop, right? Because our stomach is an empty pit by lunchtime.'

'I must have taught you *something* right,' I said.

'And now it's my turn to teach you, so let's go.'

Outcast or not, though, what Juno showed me, where she took me, it was all staged, it was all controlled, and it definitely didn't include everything. 'We can't go there,' and 'I can't show you that,' were probably the most repeated things she said over the next few hours. I saw what she, or they, wanted me to see, and no more.

But what absolutely couldn't be hidden was the real sense of a driven, united society. Within this improvised, semi-fenced, and partially gated community, there were more houses than people, although their state of repair varied massively. Some were little more than collapsing shells, now used as quarries. Others remained pristine, albeit with a lot of work needed to keep them so. And then there was the huge spectrum of everything else in between, like the three houses the Outcasts lived in.

Multi-shade tarpaulins covered many of the roofs, with two particular colours being the most common. 'Why is yellow and blue everywhere?' I asked.

'It was what we found,' shrugged Juno. 'Something must have been going on at the time, but after the Alpha Bug, we can't remember.'

Flickering memories of a war, a real war in my lifetime, feathered through my mind. Had I been a part of it before The Change, or was I just reading the signals about what was going on, supposedly safe in my bunker. I didn't know, and I shook my head to focus on what Juno was showing me.

'So what about the bridge?' I asked.

'How do you know about that?' Juno's head snapped round to look at me.

'Your settlement stretches both sides of the river,' I said. 'Right?'

'Maybe.'

'And I bet you don't use it just to get from one side to the other.'

'Well...'

'And now you're *really* giving it away.' I laughed.

Awkward silence, and friend or not, I was still an outcast, no matter how much I was one of *their* Outcasts.

'You may as well know,' said Juno. 'We use a water mill.'

Which probably sounds like nothing to you. It may even sound like less than nothing. A water mill? Is that it? What kind of old technology is that?

Pretty damn constant and clever renewable technology is what it was, which made it very valuable. And Juno, politely but firmly, wouldn't let me anywhere near it.

'You've got electricity?' I asked. She looked away and didn't say anything, although it wouldn't have taken the brains of Hypatia to work it out. 'Come on, Juno,' I said. 'I'll know it as soon as you switch on a light.' I smiled at her. 'I showed you mine, didn't I?'

'You're asking a lot,' she murmured. 'And I've been told, very clearly, what *not* to show you.'

'Did they tell you to bring me in?' I asked her, suddenly suspicious, and instantly ashamed at myself for the accusation, and then wondering, all at the same time, why I hadn't thought of it earlier.

'It's not that easy,' she stammered. 'It's not as clear as that.'

'I bet it's not,' I said. 'And I don't think Addison would have said anything, but I'm guessing Collar's been briefing every Stalker, every want-to-be Stalker, all about me. Killing me was Addison's ticket into the Stalkers, but she couldn't do it and they kicked her out for it.'

'You *do* like her?' She looked at me and I fidgeted.

'She's growing on me,' I said. 'Now that I'm getting to know her.'

'She should never even have *tried* to be a Stalker,' said Juno.

'So, what about you?' I asked. 'Did they offer you Addison's spot on the team for catching me?'

'No,' she said, avoiding my eye for the first time ever. Something wasn't right there. 'Collar can't make offers like that. She can't send us out to kill. The Stalkers react to signs, they follow tracks. She—'

'She's filled up with hate,' I said.

'Can you blame her, Alex?' asked Juno. 'After what they did. You've seen the scars. They'd have done worse if they could, and then they'd have killed her. You saw what they did to me, you knew what they wanted to do to me. You *can't* think any different. Have you seen *any* good in them, ever?'

I thought about Juno's question, then thought about all of my close encounters with the Alphas. It seemed as though their most extreme traits were all that survived the Bug. But I knew that men could be better than that; I'd seen them better, remembered them as better. Was that all gone? If it was, I despaired for humanity's future.

'Not yet,' I admitted.

'And what would happen if they got loose in here?' She turned a full circle as she spoke, her eyes taking in everything around her.

'Nothing good,' I said. 'But that's not me. I'm not one of them.'

'And I'm not Collar,' she said. 'I *did* want you to live here with us, and maybe I was being selfish, maybe I shouldn't have done what I did. But you're here now, for better or worse, and it was all my idea. I can't explain why I did it, Alex. Maybe I didn't think it through properly, but I absolutely didn't want you to be harmed, I promise. Now, do you want to see what's in here or not?'

Juno walked towards what was once a detached townhouse, although this one looked as though the roof had been partially hewn open, with great gaping holes smashed through the ceiling tiles of what otherwise looked like a still sturdy building. From the ground, I saw what looked like rafters sawn through.

Juno led me inside. 'This is where some of the Stalkers are based,' she said. On every floor, each room I peered into had two or more Stalkers. Their bows and hostile looks marked them out as different, reminding me of the way that Collar glared at me, even when I wasn't hanging upside down.

'More misfits to show around, Juno?' asked one of them.

'I thought that's what you were,' she shot back.

'Always a wise-arse.' I looked nervously at the Stalker who spoke. A super-large knife was sheathed at her belt, and she held her bow loosely in one hand, although it seemed an extension of her own anatomy. 'And what are *you* looking at?' she growled at me.

'You don't know, either, huh?' asked Juno, while I was still wondering if I should say anything.

'Get your guided tour done, Juno,' snapped the Stalker. 'Then get out of here and take your mother with you.'

'I'm younger than you, bitch,' I muttered.

'And you don't even know who yours is,' replied the Stalker, who glared at me and then went back to the open window. She was right about being younger than me, though, and we both knew it. Her lean, muscular limbs were tight and springy with youthful vitality, and I knew that however good I might have looked, I was fast losing that one thing, and that one word that had definitely survived The Change: collagen. If only it existed as abundantly as the times it was mentioned in the books I'd read.

The townhouse wasn't a place to live; it seemed more like a ready-room for armed fighters to head out at a moment's notice. 'We've got towers like these in a few places,' said Juno. 'There's a great view from the top.'

On the second floor hallway, a ladder had been bolted into place between the floor and the loft hatch. I followed Juno as she rattled up the rungs and onto a solid plank floor space, where another three Strauss sat on worn kitchen chairs. Juno and I made five, and that made it cosy. Something as simple as being cramped together, up close and personal, it took some getting used to.

The two holes that had been hacked out of the tiles and woodwork for observation had crude covers, made from ever-present yellow and blue tarpaulin, I guessed for protection from the rain. The gable ends had windows, both opened in the summer heat, and Juno ushered me towards one of them. I peered out, and over Purleyont Hames' rooftops, I saw fields. Proper, old-style fields with crops lazily swaying in the gentle breeze, and intermittent figures of Strauss farm girls tending them.

'We eat what we grow,' said Juno. 'We send foraging parties into the forest on 'fruit and root' missions, and a part of every harvest, and every bringback from outside, gets prepared and stored, just in case.'

'In case of what?' I asked.

'Anything,' said Juno. 'See? We're just like you. Belt and braces. You're not the only one who can figure things out, right?'

'Right,' I said. 'You've got the numbers to make it work. And your water mill gives you running water as well as electricity.' I looked back at Juno and smiled at her, then froze immobile as behind me I heard a knife being drawn.

'This one doesn't know how to keep her gob shut.'

'Tell it to Silver,' snapped Juno. 'And can you *see* the water wheel from here?'

'Don't even say it!' growled the Strauss.

'Oh, bitch please,' gasped Juno. Her eyes flickered back to me and she smiled. 'Alex here knows all about the place, and she has done since before you were born.'

'Hey,' I said. 'I'm not that bloody old.' I turned around and stood eyeball to eyeball with the knife-Strauss. Her cold eyes bored into me and I stared back at her.

'Just get out of here,' growled the Stalker.

'We're going,' said Juno. 'But not because of anything *you* said.'

'I didn't see any solar panels,' I said to Juno, after we were standing outside once more.

'The only Strauss who *has*,' said Juno. 'Is me, when I saw them at yours.'

'Does Silver want them?' I asked.

'She doesn't know about them,' said Juno. 'I swear it.'

So what did they want? They were giving me the grand tour for a reason, and I developed a feeling that the festival, whatever *that* was, would turn into a hard-bargaining session between me and the Strauss.

'You probably don't need it, anyway,' I said. 'You've got food, you've got shelter, running water *and* electric. Does your fence go around everything?'

'Come with me,' said Juno.

It was a ten minute walk to the perimeter, where I had another flash-memory from back at the bunker, when it *was* a bunker. Lectures I'd had and pictures I'd seen showed the old borders between east and west Europe, and it must have looked something like the scene right in front of me. Houses and bungalows and even streets suddenly stopped, seemingly erased, leaving just foundations and occasional brickwork stumps poking out of the grass like broken teeth. The roads had been completely obliterated, not through demolition, as far as I could see, just from not being used. Nature's inexorable reclamation was there to be seen, or not seen as the bricks and mortar faded away. The asphalt road was there in patches, but with each passing year, it took more and more imagination to see it how it used to be.

Unlike the stretch of fence that slashed right through half a mile of cleared grassland like a ten-foot high, mesh blade. There was a clearly trampled path on the inner edge, and I looked left and right, only to see the crosswire barrier swallowed up by the trees.

'More of this is what everyone talks about,' said Juno. 'It's what everyone wants, but it's not complete and it probably never will be. Between you and me, Alex, there's more gaps than fence. Some people call it the Trump wall, but even the ones who do can't say why.' She shrugged. 'We can't be everywhere, can't protect every way in, every approach. Where there's a fence, we patrol on our side of it, the same with the gaps in between, always looking for signs. If we see anything, then the Stalkers are sent out.'

'So tell me about the sisters,' I said. 'When you were recovering, there was a sister for everything. What's that all about?'

'It's like this,' she said.

If there was one word the Strauss liked, it was sister. Healing Sisters did the obvious. Rescue Sisters went out looking for injured sisters, mostly Stalkers, to take back to the Healing Sisters, and Survivor Sisters were like me, alive and alone in the wilderness. Senior Sisters was what you were as soon as your hair started going grey.

And those were just the ones I'd heard about.

I touched my still-auburn hair and wondered if I'd ever live long enough to be called a Senior, then smiled to myself. I had a *long* way to go before that kind of acceptance happened. If at all.

Maybe they'd call me a Sort-of Sister.

Or a Sometime Sister.

Or maybe just Alex.

Anyway, there wasn't a sister for everything. The Stalkers were just that, and it was no surprise to hear, once again, that Collar was seen by all the other Stalkers as their hero.

'If you're not one of them,' said Juno, 'then she's slightly scary.'

'Only slightly?' I asked, as Juno took me into a rotting one-time portakabin that was the Stalkers' centre. The cabin opened out into a small field that may have been a sports pitch of some kind, but was now where the Stalkers learned their drills; entry-level tracking skills and all the killing stuff they'd need once they went outside Purleyont Hames' perimeter. At the far end, an archery range had been set up, while nearer to Juno and I, pairs of Stalkers tussled together in mock fights with wooden pins instead of actual knives. They carried on as though we weren't even there, and those that looked in our direction gave us a haughty stare, as if we weren't worthy of them. Yet for all the ugliness of that near-arrogance, there was also a real group identity. They all dressed the same in their black and green leggings and tops, they clustered in groups, faced inwards, and laughed and joked together. All of their non-verbals said closed to outsiders, which out in the wilderness probably went a long way to keeping them alive. 'What made you want to be one of them?' I asked Juno.

'They're not all like that,' she said. 'It's just a show, some of them were kind. They helped me.'

'Yeah,' I said. 'Until they sent you out there on your own.'

'That was Collar's rule.'

'No shocks there,' I replied. 'Aren't you worried that Collar might take over? I mean, Silver's still the leader, right?'

'Silver's not her name,' said Juno. 'It's what she is.'

'Yes,' I said. 'She's got a bit of grey hair, so she's a Senior Sister. I get that. But then, so has Collar, right? Give it a couple of years and I'll probably have grey hair as well.'

'No,' said Juno. 'One Senior Sister becomes Silver, and it gets decided by others.'

'You mean she's elected?'

Juno nodded. 'When Silver dies, the other Senior Sisters decide which one of them should be our next leader. No one can vote for themselves, and we all respect the decision.'

'Even Collar?'

Juno nodded again. 'Even Collar.'

'So once she's voted in, she's got the job for life?' I shrugged when Juno nodded once more. 'And I'm guessing if Logan had taken over, all that would have changed?'

'You'll have to ask Addison,' said Juno. 'Today was the first I've heard about any of it. I'm not sure I'd have wanted Logan in charge, though.'

'Why not?' I asked. 'She seemed all about exploring further, seeing what's over the next hill.'

'And she also wanted to kill anyone who got in her way,' said Juno. 'You heard what Addison said about her. She'd have definitely killed you.'

'Like Collar wanted to today?'

'Like Silver stopped her.'

'True,' I said. 'She seemed quite measured back there.'

'She was,' said Juno. 'But you don't know how close you came to turning her against you.'

'She doesn't like trans women either?'

'No,' said Juno. 'Well, actually, I don't know, but when you said that the Alphas kill the people we love? Silver survived The Change with a child, a daughter. And the Alphas killed her.'

'Oh, shit,' I murmured.

'Do you need to know more?'

'No,' I said. 'I can fill in the gaps.'

'Good,' said Juno. 'So forget about Logan and focus on Collar and Silver. Silver doesn't see you as a threat, and that's her mark, her vision, that's what she is. The Senior Sisters chose absolutely right with her.'

'How many Silvers have you had since The Change?' I asked. I wasn't normally this nosey, but I just couldn't help with the questions.

'Three, so far,' said Juno.

'Doesn't seem to be a job that lasts very long.' I'd hemmed way into impolite territory, practically suggesting that Silver's days were numbered. 'So what about the next generation?' I asked. 'I mean, you want to last more than a few years, right? And I know you're not friendly with the Alphas. I mean, who would be? Certainly not me. But if you want to survive, you're going to need younger people to come along, if you know what I mean.' My hands fluttered as I tried to find the right words. 'I mean, the facts of life, right? I mean, even *I* know all about that shit, although what's the point? You *must* know what I'm talking about.'

'We do,' said Juno. We started walking once more. 'And we don't have a solution. We've talked about it. *Everybody's* talked about it.'

'Well,' I said. 'You'll need to find some way of making it work with at least some of the Alphas. Because if this whole thing is ever going to get past one generation, at least *some* of you need to get it together.'

'I know,' said Juno. '*We* know.'

'And don't look at me.' I said. 'I've been fixed one way, and I don't have the right internals for the other.'

'Haven't you ever thought about it?' asked Juno.

'No,' I replied. 'I've never had a future. And until you invited me here, all I thought about was the next meal, the next day, the next season, and staying alive long enough to see it through.' I looked back at her. 'For as long as I could.'

'And that's it?' asked Juno.

'What else is there?'

'We're all part of something bigger,' said Juno. 'And you could be, too.'

'Maybe once,' I said, remembering the bunker as it was, remembering Tanya Strauss. 'Before all this happened, sure, I was part of something. I belonged, I was accepted.' I looked around me and shuddered. 'Not any more though.'

Juno was doing it again. She knew me better than I knew myself. She knew what I wanted, what I wanted even more than a poxy trip to Greenwich. I looked at my watch, saw that it was three o'clock, and for once it wasn't enough. It also wasn't enough that I knew I was a woman. I wanted, I *needed* to be accepted as one. Juno knew it and she said it. I knew it, deep down. I knew it, but I kept running away from it.

Mainly because it was so damn impossible.

Impossible Princess, where the hell had I heard that before?

'I'm not a part of anything,' I said.

'You're wrong,' said Juno. 'And I'm right. And you'll find out tonight, at the festival.'

Chapter 16

I'd been kind of wondering all day what the hell the festival was about. And while there was some connection between the nearby ruins of Reading and a festival that I couldn't quite nail down, it didn't really fit in with the post-apocalyptic need for survival. Even though the Strauss *had* managed to cobble together a working society, along with food, energy and shelter, having some kind of midsummer solstice celebration, while surrounded by enemies on all sides who were getting stronger all the time, it was a bit like me cavorting around in a wedding dress and high heels, just because I could.

Well, there was this one time…

Okay then, so maybe the idea of a festival wasn't *quite* that bad. If you think about it, it was like giving the whole world the two fingered 'screw you' sign, a massive show of defiance.

For as long as it lasted.

What I'd been shown so far was interesting, but it didn't give me all the answers, and I had loads more questions floating around in my mind.

And maybe I'd get the answers, because during, or more likely after, the festival, I was pretty damn sure that some kind of deal was going to be made, or at least offered. Unless they really were that twisted that they'd show me all this stuff, and then kill me just for the hell of it.

They wouldn't, would they?

Collar might, but the Outcasts? No way. I was pretty much one of them already, and maybe that was Silver's plan. She seemed to run the place with a very subtle hand, and that was just one example of how she did it. If you were an Outcast, you were part of the Strauss, but at the same time not part of them. It seemed an ideal halfway house to put me into while we figured each other out, a good way to make me think that I might have a chance of belonging.

And I'll say one thing for the Outcasts, they sure fed you well. At six o'clock Juno and I walked back to their collection of houses and, without even needing to look at my watch, I was given a plate full of freshly cooked vegetables, and as a special guest treat, two huge chunks of the bread they'd worked out. It was flat and laced through with tomatoes and some serious herbs. 'Collar would love to just slit your stomach open,' said Varia, with her usual social grace. 'But we'd rather keep it full, and in one piece.'

'Me too.' I grinned back at her through a mouthful of food that sent my taste buds into overdrive.

'Who's going to the festival?' Addison asked the living room's tightly packed occupants. She locked me into her gaze for a second longer than she needed to. '*You're* definitely going.' She smiled. 'Now, who else?' Silence fell and Addison looked carefully from one to the next. She picked five, seemingly at random, then looked at me. 'They happen once a week,' she said. 'And we all get a turn at going.'

*

In the cool of dusk I found myself back in Purleyont Hames' rickety hall, but this time I was sitting down, wearing my freshly brushed camo and not in immediate fear of being shanked. This was my most eventful 8pm I'd spent without being in danger, ever. There were maybe two hundred Strauss sitting in cramped rows against three walls, dressed in faded dresses, leggings and sport tops, intervals of mix-match camo, and the odd speckle of stonewashed denim.

The sheer number of Strauss crammed into a small area was a crashing explosion to my senses. I'd lived alone, encountered occasional other humans, usually in a hostile way, and now I was sitting shoulder to shoulder with hundreds of them, all talking and at ease in each other's company. It felt weird, unexpected, scary, exhilarating, and daunting, all at exactly the same time.

The hall's far wall and middle space remained empty. I sat in between Juno and Addison, and apart from the openly hostile glares from Collar, who was thankfully nowhere near me, I was pretty much ignored.

'Don't worry about her,' whispered Addison. She'd brushed her buckskin dress and I forced myself to stop looking at her bare knees. A microsecond too late, she caught my eyes and smiled lightly as I looked away and blushed. 'Collar's always stab-staring at somebody,' she said, ignoring, or at least not mentioning, my flushed cheeks. 'Tonight it's your turn.'

'That's all?'

'That's all.' She looked at me and this time I looked right back into her large brown eyes. 'Trust me,' she said.

Collar aside, it was actually the fact that no one else was staring at me that made me feel good, as though I was just another woman in the packed hall. I looked over at the far wall and saw that it had a slightly raised platform in front of it. If I didn't know better, I'd have said it was a stage.

It *was* a stage.

There weren't any spotlights or major effects, just a handful of strip-lights which flickered from time to time when the electric didn't quite manage a constant supply. Silver stepped onto the stage and the quiet murmur of voices quickly faded to nothing.

'Welcome, sisters.' Her deep voice carried around the hall, and her midnight skin shone healthy and toned. 'Let's remember why we're here, and why we will always be here. Let's make sure we never forget why *we* control our destiny, and why no one else ever will.'

'She says this every time,' whispered Juno. 'I think it's one of those rituals you told me about.'

'Quiet,' hissed Addison. Juno rolled her eyes and winked at me.

'Rape.' Silver's voice boomed out the last word I thought she'd ever say, and I suddenly stared at her, my attention snared.

'No more,' the entire congregation chorused their reply.

'Coercion.'

'No more.' Louder.

'Control.'

'No more.' Louder again.

'Fear.'

'No more.' By this point I was joining in. Two hundred Strauss were standing and shouting back their response.

'Never again,' said Silver. 'Not now. Not ever. It's a right we defend, and it's a privilege that we've earned the hard way. Never before have all women had the freedom we have, and that freedom unites us. It makes us stronger than we can imagine, but only for as long as we remain one with each other. Remember that. Never forget that.'

Juno squeezed my arm as Silver spoke, while around the hall, silence reigned. Everyone was looking back at Silver, loyal and utterly owning the belief, being part of it, belonging to it. Never again. That's what I'd been thinking in the forest all those weeks ago. Never again was what made me kick in and help Juno.

'And having confirmed our togetherness,' said Silver, 'let us celebrate it.'

Clapping in unison started straight away, as the tightly packed Strauss swayed from side to side with the rhythm. The overhead strip-lights changed colour, from green, to red, and back again, I heard the static thump of a low-watt speaker being switched on, and the regular clapping changed to cheers and applause as a tall, curvy Strauss sashayed onto the small stage, dressed in a glittery, short black dress with long tassels, fishnet tights, and white cowboy boots.

Wow! This was a long way from the threadbare and functional clothes that I'd seen the Strauss wearing so far, and the dress fitted her like a second skin. She picked up a microphone and at the same time an old song that I thought I'd forgotten flooded out of the hidden sound system. The Strauss cowgirl looked exotic in her outfit, her body moving to the music, long limbed gold-wheat skin glowing with health. Her long black hair shone under the lights' changing colours, brown eyes twinkling with mischief and pure life. The backing music played and she lifted the microphone to her glossed lips. Lip gloss! So they *did* still wear make-up. She sang the first lyrics, and as she did, six other Strauss, dressed in a similar fashion, with tassels, sequins, and a heady mix of burlesque and line dancing, joined her on the stage. The audience cheered and clapped, and my shock at seeing live entertainment soon changed to joy at the experience. I didn't know what the hell I was expecting from the festival, and after Silver's initial words, I thought maybe more of the same. A sombre, dour and too-long reflection of how bad the outside world was, and how wonderful they were in comparison. But music, dancing, and costumes?

Costumes that I've never even imagined would ever be seen or worn again?

And Juno had kept this a secret from me in all the weeks she'd been at mine.

The music, the singing, and the dancing surf-waved over my senses. I didn't recognise the exact moment it happened, but I became as involved and carried along as everyone else in the hall. It was magic escapism from the horror outside the fence, from the brutal reality of what they, we, were all facing. I wasn't sitting down anymore, I was standing, clapping and swaying to the music, and I didn't need to see the great big grin on my face, I could feel it, I could feel the smile inside of me that lit up my whole being. Occasionally, Addison would brush against me as we all moved in time to the music, and as the chorus built, everyone in the hall joined in with the title, which, had I remembered, was slightly altered from the original, but exactly right for that moment.

'Oh yeah,' everybody sang. 'I feel like a woman.'

And I did, too. Surrounded by other women, enjoying, and positively celebrating what I was, while around me, everyone else did the same. There was no violence, no aggression, no need to fight or kill. Just togetherness and sisterhood, and a shared sense of overcoming any adversity together.

It felt amazing.

Juno was right. There was something bigger, something I could be a part of, something I could belong to, if only I wanted.

And I wanted.

As nights out go, it didn't end late. Ten o'clock by my hardly looked at watch, and as the hall emptied, Silver walked over to me. 'Be back here after breakfast,' she said, and that meant in less than twelve hours' time, because I *never* had breakfast after 10am.

Never.

Silver nodded towards Addison and Juno. 'Come along as well.' It wasn't so much an invitation as an order, and like everything done at Purleyont Hames, you thought it was simple, but there was more going on. Like the festival itself. Silver hadn't told me to be there because she wanted to treat me to a night out; she wanted to show me what it meant to be a Strauss, what it meant to be a woman, and to remind me of the part I'd played in saving Juno. Then she gave me all night to think about it. But believe me, I'd been thinking about what it meant to be a woman for a *lot* longer. And sure, I knew the Strauss saw a value in me, I knew they wanted something from me, but before I went to sleep that night in a very comfortable guest bed in the Outcasts' house, and as soon as I woke up, I really thought about what it would mean for me, to be part of them, to be accepted by them, and live among them, a woman among women.

Chapter 17

The next morning at nine-thirty, all hints of the previous night's festival had been wiped from the hall. Not that there was much. The sound system had always been out of sight, and a rearrangement of the chairs was really all that was needed. It was daytime, the lights were off, and the windows were opened to welcome the fresh summer breeze, while Silver, two Senior Sisters, and Collar sat at a small bench table on the raised platform, where last night the singers had been. Facing them on chairs at a symbolically lower level were Addison, Juno, and myself. Was it part of Silver's design, her game plan? Was she making Juno, Addison, and me go places together, bond together, like some kind of new age family unit? If she was, then it was certainly working.

Placed on the table in front of us, either as a trial exhibit or a display, I wasn't sure which, was my Glock.

'How was the festival?' asked Silver.

'I loved it,' I said. No false coyness, it was the absolute truth.

'And what did you learn yesterday?'

'I learned about the Strauss,' I said.

'The what?' asked Collar.

'It's what she calls us,' said Juno.

'And why's that?' asked Collar.

'I remember some things from before,' I said.

Collar and Silver looked at each other, then stared back at me with renewed intensity.

'No one remembers that far back,' said Collar.

'I do,' I said, thinking that maybe this wasn't the time to mention Beck. 'I used to be in the military, a communicator. I remember teamwork, organisation, weapons, and first aid. And I remember Tanya Strauss. She was my old leader. She was a strong, inspirational woman.' I looked at Silver. 'So it seemed like the ideal name for you.' I took a breath and then committed. 'Maybe I can join you.'

I sat motionless and felt the tension building inside me. My nerve endings twitched and my fingers flickered as though I'd been plugged into a long-forgotten electrical point. 'Do you want to know how to use that?' I pointed to the Glock. 'Do you want to know where to find them? Do you want to know the best ways to kill the Alphas with them? Some of them have got those as well. Do you want to know what to do when an Alpha shoots back at you? And do you want to take all of that to the Alphas and teach them that they will never rule you?'

'We can deal with the Alphas,' said Collar.

'Until they get wise to you,' I replied. 'And they've already started. They're running in groups now. Aren't you worried about what else they've got better at, because it's only a matter of time before they do. And I think you've stopped looking for anything out there that might help you.' I'd gone this far, maybe it was time to really drop the bomb. 'You're only ever as strong as you are today. What happens when you're all Senior Sisters? How strong will you be then?'

Silver's lips curled slightly. 'Some answers are harder to find than others,' she said.

'I know all about that,' I replied. 'But going out there looking for a future might actually help you find one. Knowledge is power, and if you just sit here and hope that you'll always be the biggest, or the best, or the most clever, then sooner or later you won't be.'

'Meaning?' asked Silver.

'Meaning there may be threats out there that you don't know about.' My chair scraped back as I stood up and faced them. 'And I can help you with that. A good team with the right training and the right weapons can go a lot further out, and see a lot more. I can do that, I can teach some of you to use the weapons I've already got, and then I know a few places where we can get some more.'

Well, I knew about *one* place, and I hadn't been there for years.

'We'll go out,' I said. 'And we'll see what we see. Maybe there are others like you, maybe there are groups of men that you'll actually *like*. Maybe some of them are looking for a future, looking for you. Maybe I can help you find it.'

'And that's the last we'll see of you,' said Collar. 'I've got a better idea. Leave this here,' she gestured at the Glock. 'Then go, now, and never come back.'

'Like Logan, you mean?'

Collar bit back a reply and looked at Silver.

'You know about her?' asked Silver.

'Only since you mentioned her yesterday,' I said. 'Addison told me what she knew, which wasn't much, but it's enough to know that you've had at least one rebel, one runaway.'

'She was a fucking traitor,' hissed Collar.

'She's history,' said Silver. 'I wasn't in charge then, and we do things differently now.'

'Is she dead?' I asked.

'She must be,' said Silver. 'We sent our best Stalkers after her.'

'I survived your best Stalkers,' I said. 'What do you think, Collar?' I looked at her, and she looked at the floor, then quickly around the room, and then glared pure murder at me.

'She was alive when I last saw her,' said Collar, quietly.

Silver snapped round to face her. 'That's not what you said at the time,' she said.

'We were sent out to track her,' said Collar. 'And we did. We followed the trail and we found her.'

'And it's taken you seven years to tell me?' Silver looked at Collar.

'You weren't Silver at the time,' said Collar.

'I am now,' said Silver. 'And I want to know what happened.'

'We cornered her,' said Collar. Suddenly, I was ignored as Collar was forced to explain her actions from years before. 'Hard against the river, she had nowhere to run. She said she'd never go back, she'd die first.'

'She faced two Stalkers,' said Silver. 'I wouldn't have thought she had that choice.'

'She challenged me to a fight,' said Collar. 'One on one. Addison was to play no part in it. If I won, we'd take her back. If she won, she'd go free.'

Silver looked at Addison, who nodded. 'It's true, Silver,' said Addison. 'Collar told me not to get involved. It was a fair fight.'

'Then presumably Collar won,' said Silver. 'The best of the Stalkers, never been beaten, the Stalker who cut an Alpha to pieces for trying to rape her. We all know the stories about Collar.'

'Logan beat me,' said Collar, her eyes fixed on the table as she spoke. 'Me and Addison stayed out for two days longer, looking for her, but the truth is she beat me, and I let her go.'

'*We* let her go,' said Addison.

'She'd have killed you,' said Collar, lifting her head and looking at Addison. 'There's no shame in it, Addison.' Collar turned to face Silver. 'I told Addison to keep quiet. I'd rather have lied, and died, than let anyone know I was beaten by a traitor.'

'And what if she's still alive?' I asked. 'What if she told the Alphas some of what she knew? Maybe she didn't want to.' I ran with the idea. 'Maybe they made her, maybe they kept her alive for their own reasons. Maybe she managed to find a band of followers out there who were less choosy than you are. What if she's the reason the Alphas are becoming more of a problem?'

'The reasons don't concern us as much as the reality,' said Silver.

'And that's why you need me,' I said. 'I've lived out there all of my life, and I can train a team to do the same thing. We'll go further than your Stalkers, we'll have strength in numbers, and we'll get you results.'

'When you say "we,"' said Silver, 'who do you mean?'

I looked at Addison and then Juno. 'The Outcasts,' I said. 'They don't fit in with the rest of your Sisters, so it's not like I'm poaching anyone that you think you actually need. I'll turn them into a team and I'll give them a purpose and make them useful.' I looked left. 'Juno's already been outside.' I looked right. 'So has Addison. They've got knowledge, and the others can be taught. Who knows,' I turned my gaze to Collar and winked, 'we might even come back.'

'Let's start with having you as a friend,' said Silver. A hiss of objection rose from Collar. I couldn't blame her, really, because after little more than twelve months' actual service fifteen years earlier, I was suddenly putting myself forward as a leader. I wondered what Wing Commander Strauss would think of my wild ideas. 'Once you've shown us your worth,' Silver continued, 'and when you're at one with the settlement, will that give you fulfilment?'

'What do you mean?' I asked. I knew what she meant. She knew I knew what she meant. And I knew that she knew…

'I mean,' said Silver, 'will you teach us to use the weapons, how they can be used against the enemy, and will you lead the team? Out there?'

'I will.'

'All that risk, just to become a Strauss, as you call us?'

'It's no more than I was doing on my own,' I said.

'And you want nothing more than to belong?'

A pause, and I knew that Silver had me.

'Juno taught me what I already knew but never admitted,' I said. 'She taught me that I *do* want to belong, but more than that, I want to be accepted as a woman. It's more important to me than I thought. But you're right, Silver, there's something else that defines me, something else I want, something else I need.' I took a deep breath. 'I need to get to Greenwich.'

'Where?' asked Collar. 'What the hell is Greenwich?'

'Time is at Greenwich,' I said. 'It's got, or at least it used to have, the most accurate clocks ever made, and I have to have one. I've got to try to get there. It's my obsession.' I looked at Silver and I hoped she wouldn't think I was *too* crazy. Then I raised my arm and swivelled my wrist to show them my watch. 'I've got this thing about time. Keeping time, telling the time, knowing what time it actually is, what time it really is.'

'But you've already got a watch,' said Silver.

'I've got more than one,' I replied.

'So why go to this place,' asked Silver. 'Greenwich? Where is it, even?'

'East from here,' I said. 'Southeast of London. Before, I was thinking that once I got past your settlement, I could follow the river through London and make my way there.'

'You want to go through London?' Silver's tone told me *exactly* what she thought of that idea. 'It's not a city anymore, and believe me, we're close enough to know. It's nothing but ruins and lawlessness and death. And Greenwich is surely just a name by now. Will it even be there?'

'I don't know,' I replied. 'I mean, there's a place there. At least, there *was*. It used to be where the centre of the world was, and all time was reckoned from there.'

'And you want to go there for something you've already got?' asked Silver. She looked at me and raised her eyebrows. 'That's a big risk to take.'

'I *have* to go there,' I said. I looked at my wristwatch. 'You're right, though. This tells the time, and it's super accurate. But I need more than just that. I need to know the day, the date, what month it is, even what year it is.'

'What do you need to know all that for?' jeered Collar. 'Do you only work on certain days? We know one week to the next for the crops, the seasons, and day and night. What the fuck more does *anyone* need to know?'

'I know the day, date, week, month, year,' I said. 'Even the leap years.'

'A leap year?' asked Collar.

'Okay,' I said. '*You* don't need to know all that stuff, but *I* do. Before The Change, before the Alpha Bug, it ruled my life. Everything I did was by the clock, and it hasn't left me.'

'So if you know all this,' said Silver, 'why Greenwich?'

'Because I've got an old phone that I keep charged up,' I said. 'That's my calendar, my rock-solid reference point. If my watches lose a second, the phone keeps them right.'

'But...?'

'It doesn't recharge as reliably as it used to.'

'Meaning?'

'I got clumsy,' I said. 'I tripped over the charging cable. My phone still charges up, but the cable's been damaged and it won't last forever. I can't get a replacement cable, so I need to think about replacing my phone, or, more likely, finding something else that'll do the same job.'

'I didn't know Greenwich had a stock of old phones.' Silver looked at me with a slight, almost unseen smile.

'They don't,' I said. 'What they have, or *had*, were centuries-old clocks that were accurate, really accurate. They were hand wound and gave perfect time at sea, through storms, all weathers, for months, for ever. And I want one. Greenwich is like a temple of time, and if I could get even just *one* of those clocks,' I was breathing heavily as I spoke, talking fast, and I couldn't see but I was sure my face was flushed, 'well, it would be like I could *always* tell the time, and I have to be sure. I *have* to get to Greenwich to really find out and *stay* sure.'

'And you really think these time machines are actually still there? Even now?' asked Silver.

'Yes,' I said. 'Maybe. Oh hell, I don't know. Not for sure. But I *do* know where Greenwich is.' I paused and looked at Silver. 'I mean, maybe the place got emptied out years ago, or maybe it's been ignored and forgotten, but I've got maps and a compass, and I can navigate. I can get there. I was on my way there when I helped Juno. It's simple,' I said. 'I'll train the Outcasts in weapons and navigation, and then we'll find a supply of firearms and we'll go far and wide to see what else is out there.'

'As long as one of those missions is Greenwich?' asked Silver.

'As long as the *first* mission is Greenwich,' I replied.

Chapter 18

Later that day, Silver visited the Outcasts' house and called me into the garden.

Alone.

'You're no good to me dead.' She looked at me directly, her large eyes burrowing into my soul. 'And you may not realise this, but the rest of the Outcasts mean too much to me to send them out on a suicide mission just to heal *your* obsession. Believe me on this, Alex, if you try to go to Greenwich, none of you will come back.'

'Silver,' I said. 'I *need* this.'

'No,' she replied. 'You need *this*.'

She handed me a small package, a coiled up length of black cable, still in its plastic packaging.

'Open it,' she said.

I didn't have to. I knew what it was. It was a charging cable. A brand new charging cable. I looked at it, then stared closely at the connections. My hands trembled slightly. It would fit my phone and I could keep it charged up, and I realised that I had what I needed without having to go on a nightmare trip to Greenwich.

'The clocks are at Greenwich,' I said, already losing the argument.

'The clocks *might* be at Greenwich,' smiled Silver. 'And maybe one day we'll send a team that way, but right now, can we agree that there are more pressing matters?'

'Thank you,' I said.

'For what?' she asked.

'For knowing me. For knowing what it means to me.'

'You made that very plain,' smiled Silver. 'I think even Collar worked it out. You also brought Juno back to us, for which we are thankful. And now that you don't need to throw sixteen lives away on a gesture, however important, we should focus on other things.'

I followed Silver back inside. For the price of a one metre length of cable, I'd been bought, and my life had been changed, but also arguably saved. We walked into the living room and fifteen sets of terminally curious eyes looked at me and Silver. I especially felt Juno and Addison's searching gaze, desperate to know what Silver had said. And as soon as she got the hell out of there, I'd tell them. I'd have to.

'Alex has got some thinking to do,' said Silver. 'And while she's doing that, alone, I've got some things to say to all of you.'

I knew when I was being told to leave the room.

*

Stepping out of the Outcasts' house, I was never a hundred per cent sure I could trust Silver to trust me. Not really. But what choice did I have? Sure, they *might* have just let me walk away, clutching my charging cable and never to be seen again, but there were no prizes for guessing who the Stalkers' number one target would be if our paths ever did cross in the future. And if we *did* part as anything less than friends, I knew whose concrete home they'd be looking for as an absolute priority, unless of course they were complete idiots.

Which they weren't.

So, like it or not, there was nothing else for it. I was there for the duration, and it really was the only deal on the table. I'd have to train up the Outcasts and then we'd have to do whatever mission was given to us.

And after that, it was a case of live in hope that *if* I still wanted it, one day, some day, maybe, we'd be sent to Greenwich.

But right then, I was still at Purleyont Hames, and one of the great things about being there were the several open areas that punctuated the slowly weathering buildings. Each one had a huge tree in the middle of it, an oak, a sycamore or a chestnut, a real forest giant that had been there for centuries before The Change. At any one time, you'd see a random group of Strauss just lying down and staring up at the tree and the leaves. I found one, copped a squat as the Strauss called it, lay back on the warm ground, and just looked up at the gentle sunlight filtering through the dense green canopy. It was utterly relaxing, tranquil, and despite myself, despite where I was, and despite what I'd geared up to doing, I felt my worries and concerns melting away into the earth.

'If you stay there much longer you'll turn into a tree yourself, and then you'll have the birds crapping in your branches.'

'How long have you been there, Varia?' I asked, without even opening my eyes.

'Long enough to wonder if you'd died in your sleep.' It was *definitely* Varia. 'I mean, you're almost old enough to.' I could practically hear her smiling. 'Must be why Addison likes you.'

'She does not—'

'Aren't you supposed to meet the rest of us?' she interrupted me.

'Yes.'

'And aren't we supposed to be going somewhere?'

'Do you always ask questions you know the answer to?'

'No.' She laughed. 'Sometimes people teach me things.' A solid object landed on my stomach. I grunted and sat up, then looked down at the Glock resting on my lap. 'I reckon they must trust you after all. Are you really going to get one of those for all of us?'

'That's the plan,' I said.

*

'No one has to come.' I was back at the Outcasts' house and talking to all fifteen of them. 'And to be honest, you'd probably be a lot better off if you didn't. If you stay here, you'll be housed, fed, and clothed. Out there, you could very easily end up getting killed. Or worse.'

'She sure knows how to sell it to us,' said an orange-haired Outcast with a pierced nose ring and connecting chain that ran to her left ear.

'I'll lie if you want me to, Lamp,' I said. 'But you'd find out the truth soon enough, and then you'll be back here by sunset. So what would be the point of that?'

'What are you asking us to sign up to?' asked another Outcast.

'Nothing easy,' I said. Crystal, who'd asked the question, had pale blue eyes and long, straight blonde hair. She'd been selected as a Sani-Sister, but flat out refused a lifetime of keeping everything clean. Which was weird, because she was obsessively, sparklingly spotless herself, and I could see why that role had been assigned to her. She loved to wear white clothes and I wondered how she'd take to swapping over to camo. 'We've got a hard trek to my place,' I told her. 'You'll need to shake out into two teams, work together, fight together. And out there,' I said to everyone, 'if it all goes wrong, you might have to die together.'

'Are there any reasons we might actually *want* to do all this?' asked Lamp.

'You'll be free,' I said.

'Free?' she replied. 'Aren't we that already?'

'Out there you'll be free from the Sisters,' I said. 'Free from being judged, free from not fitting in. We'll be going into the unknown, and we might find food, supplies, riches, or death, but we'll certainly find adventure. And maybe you'll find yourselves, a higher meaning, whatever.' I looked at the Outcasts. 'You've been told that you don't fit in, that no one can depend on you. Well, I say that you *can* depend on each other, and that makes you stronger than anything. Out there,' I flung my arm in a haphazard sweep that I suppose could have encompassed anywhere. 'You'll have your sisters' lives in your own hands, so if that's not fitting in with those around you, I don't know what is. I'll teach you skills you won't learn here, and whatever this world is about, outside the fence, I, we, *you*, will be the ones to find it and to see it. But know this. The one thing I can't offer you is safety, and the Alphas are making it more dangerous every day. If you want to stay here, keep your seats and that's fine. If you want to come with me, stand up and let's go.'

Fifteen Outcasts heard my words, fifteen lives were given the chance to change, and fifteen women stood up and decided their own fate.

Chapter 19

I don't know why I hadn't expected it, but my team became just that.

Mine.

All of a sudden, I was in charge and having some kind of insight into how Tanya Strauss must have felt, having other people to think about. I was now making decisions for others, as well as knowing them, and worrying about them.

And I don't know *when* it happened, or *what* exactly made it happen, but during that time I kind of stopped being a loner, and kind of started being a people person.

We were sixteen, including me, and that meant two teams of eight. Forever known as the Outcasts, an ever-changing drop-group of rejects and misfits, we became The Outcasts, our official title. We weren't Sisters, or Stalkers, and I set about creating our own uniqueness through skills that only we knew. I led them all back to the bunker, and once there, I taught them map reading, navigation, and as much first aid and medical as I'd managed to pick up over the years.

Beck, who, according to Juno, remembered all about healing from before The Change, had knowledge I wanted. Real knowledge, real experience, and I was desperate to talk to her about it, and that made her the one person I categorically wasn't allowed to.

On that point, I was right: Silver only trusted me so far, so I was left to work it out for myself, which was probably also what she wanted.

Thankfully, I had Lamp, with her carrot-juice dyed hair cut short on one side and a thin chain connecting her nose ring to her earring. She'd wanted, really wanted, to be a Healing Sister, but it hadn't worked.

'What happened?' I asked her.

'One of Beck's arse-lickers told me I had to take my nose ring out if I wanted to be a healer.'

'And you said no?'

'I put a pint of flax water in her night drink.' She grinned at me. 'She was sat on the crapper all the next day and I became an Outcast.'

'Any regrets?' I asked.

'Can I keep my piercings?'

'Sure you can.'

'None then.' She smiled.

'That's good,' I said. 'Can you read?'

'Kind of,' she stammered, looking everywhere but at me.

'Well, you're now the Outcast's medic. Read these and make Beck jealous.' I dumped a shitload of medical books in her lap and went back to training the rest.

'I've been right all this time,' said Arc, looking around the bunker with wide-eyed curiosity. Sitting on the erratically carpeted, but still cold, concrete floor, she hugged her knees to her chest and wrapped her too-long arms around her legs. 'I've always said we should be out here, exploring, meeting others like us.'

'How come they didn't listen to you?' I asked, genuinely curious, because that was exactly what they were wanting me to do, *and* with fifteen Strauss to join me.

'I was all for making friends with them.'

'For sure?' I asked.

'I actually spoke to one,' she said. 'A real Alpha. No one believes me, though. Not really.'

'Why not?' I asked.

She shrugged. 'It doesn't fit in with what they want. They want them all to be seen as enemies, as a threat. Well, this one wasn't.'

'What happened?'

'I was on a foraging trip,' she said. 'Not far from a fence line, just three of us. And have you ever got that feeling, that prickling sense in your mind that you're being watched?'

'All the time.' I smiled. 'Why do you think I'm going back out there?'

'I'm serious,' she said. 'Anyway, he was hiding in the undergrowth, looking at me. He was maybe the same age as I was, *and* he was clean.'

'Clean?'

'You know,' she replied. 'He'd had a wash. His hair was a bit of a mess, but I could see his face and he didn't smell like a dead animal, like the rest of them seem to. And he didn't look,' she flustered her arms. 'You know,' she said. 'He didn't look angry.'

'He already sounds different to the others,' I said.

'I went up to him,' she said. 'I spoke to him. He was scared; all he wanted was food.'

'So what happened?' I asked.

'I gave him the wild berries I'd picked. The other sisters came into sight and he ran away. They didn't see him and they didn't believe me.'

'Weird,' I said. 'But then again, what isn't? Maybe we'll find a few more friendly ones out there. If we do, offer your hand.'

'What?'

'I've read about this,' I said. 'It's called shaking hands.'

'Bloody hell, Alex,' laughed Arc. 'Is there anything you *haven't* read about. Your eyesight'll be worse than mine if you don't kick that habit.'

'Here.' I held out my right hand.

'Here what?' She looked at me, suddenly suspicious.

'Take my hand.'

'What?'

'Take my hand.'

'Why?'

'It's a way of showing friendship.'

'What?' she said. 'By touching hands?'

'Try it,' I said.

Arc gingerly unwrapped her arm and brought her hand towards mine, holding it in mid-air. I held her hand gently, shook it, and as I did, I looked into her eyes and smiled. 'There,' I said. 'It's called shaking hands.'

Arc whipped her hand back as soon as I released it and she looked at me. 'What does it do?' she asked. 'What does it mean?'

'It's a gesture,' I said. 'It can mean hello, it can mean you're friends with someone, it can be a way of saying well done.'

'All that from just shaking hands?' asked Arc. 'No wonder the human race went to shit.'

'The next time you meet an Alpha who you think might be friendly,' I said, 'give it a try and see if it works.'

'Never mind that,' she said. 'I'm trying it out right now.' She jumped to her feet. 'Juno! Look, watch this!'

*

I'd set aside a week for training, and then we'd be off for a firearms and camo scavenge. And in that week my stash of tinned food took a real hammering. But more than that, for the first time in years, the bunker echoed to the sound of voices and movement, almost bringing to life a building that was never meant to be homely. It was a world apart from the sometimes crushing solitude I'd lived before.

'I told you it tasted good,' grinned Juno. She sat at the kitchen table and wolfed down a slice of bacon grill.

'How long were you expecting this to last?' asked Addison, eating her own rations with the same eagerness.

'I don't know,' I said. 'But I wasn't expecting to feed half the Strauss.'

'You'd rather be back on your own?' she asked.

'Only when you keep going on about my wardrobe,' I said.

'Clothes in a box don't mean a thing,' said Addison, licking her fork clean. 'Maybe you'd look good enough to work the Festival.'

'Yeah,' I replied. 'And maybe I wouldn't.'

'I think you would,' said Addison. 'You've got the figure *and* the fitness.' She smiled at me. 'I bet you could even sing.'

'Not a chance.' I smiled back at her. 'But I can definitely talk, and for the next week I'll be talking all about navigation and moving across country.'

*

Back in the day, you'd probably have called me an armchair general, a leader in my mind, but never for real. I wished that Tanya Strauss had made it through The Change, leading, encouraging, as well as damn well telling me what I should be doing. But she wasn't, it was just me, Alex, in charge and leading the troops.

And my priority was more firearms.

Could I still get to the armoury? It had been a long time. Terrain had changed, and vegetation had sprung up everywhere. Roads were fast disappearing and paths had vanished a long time ago. Hill contours, compass bearings, and very occasional landmarks were still there, and they were a help, but not the gospel truth they used to be.

And yes, there *were* a few places where armouries existed, according to some very old maps and documents I'd read. And yes, I'd even been to a couple, but at two of them, someone had got there before me. At Sandhurst, I arrived in the middle of a years-ago winter, and the place had been skinned of all ordnance and used as an open toilet so recently that the shit perched on top of the empty ammunition boxes was still steaming.

Aldershot was even worse. Looking back, I actually should have realised it. The bigger the military site used to be, the more attention it would attract. On the map, the whole town was Army and nothing else, and by the time I'd worked up the nerve to go there, every place that *might* have stored weapons was a smoked out ruin, scoured from the earth with explosives. I *really* didn't want to meet whoever had done that.

It would have been so much easier if the bunker I'd been based at, and now lived in, had been authorised to draw weapons, but I guess that order came too late, or not at all. Instead, I found an armoury at Hermitage. Hermitage? Even the word sounds solitary, and the place sure as hell lived up to the name. Post-Change, the village was still recognisable, but the woodland claim-back was already starting, and that suited me right down to the mulching soil at my feet.

Three trips, years ago, and I liberated a Glock, a shotgun and as much ammo as I could carry.

And as long as no one else had found and rifled the place, and as long as I could find my way back, there'd be enough firearms to tool up the Outcasts.

But first, we had to get there.

It was time for some team building.

Juno was the only one I knew even remotely well, and despite her knocking me the hell out when I'd taken her back, I still liked her. She'd learned so much when she was healing and getting better, and I knew she'd flourish if she had some people of her own to watch over, so I put her in charge of her own team of eight Outcasts. And really, who better to pass on my way of thinking?

Addison? I kept her with me. I told everyone it was for her age and experience, and to build bridges after the first time we met. But I knew, and I think everyone else did as well, that I liked having her close by. Nothing was said, but there was always a look, a smile that made me nervous and happy and unsure, all at the same time. I wanted to avoid the feeling because I didn't understand it, but I also craved it.

I had no idea if these strange thoughts or feelings went both ways, and I sure as hell wasn't going to talk about it.

Juno and Addison brought plenty of positives with them, with their experience of being with the Stalkers, and knowing how to use their bows. Juno's crossbow gave the impression that it would fall to bits at any second, but Addison's pristine hunting bow looked like it had been plucked from a shop the day before.

'Do you still know how to use it?' I asked her.

'Stand against that tree and put an apple on your head.' She grinned at me. 'We'll find out.'

'No need,' I replied with a flaky smile of my own. 'I believe you.'

Until we got to Hermitage, it was Juno and Addison with their bows, Crystal with the Glock and me with the shotgun. Everyone else had knives and pikes.

Day seven at my place. Alarm call at six-thirty, breakfast at seven, and final kit check and departure at eight. Perfect, time-controlled and, in my mind at least, a normal start to the day. The whole group thing, though, threw up issues I hadn't even considered, such as keeping people quiet on the move, defusing sudden and unexpected arguments, and having to answer unending questions about the wilderness from people who'd never seen it. Travelling as a group, though, definitely gave you a feeling of security, a sense that you knew you could at least take a break while someone else was watching out for you.

But, some things stayed the same, which meant that our first trip beyond the wire was day time only. Overnight was just too dangerous, even with our numbers, even with weapons. The feral dogs didn't give a damn about coming straight at us, and one bite would almost certainly mean infection, and infection meant you'd likely die.

Antibiotics? Maybe, but only if you were back at mine, and don't count on a sensitivity blood test *or* me to pick the right drugs for the right wounds. As for Juno's post-op infection, I was lucky as hell to get it right. And so was she.

Then there were the marauding Alphas; probably less of a threat as long as they weren't in groups, but a lot less predictable. I mean, sure, some of them were single-minded and easy to outwit, but not all of them, never all of them. Like Brig, who'd left Marlo to die while he back-tracked and caught up with me.

A light, early morning drizzle of summer rain kept everything real. Leggings and base layer tops quickly became soaked, while my camo did the usual thing in the rain, doubling in weight and taking on the consistency of cardboard.

I hadn't been back to the armoury for years. I hadn't needed to. I wasn't ever expecting to have to arm my own platoon, and the bunker was already full with everything I needed. I, that is, not we. One day, I might have run out of ammunition, but by that time, I figured I'd be too old to even get to Hermitage.

I remembered the last time I went there, and it took me four hard hours of speed marching mixed with jogging. Coming back took a while longer, because carrying several thousand rounds of ammunition, weapons, and cleaning kits was bloody heavy. Even young and fit, you've got your limits.

I kept my bearings tight and checked against the hilltops and contours much more than I would have done on my own. The predicted impatience from the Outcasts didn't materialise, and then I realised that they were so utterly overwhelmed by the experience, and taking in all the new sights, mostly forest, that they didn't actually notice I had a huge rod of fear up my own spine, terrified that I might get us all lost.

But the novelty was eventually replaced by very sensible curiosity.

'Are we there yet?' asked Varia.

It was a good question, and according to everything, my compass, the map, where I *thought* we actually were, we should have been right there.

The first time I went to Hermitage, I used the motorway as a reference point. Now though, vast chunks of it had either been eaten up by nature or dissolved back to its constituent parts. Even the remains of one-time cars and trucks were now barely relics, with little more than bits of engine block remaining, and most of those now doubled as self-created plant pots.

Had I got it right? Had we made our way back there, or were we lost in the rain? I checked the compass, took a bearing against the gentle gradient, and looked even harder into a clump of saplings.

Saplings!

That was the clue. Saplings hadn't been there for long, and with a huge show of soggy confidence that I absolutely didn't feel, I strode off the narrow forest path and into the dense vegetation, willing myself to be right, and not daring to think what I'd do if I wasn't.

At first I didn't see it, but you couldn't blame me really. It was all young, fast growing trees, multiple branches and green, bunching boughs laden with big, juicy, rain-infused leaves. I pushed them aside like they were a rained-on set of ecological curtains, but every time I thought I'd cleared the undergrowth, there was another set of leaves, branches and vision-obscuring vegetation to get through. I felt myself panicking, and then, suddenly, I was through.

The new tree growth extended right up to the armoury's rough-edged concrete walls. There was no longer a trace of the paved pathways that once criss-crossed the entire area, and what might once have been tightly mowed lawns and regimented landscape had been swallowed up by nature. All the other buildings had decayed, eaten up by the returning wilderness, although the one building made for storing weapons and ammunition was understandably more robust.

The armoury's steel door had been painted drab grey once upon a time, but in the intervening years it had blistered and peeled, and a surface of rust now coated its once haughty impregnability. While everyone milled around the closed door, Juno heaved on the mottled, unmoving steel handle.

'Now what?' she asked.

'We use this.' I pulled out a massive key that slid into the hooded keyhole. 'The first time I was here,' I said, 'the door was half open.' I thought it best not to mention the rotting body that had been keeping it that way, jammed in place, decomposing and half devoured by the new, post-Change wildlife.

I turned the key. The door slowly creaked open, and specks of rust jumped from the hinges. I crept inside, where the darkness yawned a silent welcome, and then it was back to the Stone Age as the Outcasts pulled out their flints, then huddled around their religiously-kept dry kindling and got the torches going.

When I'd discovered the place, the bodies inside the armoury were still recognisable. This time, while the big predators hadn't made their way in to scavenge, the smaller ones had. Flesh and blood had all been eaten away by nothing bigger than worms and ants, and I stepped respectfully, and with a residual nervousness, over the still-clothed skeletons.

First stop was the weapon racks, and they were untouched. There were dozens of pistols, all Glocks, and five pump action shotguns, just like mine. They remained pristine, still sheathed in protective grease, while close by I found a stash of damp but unused holsters and webbing belts. I showed the teams how to connect them up, then handed them out, one for everyone. Next to the webbing belts was a pile of camouflage. None of it fitted any of the Outcasts very well, but that was a job for another day. We took all five shotguns, passing them out at random, and then went deeper into the armoury to the ammunition store.

When everything had been functioning, I knew this last, final room would have been thoroughly secure, a fortress within a fortress, and always kept locked and watched. Since then, it was just a cramped, dungeon-like chamber at the end of a dank, musty corridor.

The nine millimetre stocks were nestled inside their small, waxed cardboard boxes. I stood in the ammunition store and, one at a time, the Outcasts came in and I crammed handfuls into their packs, as well as all of the shotgun cartridges I could find. It was probably overkill, but it wasn't very often I'd have my own caravan train to load up with booty, and to be honest, the armoury was somewhere I didn't want to come back to. Maybe it was the bodies, maybe it was the sense that even here, the Alpha Bug had hit, and hit hard. It was a place of death and we were taking with us the means to dish out even more.

I checked my watch, and in the gloom I read the luminous reassurance of two o'clock. I thought about the surely haunted armoury, and then the rain outside.

'Ration stop,' I said. 'Let's make it quick.'

I set the example by bolting down my thin slice of corned beef, shuttered between two bits of delicious Strauss flatbread, which for me was an amazing innovation.

'Right,' I said, 'has everyone got a pistol?' Muted affirmatives gave me the answer I wanted. 'Has everyone got ammo?' More expressions of yes. 'Good. Keep everything secure. No touching, no fiddling, no curiosity. Once we're clear, we'll go to ground and you'll have your first lesson.'

Their expressions matched my expectations: gone from a wary watchfulness to actually *wanting* to find trouble. And that was good. It had to be. I wasn't training these women to run at the Alphas and just shout at them; they were going to have to kill them. And with pistols, they'd have to be pretty close to do it. I'd initially thought that in a fight, I'd hang back with a shotgun for fire support, but I quickly realised that I'd have to be there, in among it with them. It was the only way they were ever going to follow me.

'Juno,' I said, 'with me.'

I led her back to the armoury door. 'Make sure everyone's wearing camo, then take them back the way we came. Fifty metres past the new trees there's a clearing. You remember the things we talked about?'

'Affirmative.' She smiled at me, transparently proud of her new vocabulary and skills.

'Good.' I smiled back at her. 'You're the point. Take them there and get into all round defence. I'm on the tail and I'll secure things here.'

Juno nodded, and the Outcasts rolled up ill-fitting sleeves and filed out behind her.

'She's doing well.' While I'd been watching Juno lead her team into the foliage, Addison materialised by my side. She'd started the expedition in a base layer top and leggings, and now she was the only one whose newly found camo fitted perfectly.

'She's a quick study,' I replied.

'And you're proud of her, right?'

'All the time,' I said. 'And can't we discuss this somewhere else?'

'Yes, dear.' She chuckled.

'And don't ever call me that again.' I smiled at her, then burst out laughing as she mock saluted me in the pouring rain. 'You look good in your new outfit.'

'Almost as good as you,' she replied.

'Always better than me.'

I locked the door and we headed out, leaving the armoury empty and secure. We formed a circle on a raised patch of mixed grass and moss and faced outwards with overlapping feet. The rain was hosing down and the Glocks were getting their first look at a washed out British summer.

'Everybody pick up a magazine.' I spat rainwater as I spoke. 'Then open a box of ammunition and start filling up.'

We really should have done this back at the armoury, but the whole place spooked me, so instead we did it in the rain. Shiny cartridges slipped into magazines and sat there like fat, brass coloured slugs. Everybody had their own pack or set of pouches, as well as multiple pockets in their newly-donned camo, and the rapidly filled magazines quickly disappeared into them.

'Now,' I said. 'Everybody, take a full magazine, and load. Remember how they go, you can't put them in the wrong way. Watch me.'

I slipped the magazine out of my Glock and held it up. Then, with the pistol in front of me, I slid the magazine into the empty housing where it clicked home. 'Everyone do the same.'

I watched and they followed. 'Listen for the click, feel the click. Good.' Here's where it got dangerous. 'Grab the slide.' They'd all seen this, watched me do it on the demos I'd shown them during the rest breaks that morning. Sixteen hands grabbed sixteen Glock slides.

'Make ready.'

Sixteen sets of working parts were placed under tension, and sixteen bullets slid into sixteen chambers. This wasn't how it had been done before, but this wasn't before.

'Back in the holsters,' I ordered. 'We'll be firing live once we're back home.'

Despite the rain, despite the looming sense of danger at being out in the wilderness, I felt it. The Outcasts were armed, they'd a had very rudimentary training, and they were also a team. Well, two teams if you wanted to be pedantic. I looked around and saw firmly set jaws, eyes instinctively looking outwards, and movements that only a few minutes earlier were soft and unsure, now became firm and precise.

'Let's go,' I said.

A mile from the armoury, the low-branch vegetation thickened up and we closed together for visibility. My mind drifted to the next waypoint, and I worried about keeping the maps dry in the rain. I was already half thinking of the warm water wash and a change of clothes waiting for me when a round stone, half the size of a football, whistled through the air. I looked at it in a silent, semi-dreamlike state. I saw it and I didn't, knowing what it meant and not wanting to accept it.

The stone skimmed past my rain-soaked eyelashes, smacked against a tree trunk and then bounced viciously backwards, hitting Crystal's head with a nauseating crunch. Without a sound her eyes rolled back, her limbs turned to fondant, and she collapsed to the saturated ground. For exactly two seconds I stood there and simply stared, then everything I'd read, learned, planned, and remembered suddenly kicked in. I felt the reset switch flip over in my mind, and time slowed down.

'Enemy!'

Chapter 20

Huge gouts of adrenaline surged through me, and even then, with all of this happening, I wished my voice was an octave higher and I could scream. As it was, my deep tone was still loud enough to cut through everything and generate a satisfyingly instant response. Everyone laid down and faced outwards while multiple, disembodied howls soaked through the sodden trees and undergrowth.

'Keep down,' I ordered. My hearing felt as clear as an alpine dawn, my eyesight more precise than an eagle's, and I felt as young and invincible as I did when I was nineteen. 'Everyone look towards the trees,' I shouted. 'Hold your fire until I say, and as soon as you see someone, call out. Lamp, see what you can do for Crystal.'

More stones sailed through the air and landed with wet thuds in the soft grass. 'Has anyone seen the enemy?' I called out. No one replied. 'Listen in,' I said. 'I want one of them alive.' A softly voiced growl flickered around my circle of half-concealed Outcasts. 'Juno,' I said. 'Your team stays here.' I looked over my shoulder at Crystal, lying still and cold, blood oozing from her temple where the stone had hit her. 'Talk to me, Lamp,' I said. 'How's she doing?'

'She's got a pulse,' said Lamp. 'Dressing applied, slow bleeding. Unconscious. Not much else.'

'We're not leaving her behind,' I said. 'I need her walking out of here, understand?'

'What about the Alphas?'

'You just worry about Crystal,' I replied. 'Everybody. Pistols out,' I ordered. 'If you see an Alpha, point and shoot.'

I saw the stone that had decked out Crystal. A large bloodstain now coated one side of it. I hauled up to one knee and hurled it as far back as I could. 'My team,' I said. 'With me.' The stone disappeared into the undergrowth, and I crawled in the other direction. Lamp stayed behind and I had six Outcasts with me. Would they be enough?

I slithered off at a tangent to where I thought the Alphas were, then peeled right. This was risky. I couldn't see them, they couldn't see us, and we were just about to start shooting. There were lots of things going on here that I really hadn't thought about.

I knew enough to keep low and, in single file, we crawled in a wide circle through rain-soaked undergrowth and up a slight incline. I could hear deep, grunting voices ahead and I froze.

'They're just ahead of us,' a voice whispered in my ear and I saw that Varia had appeared next to me. 'I've seen them.'

'How many?' I asked, wondering if she'd do her usual thing and exaggerate.

'Loads of them,' she hissed. 'We'll never kill them all.'

'You'd better hope we do,' I replied.

'Can we cut their peckers off?'

'No.'

'But—'

'No!'

I put the rest of my team in a line facing the noises and then started to crawl forward.

'Where are *you* going?' Addison gripped my shoulder.

'I've got a plan,' I said.

'Well, what is it?'

'No time to explain,' I replied.

Actually, there was plenty of time to explain, because it was the quickest, dumbest plan going, simply a surprise ambush and hopefully shoot them all before they realised I was there.

'Be careful,' said Addison.

I smiled at her and crawled forward, as quietly as I could, but who was I kidding? If the Alphas had an ounce of sense, they'd have made me straight away. Maybe we were all still learning, or maybe they *did* think with their peckers.

There were three of them, positioned with their backs to us. Just three against sixteen. But it was three Alphas who were now working as a team, and that was a curve ball we didn't want.

Two Alphas were hiding behind a fallen tree trunk and throwing stones at Juno's squad, while a third knelt over the natural parapet, gave unhurried, whispered orders, and tried to guide their aim. This was a co-ordinated effort, with a leader, specific roles, and operating from behind cover. We needed to know a lot more about this shit, but first of all, we had to survive the encounter. I pulled levelled my Glock and aimed for the Alpha who was guiding the others. He'd have been ideal as a prisoner, but I didn't want him escaping and he was also far too dangerous to leave alive.

Alive.

Before, I'd have kept low and disappeared my way out of there, with maybe a barrel or two from the shotgun, fired as a random deterrent, but never used for killing.

Not anymore. The Alphas' trap had already given them one casualty, and if I didn't kill these Alphas, they'd kill us. Now I was aiming for the central body mass with the express intent to kill. This was survival; this was protecting my team.

I was five metres away from them, on raised ground behind them, and I couldn't miss. I fired two shots, so close together they almost sounded like one, and the lead Alpha was dead before he even knew he'd been hit. There wasn't any blood, not even the small haze that I'd expected to see from the entry wound. He just tensed and fell forward, his spine shattered and his filthy, ragged clothes soaking up any blood that would normally have showered outwards. The effect on the other two, though, was electrifying. They heard the gunshots and their gaze quickly shifted from their dead friend to me. Shock spread across their faces, their cohesion dissolved like melt-water in the sun, and they both sprang to their feet and ran, barrelling straight towards Juno's team.

'Team Alex,' I shouted. 'Get down.'

I flopped down on the wet forest floor and heard the whip-crack of multiple gunshots, followed by raindrop stillness.

'Juno,' I shouted, still lying flat in case any more fingers were on triggers. 'Is the area clear? Are you safe?'

'Two dead,' she called back.

'Ours or theirs?'

I heard the laughter first. 'Theirs. No prisoners.'

I stood up and retraced my team. 'Come on,' I snapped. 'We've been shooting and making noise. That's going to bring every Alpha for miles around down on top of us.'

'Then we'll kill them,' said Varia. She stood up and fumbled with her webbing belt. 'I've seen loads of them now. They don't scare me.' I cringed as she holstered her pistol while still holding the trigger, and I kept my eyes closed, waiting for the bang and a nine-toed Outcast.

No bang.

'Follow me,' I said. 'Now.'

I'd just killed someone for the first time. I should have been a sprawling mass of emotions, but as much as I wanted to stop right there and think about it, I knew I couldn't. Others were thinking and feeling the same, and I was responsible for all of them.

We ran back the way we'd crawled out, low lying leaves brushing against our already sodden clothes and I didn't even notice. At the harbour area I saw Lamp kneeling over a still comatose Crystal, while Juno's team knelt in an outward circle. At their centre were two dead and very bloodstained Alphas, track marks on the wet ground showing where they'd been dragged from. One of them wore the usual ragged Alpha garb, torn and filthy overalls, while the other drew my attention. He was equally bullet-ridden and loose-limbed as only the dead can be, but it was his clothing that instantly marked him apart. He was dressed as some sort of priest.

A priest?

And that was the last thing I expected. Because while the Alphas didn't exactly have a uniform, they all tended to wear distressed remnants of anything that came to hand.

Apart from this one. Strange didn't even come close, and I thought *I* was weird.

'What the hell is this with his clothes?' I asked.

'I don't know,' said Juno.

'Me neither,' said Addison. She smiled at me. 'I bet even Varia hasn't seen this loads of times.'

'Greta, Arc,' I picked the two nearest Outcasts at random. Greta was small and quick, Arc, long-limbed and gangly. 'Search those two lumps of meat,' I said. 'Let's see if they can't still tell us something.'

Searching the dead like it was nothing, except it wasn't nothing. Greta and Arc looked pale and upset, but they didn't hesitate as they went through two sets of worn out, bullet-holed and bloodstained clothing. The first dead Alpha had nothing, not even a knife. Half-healed cuts and borderline malnourished body spoke of the usual harsh life in the wilderness. The priest, for want of anything else to call him, was equally thin, but showed no wounds or scars. He carried two rudimentary bandages, a creased paper diagram, and an unopened pack of sutures.

Sutures!

Anyone who didn't know what they were or how to use them wouldn't have hold of them, but this dead Alpha did.

Running in teams, giving orders, medical back-up.

Things were changing.

I looked more closely at the diagram. Shit. This wasn't a diagram, it was a map. Well, part of a map, but a specifically cut part of a map. I squinted at the paper in the hosing rain, hunched over it to stop it becoming waterlogged in the deluge. It was a hillside. I'd have recognised those light brown contour lines and numbers anywhere. This strangely dressed but still dead Alpha had part of an Ordnance Survey map on him.

But why?

Time to think later. Right now, we had to move. I knelt down next to Lamp. 'How's Crystal?' I asked.

'She's coming around,' said Lamp. 'And she's stopped pissing blood. That direct pressure stuff really works.' Lamp's hands were pressed against both sides of Crystal's head, as though she was squeezing a ball. One of her hands was over the impact site and washed through with rained-on rivulets of blood. Crystal lay on her back, swaddled in donated camo. It would keep her warm and protected from the rain for as long as it took for the layers of clothing to become soaked through, and then hypothermia would add to the shock, and it didn't look good from then on in.

Welcome to reality, I thought to myself. *Welcome to leadership. You wanted it, now deal with it.* I forced my thoughts away from the worst case scenario. Crystal was still alive. This was the real world, real life outside the wire, and people were always going to get hurt. Hurt, yes. Dead? No fucking way.

'Can she walk?' I asked.

'She'll need help,' said Lamp. 'Unless you want to wait two hours.'

'No chance,' I said. 'Arc, Varia, get either side of her. You're her legs and we're leaving. Single file apart from Crystal, Lamp, and whoever's helping Crystal walk. You four stay in the middle. Everyone else, eyes open. We've got distance to cover and we're heading straight back to my place.'

'Hey.' Addison appeared at my side. She touched my arm lightly and I looked at her. 'Are *you* alright?' she asked.

'I'm not the one who got hurt,' I said.

'That's not what I mean and you know it. You took a life today, and that's a big thing, it's a huge thing.'

'I know,' I said.

'Talk later?'

'You bet.'

'What's a bet?'

I smiled. 'I'll tell you when we get back. Outcasts!' I snapped out the order. 'Let's go.'

Crystal was walking, but only just, and it was more from the joint engines of Arc and Varia than her own feet that got her out of there. But at least it raised her consciousness as well as her blood pressure. If it didn't kill her, maybe it would force her to recover.

*

With dusk slowly settling, the stony ground and birch trees surrounding the bunker blissfully emerged from the wilderness.

'Not *this* again,' muttered Varia. I could kind of see her point as we lay down in the pissing rain, spitting distance from warmth and shelter, and watched. 'They won't just wait here to ambush us,' she said. 'I've seen them loads of times, they're not that patient.'

'Maybe they're out there, but they're just asleep,' I replied. '*I've* seen that before.'

I looked back at the bunker, scanned for any sign, listened for any sound. Everything looked clear, but I could feel the lurking, unseen night dangers closing in on us.

'For fuck's sake, Alex,' muttered Varia. 'Just have great big pits with spikes in them if you're that worried about getting raided while you're away.'

'I tried that already.' I chuckled. 'And I nearly fell into the bastard thing myself.'

'I had no idea you were so bloody blind,' she replied. 'Best you stick to your blades of grass and stone piles.'

I led the Outcasts over the clear ground, unlocked the door and counted us all inside.

'Greta, Addison,' I said. 'Take the windows, stay alert, and keep checking outside. Lamp, get Crystal into the medical room. Stay with her, she's your responsibility. Juno, everyone else rests. Organise a rota and make sure everybody takes their turn at sentry duty. If they're not on guard, they get dry, they eat and they sleep. Once I've seen to Crystal, we'll talk about today, and figure out what we need to do better next time.'

I walked into the med room and saw Crystal lying on the canvas camp bed. Lamp had released her vice-like hold on her head, Crystal's wound had stopped bleeding, and she had a swelling the size of a ripe strawberry. It could have been a fracture, but I didn't have an x-ray machine, so what the hell did I know?

'What do you think, Lamp?'

'Shit on a stick, Alex,' she gasped. 'You're asking *me*?'

'Are you the team medic or not?' I asked.

'Well...'

'Well, nothing,' I said. 'We weren't ready for that contact today, but we still dealt with it. And you might think you're not ready to help Crystal yet, but unless you make that leap and just do it, you'll never be ready.'

Lamp's lower lip trembled and I cursed myself for being so utterly crap at speaking to people. I never said it right.

'You're not alone,' I tried again. 'I'm here, we've got all of my kit to back us up. You know more than you think you do, Lamp.'

'Truly?' she whispered.

'Would I lie?' I smiled. 'So, tell me what you know about Crystal, tell me what you've done, then tell me what you're going to do.'

'She's exhausted,' said Lamp. 'That was one fucking big stone that hit her, and she's lucky to be alive.'

'So she's got a head injury,' I said. 'What else?'

'Nothing,' she replied, her voice firming up. 'And stop trying to trick me. While you were fannying around with that weirdly dressed Alpha, I was doing a full body check on Crystal. Apart from her head wound, she's tip top.'

'So what did you do?' I asked.

'Direct pressure with a field dressing, then once the bleeding stopped, I checked the wound.'

'You must have really pushed that dressing into place,' I said. 'All I could see were your hands. So, direct pressure, then check the wound. Was that the right way around?'

'I don't bloody know,' said Lamp. 'And nor do you, Alex, but she's still alive, so I couldn't have gone too far wrong.'

'Good answer. What next?'

'I checked her eyes for dilation pop-out. They're equal, reacting to light, and now I just hope to hell she wakes up.'

'Brilliant,' I said. 'I'd have done the same. What's important is that we didn't lose her out there. And now that we're back here, we can throw everything we've got at her.' I looked at Crystal; she was sleeping and softly breathing. I leaned against the wall and folded my arms. 'You're the lead medic and I'm your helper. Tell me what to do, and tell me what *you're* going to do.'

Lamp looked around the medical room and whistled softly. Then she grabbed the sphyg and wrapped the cuff around Crystal's arm.

'Observations tell you a lot about your patient,' she said. 'The Healing Sisters said the same thing. Look at the skin colour, the breathing, what they say, how much they eat, drink and piss.'

'That's all good.' I smiled at her. 'So what about blood pressure and pulse?'

Lamp squeezed the rubber bulb and the cuff tightened around Crystal's arm. I gave her the stethoscope. 'Plug it into your ears,' I told her. 'Put the diaphragm here.' I placed it on the crook of Crystal's elbow. 'Squeeze here, look at the needle here, release the pressure here. When you hear the pulse, that's your top reading. When you can't hear it, that's your bottom reading.'

'A hundred over forty,' Lamp murmured. I wrote down the numbers. 'That's low,' she said.

'We'd be more worried if she was up and running around with those stats,' I said, 'but she's laying down and relaxing. It's low, but we'll take it. Then we keep checking, and that's another reason why we need accurate clocks and watches.'

'*That* again?' Lamp rolled her eyes, then watched me as I put in a cannula and started a bag of fluid.

Crystal stabilised, and that was a good thing, but it still wrecked what I'd hoped for, which was a night of reflection, talking about what had happened at the armoury, learning, and then improving for the next time. Instead, I didn't sleep at all as I made sure the sentries stayed alert, then saw to it that everyone else ate and slept, while still rotating myself through sentry and medical overwatch.

Addison became my shadow as I went from one room to the next. She mirrored my checks, talked, reassured, and did a much better job at it than I did. She looked at me, and the lines around her mouth relaxed slightly.

'Any movement out there?' I asked.

'None,' she said. 'How's Crystal?'

I felt all eyes turn to me as Addison asked what everyone else wanted to know. 'She's stable,' I said. 'Lamp's got her and she'll be fine. One more scar for the Outcasts, and nothing for the Alphas.'

'My sentry shift has finished,' said Addison. 'And we need to talk. You have to tell me what a bet is.'

We crouched down in the hallway next to the kitchen.

'It's a promise,' I whispered, sitting as close to her as I dared, and using the pretence of having to talk quietly as my excuse, if she ever asked.

She didn't ask.

'A promise?' she looked at me with a creased forehead and her dark eyebrows nearly joined. 'Really?'

'I promise.'

'You promise?'

'You bet,' I smiled at her.

Hey, I remembered some stuff and I've read *some* books, but I haven't read *all* of them.

Another reason I didn't sleep that night was because I kept questioning my own performance, my leadership, about how I'd let Crystal get hurt in the first place. I felt like it was all on me, all my fault, everything.

Just before dawn, Lamp came looking for me. 'Crystal's awake.'

I sat upright from my spot at the window, shook myself like a wet dog and barrelled into the medical room.

Whatever it was that made me think about even having a med space, I was never so grateful. First Juno, and now Crystal. And even if me and Lamp weren't proper, real medics, what little we did know and what little amount of years out of date equipment I had squirreled away, it helped.

'Christ, Alex,' said Crystal. 'You look like shit.' She was sitting up, and a chunk of her long, ivory-coloured hair had been shaved and replaced with a very ungraceful sticky dressing. She was even paler than normal, but she was smiling.

'It's been a long night.' I smiled back at her.

'Well,' she said. 'You'd better smarten yourself up before we go back to the settlement. I don't want you showing us up looking like that, especially after you taught Lamp as well as you did.'

I laughed. The night's exhaustion sloughed away from me, and as the dawn glimmered over the trees, I realised that we were no longer a disparate bunch of Strauss misfits, and while we might have always been outcasts, now we were Outcasts that belonged to each other.

Chapter 21

As much as Silver might have tried, and as much as Collar really would have tried, it simply wasn't possible to give up the bunker. And it wouldn't have been a good idea, either. Silver would have understood, and Collar would have as well, although she'd never say it.

The Outcasts set up a permanent presence there. Sometimes we ferried back to Purleyont Hames in small numbers, mainly to let Silver know we were still alive and making plans and preparations, but also to reassure Collar that we hadn't disappeared to form our own base somewhere else. And now that we had firearms, we had to learn to use them properly.

Outside of the Strauss boundary, the bunker was a secure location. Our only secure location. I smiled at that thought, a small but tangible acknowledgement that I wasn't just thinking in terms of my own existence. And besides, the place had a working vegetable garden, a weapons store, and medical facilities. My books, along with my girl-stash of clothes and make-up, had all been moved back to Purleyont Hames. It felt a bit like giving something up as a hostage, but I had to do *something* to prove that I wasn't about to do a runner.

And so, as my possessions emptied out and the Outcasts moved in, the bunker became less about me and more about us.

*

'Why do we have to bother with all of this?' asked Varia. It was always Varia asking the questions, and by now I expected it. What was bothering her this time, quite reasonably, was why she had to squelch along a meadow floor on all fours just after it had been raining. All of the Outcasts were wet, and now they were getting filthy, and their camo was getting wetter and heavier by the second.

'Because we need to get close,' I said. 'We need to be unseen. The sooner they see us, the sooner they try to kill us.'

Varia grumbled but carried on crawling forward. I'd heaped a pile of ready-chopped firewood into a mound at one end of the field, and it became the imaginary objective in as many varied scenarios as I could devise.

'Incoming fire,' I shouted. 'Team two, hold. Team one, move left.'

I'd quickly discovered that being in charge was really hard, even with simple evolutions, even when there weren't actually any real enemies. In my mind were all sorts of complicated what-ifs, and I then had to translate that into simple orders and movements for the teams.

Decisions. None of my memories and none of the books I'd read *ever* prepared me for that.

'They're armed,' I said, making sure I stood behind everyone. 'They're shooting at you and they want to kill you, so put down some fire.'

Spaced shots popped out from the static team. It was a world away from the sudden, short-blast cacophony of noise that the dead Alphas had faced back at the armoury, but as long as it kept their heads down while we worked closer, it would be enough.

When it was for real, the shotguns would be used, but I had to temper training with supplies. Get them used to the pistols, get them used to firearms, and then I'd figure out who'd be best with the shotguns, once I'd worked out how to best use them.

Even more decisions.

While the team giving covering fire stayed put, I followed the second team as they snaked sideways. I'd left random logs on the ground to represent vegetation and slowly, half of the Outcasts moved forwards. It was a basic take on the flank attack: keep their heads down and then come at them from the side.

I switched people around, giving everyone a chance to take charge. 'But *you're* in charge.' Greta looked up at me as her team approached the slowly disintegrating pile of damp firewood.

'And what if I get hit?' I asked her. 'What if I get hurt, like Crystal did? We can't ever stop if we lose people.'

Greta's team were at right angles to the wood pile. She wore a bright pink hair band around her thick brown hair. It was a simple way to identify the team leader.

'You're giving the orders this time,' I said. 'You decide what to do.'

Greta nodded, kept her pistol pointed at the target, and pulled out a whistle. Quite why I'd thought to stash a whole load of them, I don't know, but they were really proving their worth as simple communication tools. I kept the whistle blasts as simple as possible. There weren't any codes, or sequence of blasts, it was just one long whistle tone, which meant everyone moved to the next drill.

And if it was a whistle on a flank attack, it meant stop the covering fire, the flanking team are going in.

Greta sprang to her feet and screamed out a challenge. It was a wordless, innate and individual sound, and the rest of the team followed her, screaming their own rage-war battle-cry. They ran forward in a line abreast, scanning the ground in front and looking for targets. Once they got closer, it was aimed shots into whoever they found.

'Kill them all,' screamed Greta. She held her Glock close to the woodpile and fired into the rapidly splintering logs. She controlled her group, checked the enemy position for signs of life, then brought everyone to ground in a circle, pistols pointing outwards. Then it was one more whistle and the covering team scampered forward. Georgia brought them in and they formed a circle next to Greta's. For real, if time allowed and there were no more enemies to see, ammunition would be counted and spread around, injuries checked, more enemies located. If there was still a fight going on, the next assault would be planned.

If, if, if. That was the one word haunting me.

'Good work, team Greta,' I said. She looked up at me, covered in mud splats, her mouth clamped shut and a killing look in her eyes. Whatever bunch of bastards she'd imagined the pile of firewood to be, in her mind, they were still out there. 'What happens next?' I asked.

'Help the hurt and finish the job,' she said.

'Help the hurt and finish the job,' repeated everyone else.

'And we don't leave anyone behind.' I joined in with the final line. 'Because at Greenwich,' I said, 'we'll all be a long way from home.'

'Get a load of Lara Croft here,' laughed Greta. The Outcasts stood up and we walked back to the bunker.

'Who's that?' asked Crystal, wiping mud from her face.

'Lara Croft?' said Greta, stowing her Glock and then patting the holster. 'She was some antique dealer that went around the world looking for old artefacts. She wore a funny hat and had a gun and a whip.'

'Alex hasn't got a whip,' said Crystal. 'Or a funny hat.'

'No, but she's got a gun and she's looking for old stuff. Is that close enough for you?'

'And why do you need to go to Greenwich anymore, anyway?' asked Addison. For once she was as mud-stained as the others, yet somehow still managed to *look* clean.

'I don't know what you mean,' I said.

'You know exactly what I mean,' said Addison. 'Silver gave you a charging cable already, which means you've got juice for your phone. You don't need one of those stupid clocks, and we don't need to risk our skins to help you get one.'

'Those clocks aren't stupid,' I said. 'When you see one, you'll understand.'

'Will you dress up for us if we go there with you?' asked Addison, smiling at me in a way I was finding hard to fight, and she knew it.

'You'd risk your life to see me in a dress?' I asked her.

'Depends on the dress,' she replied.

Chapter 22

'But where?' I asked no one in particular.

Ever since we'd killed the Alphas outside the armoury, we'd been poring over the scrap of map we'd recovered, and it was tantalising in its vagueness. Three Alphas working together, one of them giving fire control orders to the stone throwers, one of them dressed like a priest, *and* equipped with sutures and carrying part of a map. The sutures I could understand, that was easy. He was there to patch up any injuries. But the map? Was it a token, a sign of importance, was it a pass, to allow him past a barrier?

Or was it there to identify a particular point?

But if that was the case, where the hell was the rest of the map? Because on its own, showing just a little scrap of land, it could literally be anywhere.

One thing was for sure, though. We absolutely couldn't ignore it.

'There's definitely a hill,' Juno's finger traced the contour lines. We were crowded around the creased scrap of paper, which was laid flat on the kitchen table. All sixteen of us followed Juno's narrative. 'That's a forest, and this is a road and this is a tower.' She pointed to the two features.

'But it doesn't give us a location,' I said.

'We *have* to find it,' she replied. 'That Alpha was something different, way different to anything we've ever seen before. And if they've got a base, and they're ambushing us near a weapon stash, we need to know about it.'

Juno was right. I sighed and stood up, collected my entire collection of ordnance survey maps and passed them around. 'Let's try and narrow this down before we do anything else,' I said. 'If we can agree on a location, we'll go there and see what we can find.'

*

In the end we found three possibilities, so we put them to the vote, chose one of them, and we had a mission. We were going to go where we *thought* the map on the dead Alpha was showing, and we'd see if there was anything there. Even if there was nothing, it would test our movement across country, our navigation skills, and if we came across any Alphas, we'd be tested on a whole load of other stuff as well.

I looked at the Alpha's map, then the Ordnance Survey more closely.

'Holy shit!' I said. 'Green Man Common. We're going to Green Man Common.'

I'd heard about that place, somewhere, somewhere in my mind.

'What the hell is that?' asked Addison. 'It doesn't even sound real.'

'It's real,' I gabbled. 'It's real.' I leant over the map that was laid out on the kitchen table and Addison stood next to me, her limbs lightly brushing mine as she followed my wild finger-stab on the map.

'Are you sure that's what it says?' she asked. 'The writing's a bit faded.'

'It has to be,' I replied. 'The place is a legend.'

'What's so special about it?' Addison looked more closely at the map. 'Looks like a green space to me.'

'It used to be a fortress, a security base, something like that,' I said. 'A long time ago, a really long time ago. I'm not quite sure, but it was somewhere with real power.'

'And?'

'And a group of women,' I said. 'All of them heroes, they marched to this place, unarmed.'

'Were they killed?' asked Addison.

'No,' I replied. 'They won, they defeated the men, and Green Man Common became a symbol of peace winning out over war, of life winning out over killing.'

'Or women winning out over men,' laughed Addison. 'I can see where you're going with this.'

'No,' I said. 'This was talked about, *she* spoke about it.'

'This leader of yours? Tanya Strauss?'

I nodded. 'She spoke about it like she was there, almost,' I said. 'She said it was what made her want to join up in the first place.'

'And we just chose to go there?' asked Addison.

'Near enough,' I said. 'Green Man common is here.' I pointed to an area of flat, low-lying ground on the map. 'And we think that section of Alpha map is here.' My finger moved to a hilltop overlooking the common.

'And why wasn't this fortress on the hilltop instead?' asked Addison. 'It would have made a lot more sense if it was.'

'Maybe it was,' I said. 'Maybe the women lived on the common, met on the common.' I shook my head in frustration and cursed my incomplete memories. 'I don't know the whole story, I just don't.'

'And you think we'll achieve what they did?'

'Maybe,' I said. I turned and looked into Addison's soft brown eyes. 'Depends what we find.'

Addison returned my look without speaking, a slight smile tugging at her lips. 'Then we'd better get ready,' she replied.

*

It was always going to be an early start, and even though I expected the tinkling, pre-dawn alarm from my phone that now did everything except take calls, I couldn't help a small bit of sleep-deprived grumpiness.

'That's *your* rules with the time keeping,' smirked Addison, her black hair sleek and tidy in her long ponytails, her camo crisp, clean, and smoothly fitting her. Addison seemed to look good, smart, and well-groomed no matter what time it was. In contrast, I grumbled, shivered slightly in the early morning chill, and pulled on my own wrinkled camo.

Birds sang in the nearby trees and the sky lightened. Shapes took on colour and the surrounding forest became less than silhouette. All around me, the Outcasts stirred and got ready. Muted whispers as newly made teams chatted and checked each other's kit. They were gelling, coming together, and it was good to see.

'Weapons check, ammo check,' I said. 'The last thing we do before moving.'

'The last thing we do before moving,' they chorused back at me in soft whispers. Everybody was talking quietly; they didn't need to be told, and that was good, too. I checked that my Glock was securely holstered, ammo pouches laced shut, and that I had good supplies. Everybody carried water bottles and rations. My tinned food stash was being rapidly depleted, but it was worth it to keep the team viable, and a replenishment mission was now climbing to the top of my to-do list.

The bunker's main corridor was now packed with tooled up, cammed up Outcasts. I unlocked the front door and we slipped out into the new day in single file. I wasn't in the front and that was planned. Everything I learned and already knew, I was teaching to the Outcasts, and to let them know I trusted them, they'd be taking turns at navigating, using both map and compass.

And they were fast, too. While I didn't know exactly how old I was, I was damn sure I'd never see thirty again, but no way was I going to be the one to slow the pace, and I dug deep into my own reserves and stepped out.

We stuck to the forest paths, occasionally finding decaying fence posts and crumbling brick walls, now being used as obstacle courses for red and grey squirrels. But as much as we were travelling tactically, with no talking, always looking outwards, sixteen people on the move was always going to make *some* noise, so it was a hedgehog circle of outward pointing Glocks at every pit stop.

The woods were alive with sounds now that nature had reclaimed the world. Birds sang with different rhythms through the day, as though they alone were the only creatures to be heard, while on the forest floor, bushes and low-lying vegetation constantly shifted as unseen company moved past us. Occasional growls, snuffles, and grunts gave the foliage its own distinctive, disembodied voice.

'Landmark!' Lamp shouted out from the head of the column. We moved into a defensive circle and I scampered over to Lamp.

'What have you seen?' I asked.

'Church tower,' she said, flicking her orange hair clear of her eyes. 'Half right through the low trees.' She pointed into the distance to emphasise what she'd seen, and she was right. I had to squint through the light green leaves to see the pale stonework, and then I had to reach for my binoculars to make out a square-built tower that had survived the centuries. Lamp had spotted it with eyes and nothing else, and on the move as well.

'That's a good spot,' I said. 'My team, stay put. Juno's team, on me and watch how Lamp puts us on the map.' Lamp shot an anxious, wide-eyed look at me. 'Hey,' I said. 'You found that tower before I even knew it was there. If you can do that, you can do the rest. I know it.'

Lamp nodded shakily and pulled out the map. 'Compass,' she called. Greta crawled forward, pulled out a chipped Silva compass and took a bearing. The needle held north as though it had just been put together at the factory, and Greta squinted at the dial and then looked through to the tower. She lowered the compass onto the map that Lamp had placed on the forest floor, and married the two together.

'Map is orientated to the compass,' she mouthed the words like a robot, then looked around to see if there were any more landmarks. 'This is where we are.' She pointed to a spot on the map.

'Excellent work,' I said. 'Lamp, stay put. Juno, choose a pathfinder for the next leg. Lamp, hand over the route to them.'

With a slight rustling of undergrowth, both teams swapped places and Lamp handed over the location to Arc. 'This is where we're headed,' she said, concluding the switch. 'It's your route now.' Lamp and Arc shook hands.

I smiled. On its own, the handshake was nothing, but I knew it meant more, and I was secretly pleased at the small monster I'd created in team building.

At a forest clearing, a remaining roadside or marshy riverbank, each stop and waypoint was the same, including the handshake. Food and drink were taken quickly and cold, and not one Outcast complained when we sprawled in the wet undergrowth, or when a chill wind brought even more squally rainfall onto us.

But wherever we were going, we were never going to do it in a day. And that was a problem, because daylight gave most living things a kind of equality, an ability to use your strengths, whatever they were, to some kind of advantage.

Not so at night, especially with the feral dogs. In the daytime, they were relatively easy to get around. In the dark, you'd never see them in time to get a shot off.

The answer was simple enough: sleep in the trees and you'll be safe from everything on the ground, which meant sixteen hammocks in the trees, and that's where we stayed all night.

Not that we slept right through. When you're out in the wild, as soon as the loudest animal in the forest is awake and squawking, so are you. Surrounded by the birdsong all around me, I looked at the luminous dial on my watch, which gave me just past three o'clock.

Dawn slowly emerged. We scrambled out of our hammocks, laced up our kit, and with Greta taking the first lead, we moved off in single file. Our target point for the day was a hill with a tower at the top.

Chapter 23

'Up there,' said Juno.

We lay in a circle just inside a treeline at the base of a hill, and even from here, a rusting metal radio tower was still visible. One of the spars had corroded right through and it wouldn't be standing for much longer. Already it leant over at a crazy angle, and whatever it had been put there for, it was now just a landmark. Open grassland ran smoothly up the lower half of the hill before becoming forest once more.

There was no way I could know without seeing it on the map, but somewhere around here was Green Man Common, the legendary open area of grassland where once, unarmed women had defeated a bunch of armed men. If I was looking for some kind of sign, though, it wasn't there. All I could see now was mixed forest and pasture, just another small piece of wilderness.

It was a typical summer day, mixed cloud and blue sky. The birds gently twittered to each other in among the treetops, while at ground level, I looked past the open meadow. We were a day and a half out from the bunker, and even further from Purleyont Hames. I hadn't been this far away from my base in years.

'It could be the place,' I said. 'But what happens if we don't find anything?'

'We'll find something,' said Juno. 'They didn't have that map on them for the hell of it, right?'

'Then we need to start being a lot more careful,' I replied. 'No more talking unless we're in a defensive circle, and everyone stays in sight of everyone else.'

The clear ground between us and the hill's upper slope beckoned like a siren on the rocks. It was no more than a hundred and fifty metres wide and we could be across it in less than a minute. But to do that when we were potentially this close to the bad guys? Not a chance. I looked left and right and saw trees skirting the small pasture.

'Take your team and follow the treeline to the right,' I whispered to Juno. 'Stay under cover. I'll go left and we'll meet up on the other side of the grassed area. Do you see that pine tree straight ahead?' I asked her. 'All on its own, surrounded by short growing ash?'

'*That's* the rendezvous?' she whispered. 'A little obvious, isn't it?'

'I can tell you had a good teacher,' I chuckled. 'Twenty metres uphill from that point, go to ground, and we'll plan our next step from there.'

Rising to our knees at the same time, Juno and I peeled off in opposite directions, taking our teams with us. The vegetation was mixed pine and deciduous, which probably meant that at one time it was a pine plantation, although now the conifers were gradually being eased out as nature made the calls. I could still smell the pine needles on the lower slope, but as the gradient steepened, the small-leafed ash trees took over. Our eyes flickered everywhere for signs of Alphas, sounds of feral dogs. All I could hear, though, was the benign music of nature; the soft wind rustling though the foliage, and the gentle, wordless songs of birds. Our own footfalls were as quiet as we could make them, and any noise we made was swallowed up by the gently yielding soil that was overlaid with a thick mulch of last winter's leaf-shedding.

We moved slowly and cautiously. I replayed in my mind the ambush after we'd left the armoury. Could I have prevented it? Should I have seen something, a sign or a sound? Was I leading us all into a trap right now? My chest tightened and I started to imagine suspicious movements behind every tree trunk.

It took exactly seven minutes for my team to edge around the grassland and sink into a defensive circle at the rendezvous. Twenty-seven seconds later, Juno's team were alongside us, two circles of Outcasts, and I felt a bit better.

But not by much. Every step now was a step closer to…what? I didn't know, but if the map was accurate, and if it was leading us somewhere, and if we'd deciphered it correctly, then we might come across Alphas. Maybe they'd be regular ones, maybe they'd be dressed like priests.

And if they were, then this time we'd at least *try* and get one of them alive, and find out what the hell they were all about. Juno's team would stay put as a back-up, and secure the harbour, while I'd lead my team up the hill to see what we could see. Once we'd done a quick recce, it was back down the hill to make a final plan.

Time to move, and thought-sludging fear addled around my mind as I slowly and carefully led my team up the hill. I scanned through the trees as far as I could see, strained my ears, listening for everything, anything.

A twig snapped up ahead and we dropped to the floor. I knew all about that sound. It was the one warning you might get. It was the last warning you might get.

I didn't know if it was a human or an animal coming towards us, but as the footsteps got closer, I realised they were evenly spaced and deliberate. Then I heard the slow, heavy breathing. It had to be humans. Silently, I slipped my Glock forward, suddenly wishing I'd brought the shotgun.

The footsteps stopped. My nerves screamed tension within me and it felt like my whole body was being stretched and squeezed at the same time. I looked over the Glock's barrel into a beard of ferns, as visually impassable as if it had been virgin forest that was hundreds of years old. Suddenly, the vegetation parted and I saw two figures, two pairs of legs, close together, both wearing patched up priest's cassocks. Then I heard their breathing, deep, laboured and as ragged as their clothing.

'Are we far enough away?' I heard one speaking with a hoarse whisper.

'We've lost them for good in this bush.'

'They'll kill us if they find us.'

'They're jealous if they find us. And we won't be sold either, no matter what they say, no matter what Sentinel tells them.'

Sentinel?

The two figures advanced forward a few more steps, and I could see two slim Alphas, holding hands and standing so close they were practically sewn together. They stopped and faced each other, hands touching, and then I heard the unmistakable sound of a kiss. I looked up and saw that even if we'd rampaged around them and fired off all our weapons, these two were oblivious to everything apart from themselves. I'd seen Alpha urges before, but never love, never tender passion, and never towards each other.

I guess it still happened, and clearly it did. It just didn't fit in with their usual style. Maybe there was hope for them after all.

No time for philosophy though, and these were the weirdly dressed anomalies that we needed to learn more about. They'd said enough to tell me they were probably fugitives, and if that was so, then they were the ideal people to get information from.

Sending back a hand signal to the others to stay still, I snaked forward, suddenly owning the skills for sneaking up on people. Within seconds I was close enough to reach out and untie their shoelaces, and still they didn't know I was there. If anything, they were even more into each other as the seconds passed. I stood up and placed the Glock barrel against an Alpha temple.

'Don't make a sound,' I whispered.

Two grimy, cassock-clad males, with knotted matts of black and auburn hair, stopped in mid-kiss, and two pairs of terrified eyes rolled towards the Glock, then me. I walked around them so that I was uphill of them and facing south. Uncertainty and fear was stamped on their faces. Their rapid head movements, their trembling fingers, and their absolute compliance spoke of their sudden terror.

I pointed the Glock and herded them downhill. The rest of my team rose silently from the ground and circled the two captives. We hustled along, quicker but also a bit noisier than I'd have liked. As I walked them down the slope, I got back into it and appraised our concealment techniques. Juno's team lay flat on the ground in their camo, and in among the undergrowth, they were practically invisible. I shoved the two Alphas to their knees.

'Juno,' I whispered, and she ghosted into view next to me, staring inquisitively at the two Alphas.

'What are we going to do with them?' she asked. They stared at her, clearly petrified as they gaped at the crossbow on her back.

'Information,' I replied.

Juno cast an amused look at me. 'They won't tell us anything,' she said. 'They're Alphas.'

'They'll tell us everything.' I smiled, grimly. 'They're on the run.'

Chapter 24

The two Alphas crouched in the expanded circle as both Outcast teams formed a defensive ring around them. Everywhere they looked showed the same impenetrable barrier of no escape. But they were still alive, and they knew they had something to bargain with.

'On the hillside, you said they'll kill you if they found you.' I said to them. 'Why would they do that?'

'Kill *us*?' sneered the black-haired one. 'It's *you* they'll kill, a bunch of cannibal bitches you are, and being killed is all you're good for anyway.'

'Cannibals?' hissed Juno. She leapt forward and grabbed one of them by the throat. 'What do you take us for?'

'For what we've seen,' he replied. His voice was shaking. In fact, his whole body was shaking, and you couldn't blame him for being scared, but despite that he returned Juno's perfectly acted out accusing stare, eyeball for eyeball. 'You're nothing but savages,' he said. 'We've seen the bodies of our own after you've finished with them, we've even looked after the survivors.'

'What's on top of that hill?' I repeated.

'All that's here is the healing house,' he replied. 'Nothing else. They've learned, they've worked out not to have too much in one place, in case bitches like you come along.'

'Yeah,' said the other Alpha. He was similar to his friend, only with auburn hair. 'We know all about you. Sentinel told us. So go ahead and kill us right now, why don't you?'

'I won't kill you,' I snarled. 'I won't kill either of you. But if one of you doesn't talk, we'll sure as hell torture the other one.'

That got their attention. It was a low trick, but it worked. They were a thing, they had stones, and if it was only themselves facing the pain, I knew they'd die before they talked. But if we hurt the one they loved?

We wouldn't, or at least I wouldn't, but they didn't know that. I holstered my Glock and pulled out my knife, then stepped towards them with a mad, killing hate in my eyes.

'Alright, alright,' said the black haired one. 'What do you want to know?'

Was I convincing or what?

'We want to know everything,' I said. 'But first of all, why would they kill you if they caught you? You're one of them, right?'

'Do we look like them?' asked Black Hair. 'Do we dress like them? We heal them, and that's as far as it goes.'

'What do you mean?'

'Oh, bitch, please,' he replied. 'You saw what we were doing when you took us.'

'So what?' I said. 'So you were kissing. Big deal. People do it all the time when they like each other. What are you supposed to do, wait for a woman to come along?'

'*That's* the only thing some of them remember,' said Auburn Hair. 'Some of them, enough of them, they think it's the natural order, they think it's the only way.' He shrugged. 'Anyway, Sentinel's set the law, so you do what you have to if you want to survive. And if you've got to keep things secret to keep on breathing, then that's what you do.'

'Who the hell is Sentinel?' I asked.

'He's the boss,' said Black Hair.

'The boss?' I looked at Addison, who raised her eyebrows.

'Yeah,' said Auburn Hair. 'He's been on the scene a few years now, got his own set of followers called the Inquisitors. They make the law, they enforce the law, and they forbid different love.'

'Different?' I asked.

'Like us.' He looked quickly over to Black Hair. 'And they won't allow the Judas Priests to have *any* love. They say that if we care too much about each other or anyone else, how can we care for the sick and wounded? Why do you think we were running in the first place? We've had enough of their shit.'

'What the hell are the Judas Priests?' asked Juno.

'Us.' Auburn Hair thumbed his pigeon chest with a stubborn pride.

'Yes,' said Black Hair. 'We'll either heal you or hell you. Something like that. Anyway, it's what they call us, it's what they teach us.'

'They taught you to heal people,' I said. 'Isn't that a good thing?'

'Depends who you have to heal,' said Auburn Hair. 'The Alphas control the hill and Sentinel controls them.' He glared back at me like it was my fault.

'This hill,' I said, nodding towards the hilltop. 'Is that where you do your work?'

'It's where we get instructed as well,' nodded Black Hair. 'The old ones teach us what to do. They know how to do it. They've always known. They give us these clothes and that's our lives decided. They say that's how it was before.'

'They remember the past?' I asked them.

'They say they do,' said Auburn Hair.

'You're going to show us this hill,' I said to the one with black hair. 'And I don't want to hear you saying no, because if you don't, we'll kill your friend. And as for you,' I tuned to Auburn Hair. 'If you're anything other than right here and behaving yourself when we get back, I'll kill *him,* alright?'

I gripped Black Hair's scruff and pushed him up the hill. 'Do it sensibly,' I told him. 'Betray us and your friend dies. Juno,' I said. 'Do you want to see some Alphas?'

Three of us crept up the hill. Black Hair was effectively leashed to us because of our hostage, and although that gave him more reason than us to do a good job, it didn't make creeping up on an Alpha stronghold any less scary.

'What the hell is your name, anyway?' I whispered.

'Juniper,' he replied.

'And your friend?'

'Sumac.'

Juniper led us past the spot where I ambushed him and Sumac, then switched right through a thick undergrowth of thorn bushes, which then turned into a wall of thorn bushes. They'd been planted and cultivated into a natural barrier, creating an impenetrable barricade that was also camouflaged, simply because it was natural. There was no demarcation, either, like the intermittent fencing at Purleyont Hames, or the pictures I'd seen of the Berlin wall. Trees and shrubs grew in and around it, and in places it weaved and interlinked, turning itself into a kind of thorn bush maze that I'd *never* want to be lost in. Anyone trying to get in would soon find themselves stuck, with no way out. It was simple and complicated at the same time, and it was brilliant.

Juniper stopped, turned back to me and Juno, and signalled for quiet. He led us along the thorn wall, and through the links between bushes. Pulling turn-backs and taking sudden corners, we quickly became disorientated.

He dropped to the ground and Juno and I instantly did the same. He then pressed himself into the forest floor and slid underneath the thorn bush, avoiding the tanglehooks and bristles by millimetres. Following him, my vision was limited to just in front of my eyes, and when I chanced a glance ahead, all I saw were Juniper's worn bootsoles.

We crept up to another thorn wall, then snaked right and up a slight incline. The vegetation cleared and a rotting portakabin appeared out of the undergrowth. I looked left and right and three, maybe four, similar prefabricated buildings sat in the wooded clearing, all of them slowly decaying.

We crept up to the nearest one, and then, lying flat, I looked up and saw a small, stained window. I turned to Juniper. He nodded and pointed towards it.

I looked at my watch and gave myself sixty seconds. Not very long to see what was going on, but long enough to be seen by a sharp-eyed Alpha looking in the right direction. I silently rose to my knees and peered through the window.

Chapter 25

Wow. This was healing on a collective, community scale. Much bigger than my one woman side show, and, I had to admit, more informed and precise. I looked wide-eyed at a row of rickety beds beneath an intermittent and sometimes leaking roof. The beds were made from assorted materials and patched up to various stages of only just supporting whichever poor bastard was laying in them.

And what struck me most were the numbers. If I hadn't seen the two hundred Strauss crammed into the hall during Festival, I wouldn't have even thought there were this many people still alive. What was probably only twenty prone and seriously ill Alphas, to me looked like there were twenty times that many, all packed together and all being attended to by a healer in a cassock.

Some of the wounded lay still, some writhed in what appeared to be a lot of pain. Alphas dressed the same as Juniper and Sumac, and equally grubby, flitted between them. A low hum of background noise floated towards me; murmured words that I couldn't quite make out, gasps of pain and snarled orders. As I watched, one of the Alphas was hastily rolled from a narrow, rickety bed and on to a stretcher, and three straining healers carried him away from my line of sight. Then my minute was up and I lay down.

'Your turn,' I whispered to Juno. 'One minute. See what you see and then we're out of here.'

Juno rose to her knees and I scanned left and right, then looked behind, watching and listening for trouble. Nervousness scraped along my spine. I chanced a glance at my watch. Juno's minute flashed past and I tapped her foot, then faced Juniper and jerked my head, the universal 'let's get the fuck out of here' gesture which had survived The Change intact. Less than sixty seconds after Juno had used up her sixty seconds on recon duty, we were crawling under thorn bushes and heading back downhill.

It seems weird, within an absolute world of weirdness, but breaking contact and moving away from the Alphas was actually more scary than going the other way. With every crawl, crouch or step, I felt a prickling sensation all over my body. I expected and dreaded the crashing impact of a sharp blade, a bullet, or even the terminal connection of a flying, heavy body in the shape of a vengeful Alpha slamming into me, ending my escape, and at some point after that, probably my life.

Consequently, my senses were on double secret, high energy overload. My head flickered in all directions like a meerkat on steroid-coffee, and once we were through the thorn barrier and I was standing, it felt as though my footsteps were somehow barely touching the forest floor in a dance of inspired soundless movement. I'm sure that in reality I moved no differently on the way back as I did on the way in, it just felt like I did.

We reached the hillside rendezvous and I saw the comforting sight of the Outcasts. Lamp and Crystal knelt guard over Sumac. 'Are we done?' asked Addison.

'Until tonight,' I replied.

Chapter 26

Dusk settled around us, and we were good to go. 'Right,' I said. 'We've got these two for information,' I nodded to Juniper and Sumac, 'and our job for tonight is to get a shit load of supplies. Juno and I have seen the place. There's only one way in and out. It's guarded, but not all the time. Is that right?'

Juniper and Sumac nodded nervously and, once again, they clung together like two winter pigeons on a fence. I was starting to like them. As long as they stayed on side, maybe we could be friends. After all, we weren't going in there to kill anyone.

'Okay then,' I said. 'We take the gateway and we hold it, then we go in and keep the healers calm *and* quiet. Juniper and Sumac will point us towards their supply stash. We take as much as we can carry and we're gone.'

'What about the sick and wounded?' asked Juniper.

'We don't harm them,' I said. 'We don't touch them. We don't even go near them. We're not here on a kill and burn mission. We know where the place is, and we know about those weird clothes you wear, so we've got what we came for.'

'The wounded need those supplies,' said Sumac.

'So do we,' I said. 'And so do our people. So you two need to do exactly what every one of us has done, and that's pick a side.'

'Look,' said Juniper, 'we didn't ask you to kidnap us.'

'Yeah,' said Sumac. 'We were doing fine 'til you came along.'

'Sure you were,' said Addison. 'You said it yourself, you'd have been killed or sold if you stayed, and out here you'd be two runaways in the wilderness. Face it, you wouldn't have lasted a day. At least with us, you've got a chance.'

'What if some more of us want to join you?' asked Juniper.

'You think so?' I asked.

'There might be one or two.'

*

However much some of my ideas still weren't mainstream, I'd managed to inject a bit of timing into our assault plan, and no one was arguing. One minute after we took the entranceway into the healing house, we'd go inside. Juno had my spare watch, and this had to work to the second.

We crept up the slope as a half-moon gave some partial light, then we waited at the thorn barrier. Juniper guided us closer, and then gave the signal just before the gap in the thorn wall. We silently sank to floor level and I watched the empty space. Christ, we could have just walked in there.

Until an Alpha suddenly loomed out of the night. He was the biggest bastard I'd ever seen, and in all my many years of avoiding them, and now occasionally killing them, I'd seen some big 'uns.

Addison knelt next to me and I heard the slight, almost inaudible creak as she pulled back on the bowstring.

One more second, still time to walk away.

No chance.

There was just enough light to see the arrow thunk into the Alpha's neck, and he dropped without a sound. Even as he was falling we moved, creeping forward and sealing the entranceway. I slipped the Glock into my hand and, in the blanket-wrap darkness, felt rather than saw my team fan out on either side of me. Addison yanked the arrow free from the dead Alpha.

'Good shooting,' I whispered.

'Silhouette against a shadow background,' she replied. 'You're lucky I hit him at all. The next job we do is in daylight.'

'Juniper,' I said. 'Say here. Sumac, take us inside.'

One thing I'd already learned was that delegation could only go so far, and some things, you absolutely had to do yourself. *Your troops won't die for you if you won't die for them.* It was always Tanya's words that stayed in my memories, that told me what I should do. And what I had to do was go into this healing house myself to lift their supplies and maybe bring a few weirdly named healers with us.

Maximum risks went to the maximum leader. Were those Tanya Strauss's words as well, or was I making stuff up because I was scared?

I led my team past the thorn barricade and into a damp-rot portakabin that amazed me by still being upright. My boots squelched on permanently wet plywood flooring, and I heard Sumac's whispered directions.

Ahead, I saw a faint glow, flickering light from a primitive flame-torch. They'd gone back to organics for illumination, so no electricity here, or seriously restricted if it was.

Which was fine by me, as long as they had medicines and maybe some surgicals as well.

'What do you want?' whispered Sumac. 'Supplies or people?'

'Supplies first,' I said. 'But if we come across any of your mates, we'll give them the choice to come with us.'

'I know what you want,' said Sumac. 'Follow me.'

We walked past a barely lit room crammed with stretchers and canvas camping beds, each one taken up by a sleeping Alpha. I saw silhouettes of healers flitting between, touching bare limbs and checking for pulses, utterly absorbed in their care and either ignoring, or not noticing, us.

Sumac led us towards the glowing light and a small room. He turned back to me and held up four fingers. I returned the gesture and pointed to the room.

Four people inside.

Four healers.

Four Judas Priests.

Four potential enemies.

Holding the Glock in front of me, I took a deep breath and stepped into the room.

Four cassocked Alphas, sitting on four worn-out chairs, looked up and then the rest of my team flooded in behind me.

'Nobody moves,' I said softly, wondering if I was even heard over my own trip-hammering heart. 'Nobody speaks.'

'How will you know if we're on your side if you don't let us speak?' asked one of them.

In the gloom I faced a short, wide-built healer with a thick shock of white hair that followed the outline of his round face. His voice, while quiet, was high-pitched and floated around the small, cluttered room. He spoke in a strange, somehow familiar way, something I'd not heard for a long time. An accent.

'We need supplies,' I said. 'And you as well. Are you in?'

'She's for real, Chive,' said Sumac. 'She's got people and weapons, and she can get us out.'

'You think?' asked Chive. 'You're dreaming, Sumac.'

'Sumac's already decided,' I said. 'And Juniper's with us as well. So what about you? My name's Alex, I'm in charge of this expedition, and if you want, we can take you to a safe place.'

'Safe,' he snorted and stood up, wiping his hands on his grubby cassock. 'Safe from them? Safe from Sentinel? You must be joking.'

'Do you want to stay here?' I asked.

'No, he doesn't,' said Sumac. 'And nor do the others.'

'So, the two queers went over to you, did they?' asked Chive. He slowly shook his head. 'Can't say I blame them, pair of fucking perverts. The Alphas were going to castrate them anyway.'

'And you're talking about staying?' I asked.

'It's Sentinel's orders,' snapped Chive. 'And what Sentinel wants, Sentinel gets. Whether it's slicing someone or selling them to some tribe only he knows about, it doesn't matter, because it'll happen. There's nothing *I* can do about it.'

'This guy's name seems to be on everyone's lips around here,' I muttered. 'And we don't have time for this. Stay here or take a chance with us. Time to decide.'

'That's not something I've had to do for a long time,' said Chive.

'Can you remember the times before?' I asked.

'No,' he replied. 'I woke up from the Alpha Bug in a prison. I bet you bloody well didn't.'

'What's a prison?' I asked.

No, really. I didn't know what one was.

'Exactly,' said Chive. 'You've got a lot to learn about power, girl.'

'Look.' I levelled the Glock at him. 'Stay or leave, but make a bloody choice and save the talk for daylight.'

'They've been alright with us,' said Sumac.

Chive shrugged. 'Without us here, half of the wounded will probably be dead by dawn, and they're the only reason we're being kept alive.'

'Yes,' I snapped. 'And now we're keeping you alive. So here's your choice. Load up with gear and take a chance that we'll be a lot fairer than the bastard Alphas, or stay the fuck here and don't bloody moan about it.'

'What do you think, lads?' asked Chive.

The three other healers sat silently in the gloom. They looked at Chive and seemed to be waiting for him to decide for them. The seconds ticked by and my nerves screamed out at me that we needed to be going. This was taking too long.

Chive turned to the other three. 'Hale,' he said. 'Load up with splints and dressings. Beam, I want pain control and antibacs; Goster, get me fluids and spikes. All three of you back here in less than one turn and if you say anything to anyone, *I'll* rip your tongues out, never mind Sentinel and his bloody inquisitors.' He turned to face me. 'Will that do?'

'Alex,' said Sumac. 'Wait for us at the gateway.'

I paused before moving.

'He's right,' said Chive. 'You're a whole bunch of armed strangers and if you don't get out soon you'll be seen. Then we're all dead. Is that what you came here for?'

'You can trust us,' said Sumac. 'If *that's* what you're worried about.'

'Go,' said Addison. 'I'll stay back and watch them.'

'But—'

'Go.'

I didn't like it, but one armed stranger was the compromise, and a lot less noticeable than eight.

'We're just outside,' I said. 'One shot and we're back here in seconds.'

'I know,' whispered Addison.

I led my team, minus Addison, back outside, our footsteps on damp, creaking floorboards the only noise we made, and quiet murmurs from the wounded, bed-bound Alphas were the only sounds we encountered.

Outside, I knelt next to Juno at the thornbush gateway and my team fanned out either side of me, quickly becoming invisible in the darkness.

'Where's Addison and Sumac?' asked Juno.

'Inside,' I replied. 'We've got four more runaways and they're loading up with supplies right now. They'll be out real soon.'

I hoped.

Uncertainty flowed through me like a bad news caffeine hit. My attention was now pulled in two directions. I was straining my eyesight and trying to be alert for any mobile Alphas, but I was also listening behind me, trying to make some sense from the disembodied voices I heard, voices that were a lot deeper than the ones I'd been hearing recently.

I felt my nerves stretch tighter than a single-strand spider-thread holding a dead weight. What was going on in there? Had Sumac turned? Was there a fight? Was Addison in danger? Was she still alive? Suddenly I had an image of her, slashed and mutilated by an ambush of Alphas, and then they were coming for us, coming for me, slowly getting closer in the darkness, approaching from front and behind, and we couldn't see them, there was nothing we could do, they were coming for us and they were going to kill us, but only after they—

'Let's go.' Addison slapped my shoulder and I nearly screamed. 'Are you staying out here all night?' she whispered in my ear as I gathered together my scattered wits. 'The first Alpha that turns up here, they'll be after us. For all we know, one of those Judas Priest oddballs is running away right now to warn them. We need to go. Now.'

We moved quickly down the hillside, edged around the open meadow and moved fast. A quick bearing from the compass' luminous plate was all we had, but it was what we had, and it would get us in the right direction. At that point, leaving Green Man Common a long way behind us was a lot more important than exact bearings.

We headed east. There were risks either way, but we'd agreed to move at night and sleep during the day. There was a danger of getting lost, a risk of losing people, and a real chance of someone getting hurt in the dark. But it was also less likely we'd be found or attacked by vengeful Alphas, and if we could lose ourselves in the night, we'd be long gone and way ahead of them by daytime.

Or so we hoped.

*

'Supplies in the centre,' I said. Dawn was slowly lighting up the forest with mellow sunbeams sending warm corridors of light through the beach and oak leaves' green freshness. The Judas Priests thankfully dropped their loads and, slicked with my own sweat from walking hard all night, I was glad it wasn't me carrying them. With the daylight getting stronger, I looked at our new friends.

They were all dressed exactly the same as Juniper and Sumac: grimy, ill-fitting cassocks stopping at varying points between knee and ankle, mis-matched and rotting footwear that was barely stuck together, and knotted, unwashed mop-like hair that could almost double as head protection. Three of the newly seen healers, Hale, Beam and Goster, were as thin and malnourished as Juniper and Sumac, while Chive, several years older, had clearly been better fed and was the only one whose rounded mid-section tested the cassock's stitching.

'You want us to sleep on top of that?' asked Chive, looking at the pile of discarded medical plunder.

'No,' I snapped. 'Shin up the nearest tree and get some sleep. You know how to use a hammock?'

It was the least we could offer them. They'd been carrying fluids, medical instruments, and as many out of date medications as they could cram into their cassocks for the last several hours. They'd earned as decent a night's sleep as we could give them, while the Outcasts took turns standing guard.

Hours later, and as dusk softened the forest outlines, Chive climbed down from the thick-trunk oak he'd been sleeping in, while at the same time managing to untangle his hammock with surprising skill. 'Sleeping in a tree,' he muttered. 'I knew you lot would show us the promised land.'

'This is nothing,' I said. 'Wait 'til you see the Sisters.'

'Oh,' he chuckled, 'family thing, is it?'

'Something like that,' I replied. 'And what's that accent all about?'

'Heard it before, have you?' asked Chive.

'Somewhere,' I said. 'But I'm damned if I know where.'

'Me too,' he said. 'I just wish I could find someone else who spoke the same way, maybe they'd know.'

'We've lost one,' said Juno.

A shock-bolt flashed down my spine. 'What?' I gasped.

'It's Hale,' said Juniper. 'He'd been muttering all last night on the march out here, and when I woke up he was gone.'

'Shit,' I said. 'Did he take any of the supplies?'

'I don't think so,' said Juno.

'Hale's gone right back to Papa,' said Chive. 'And once he spills his shit, the Alphas will organise a pursuit group.'

'And what about you two?' I snapped at Beam and Goster who were untangling their hammocks with a lot less skill than Chive. Beam peered nervously at me from beneath a grubby blond fringe, knotting his fingers together, while Goster's dirty face was tracked with tears.

'They're still here, aren't they?' snapped Chive. Hale and Goster did a head-switch between me and Chive. I looked back at them, actually impressed that despite their beanpole builds, they'd both shouldered heavy weights through the night and not complained.

'You gave us food,' Beam chirped in a small, barely audible voice.

'No one's hit us, either,' added Goster, and they both went back to slowly folding and stowing their hammocks.

'Oh, Christ,' I gasped. 'Not another bloody double act.'

'I knew you'd see it their way.' Chive looked at me and grinned.

'Just bloody well load them up,' I said. 'If we put enough weight on their backs they'll be too damn knackered to run away. Leave Hale's share on the floor. I'll spread it among the Outcasts.'

'You won't,' said Chive. 'You've got enough to do with your navigating, and any fighting, if it comes to that. Leave the humping to us. That turncoat isn't on you, and we'll manage.'

I looked curiously at Beam and Goster, who'd shifted to strapping Hale's bags of supplies around their emaciated, cassocked bodies. 'Are you sure about that?'

'They're not doing it for *you*,' he said. 'This is pride, Priest style, and we'll earn your respect our way.'

Goster slipped on the damp undergrowth. He fell over and the weight of his load pinned him to the forest floor. He clenched handfuls of wet leaves and tried to push himself up to his knees. Arc broke out of sentry formation, knelt next to him, and took the weight of his pack. His legs shook with the effort and his face was screwed up and silent. Slowly, and with Arc's help, he stood, rearranged his load, and looked back at me with a sullen resolve.

Arc reached into her pocket, unwrapped a slice of bacon grill and offered it to him.

'Try some,' she whispered. 'It's full of protein.'

'What's protein?' he asked.

'I don't know,' she smiled. 'But I think it helps your night vision. Do you want to shake hands?'

'What?' asked Goster.

'Don't worry, lads.' Chive smiled at Beam and Goster. 'If she was hungry, it's me she'd eat. You pair are too damn skinny for them to kill.'

I suddenly saw a depth to Chive, the way he spoke to Beam and Goster as though he was talking to his best friends, while at the same time laughing at himself. It was subtle leadership, and I wished it was a skill I had. It was *definitely* a skill that Tanya Strauss had.

We moved out under the secure blanket of darkness, but more carefully, more slowly. It wasn't until the third day out from the bunker, as dawn began to slowly spread across the late summer sky, that I recognised the land, and I knew we were about a mile away from safety.

But why was there smoke rising from the same direction?

Chapter 27

It was my home, and I felt my insides being squeezed at the thought it being attacked, burned, violated. I held my hand above my head, made a circular motion, and we huddled the Judas Priests into a protective cordon and looked outwards.

'What's with the smoke?' asked Juno.

'We're about to find out,' I replied.

'Shouldn't we get these healers back to the settlement first?'

'We need to find out more,' I said. 'Varia, you're with me.'

Varia and I scuttled into the trees, the low-lying leaves brushing wet against our arms and legs as we made a bead for the smoke column. 'What do you think it is?' she asked.

'I don't know.' Scanning the dense undergrowth, I held out the Glock and once more wished to hell I had the shotgun.

We traversed a belt of thick woodland close to the bunker. The trees and land contours were all known to me, and I even recognised the sun's angle relative to my surroundings. It should have felt good.

We got closer still, and I slowed instinctively. Varia shifted over to my side. She drew her pistol, and with weapons levelled, we crept forward.

There was movement among the stony ground, and the hairs at the back of my neck that were free of my now ragged ponytail took on a life of their own. My heart rate sped up and my stomach churned. I stood still and held out my hand, palm downwards, and we both sank to the ground, then slowly, very slowly, inched forward through the low lying ferns.

Movement, and fire, and fear, were the two things I saw and the one thing I felt.

Two Alphas prowled around the clear ground in front of the bunker, both in their usual filthy, one-time denim and coats. It was practically a uniform, although these two also wore grimy red sashes, something I'd never seen before. One of them was intermittently bashing on the locked bunker door and poking a bonfire, on which burned the remnants of my bean poles and plant trellis. The other one walked aimlessly around and then returned to a nearby birch tree.

And tied to the tree was a Strauss. Ragged, bleeding, and clearly in pain.

Fear and anger fused through me. 'Get Addison and Nalda,' I whispered.

'We don't need them,' said Varia. 'We can easily take these two. I've seen it loads of times.'

'Sure we can,' I replied. 'But we'd also have a dead Strauss, if she isn't already. We need to do something fast and smart, so get Addison and Nalda, and bring them back here.'

'But—'

'Now!'

Varia slid backwards and then disappeared behind me. I looked at my watch and calculated how long we'd been gone, and how long it would take Varia to get back here. I had about forty minutes to think of a plan that would hopefully end up with two dead Alphas and a live, rescued Strauss.

*

Thirty-seven minutes later, and lost in a daydream of considered possibilities, I stifled a sudden yelp of alarm as I felt a hand brush against my leg. I spun around, gripping the Glock, and saw Addison, Nalda, and Varia.

'You told me to be quick,' whispered Varia.

I nodded, then gathered my scattered thoughts. 'Does anyone recognise that poor bitch out there?' I looked at her again; her red sand hair was matted with her own blood, and her face hung listlessly as the two Alphas walked around her and occasionally kicked the bunker's door.

'That's Gabrielle,' gasped Nalda. 'Shit, is she alright?'

'She will be,' I said. 'We're going to get her out of there.'

'Tell me what to do,' husked Nalda, and I knew I'd picked the right person for this job, although I didn't know they knew each other.

'Here's what happens,' I whispered.

Two minutes later, exactly two minutes later, I emerged from the trees at the bottom of the hillside, a long way from Gabrielle, but closer to one of the Alphas. At first he didn't see me, although it *was* still stupidly early in the morning and I was wearing camo against a low-light background. 'Hey!' I shouted. 'Hey, you stupid fuck. Over here!'

Suddenly, I had his attention. He quickly realised I was a lone woman, and a broad grin spread across his squashed-face features. He fished into his jacket pocket and pulled out a butterfly knife, then walked towards me. 'Watch her,' he shouted over his shoulder at his friend. 'I've just found another one.'

He *found* me? Yeah, sure he did.

Then, with a single-hand fluency that both surprised me and made me a little nervous, the butterfly knife blurred between his fingers, folding and unfolding with delicate precision as he stalked towards me. 'Run, girl,' he shouted. 'Run, and you might get away. Don't make this too easy for me. Make me chase you. Please.'

He liked a challenge, and that was fine by me. I was about to send them his way in sackloads, but before I did, I had to make sure we had the other one covered. My trip through the bushes was designed to give Addison and Nalda time to get into position, but with a Strauss life at stake, we all had to be sure.

And he was moving fast. A lot faster than I thought he would.

To be honest, once I realised he didn't have a gun, I was a lot safer. But I still needed a bit more time, so there was nothing to be lost by playing up to his worldview. 'Let my friend go,' I shouted, then turned and ran.

Behind me, I heard the Alpha's bull laughter. He was big, he was strong, and he could run, but I was fleet and had the edge on him. In his mind, that wasn't a problem, I was just some prey to chase down. If I got away, they already had one to play with, and if he got me, they had one more. In his eyes it was a win-win.

To keep him happy, I ran around the stony open area. It gave his friend something to watch, and I needed their eyes on me, just for a few seconds more.

Then I saw it. Addison broke cover and aimed her bow. Old technology it might have been, but it was quiet and had a longer range than my shotgun, which I didn't have anyway.

Addison's fingers brushed against her ear and I knew the time had come. I pitched forward, my movements suddenly uncoordinated, and I landed in a heap on the damp grass. Both Alphas roared, anticipating another capture. I rolled onto my back and several things happened at once.

Addison's arrow moved faster than I could see it, but I clearly heard the solid thump as it punched into the guard Alpha and threw him to the ground. Addison and Nalda were already on their feet and running towards Gabrielle. The other Alpha hadn't heard or seen, his attention still on me, and as he stormed closer, I pulled out the Glock and pointed the barrel straight at him. He checked for a second and I pulled the trigger, only to feel its unexpected resistance.

The Glock didn't fire, the Alpha was still alive, and he was coming towards me with his knife. I dropped the Glock and reached for my own blade, but as I fell, my belt had shifted and it was sitting underneath me. The fluid movements I'd practiced weren't so good when I was on the ground, wet, and faced with a fast approaching Alpha.

We both did the maths and there was no way I'd pull my knife free before he was on me, but I still tried. I looked up, wide-eyed, as he hurtled closer. He gripped his knife, lips pulled back from rotten teeth in an exultant snarl of victory, and he leapt through the air in an effort to land on top of me and skewer me to the ground.

But as his feet left the floor, his head exploded in a red cloud of blood, bones and brains. I saw it all happen, almost in slow motion, and *then* I heard the sharp crack of a pistol shot. The Alpha's movements suddenly lost all cohesion, his forward leap disintegrated along with his head, and he dropped to the floor. His mangled face made a plough in the earth as he came to a stop at my feet.

I stood up, my legs trembling and my eyes fixed on the steaming gore that oozed out of the Alpha's destroyed skull. I felt my last meal churning around my stomach and became acutely aware that my hands were also shaking.

Where had that shot come from?

Still scrabbling for my knife, I looked away from the dead Alpha and saw Varia standing there, looking at me, her feet spaced apart, leaning forward slightly and both arms outstretched, hands still clamped around her Glock's handle. Like me, she was shaking, and like me, her eyes were wide open, her lips trembling and her normally healthy looking skin a sickly pale, even beneath the grime of half a week in the wilderness.

Sick, scared, appalled at what we had done, our eye contact said we felt the same way.

Do something. Do something. She feels just as bad as you and she's just killed someone.

'Thank you,' I said, and I could hear my voice shaking, gravelly and a lot less decisive than it had been recently. 'You saved my life.'

'Is he dead? Is he dead?' Varia's voice was high and her words tumbled out. She started shaking even more. I walked over to her and, standing to one side, gently lowered her arms and guided the Glock back into its holster. She flung her arms around me and her breathing heaved in huge sobs. This wasn't the brash, sure of herself Varia who said she'd seen everything loads of times. This was Varia, who'd just crossed the killing threshold for the first time, and it was something we were all learning. Whether you liked them or not, whether you had to or not, someone was now dead because of you, and it still hurt.

And maybe that's why we're different to them, I thought, *maybe we're still human where it counts.*

Maybe.

'He is one hundred per cent dead,' I told her.

'He was going to kill you,' she whispered.

'Not with you watching my back,' I replied. 'You covered a lot of ground in a short time to get close enough for a head shot.'

'I was aiming for his chest.'

'That can be our secret,' I told her.

I gently untangled her grip, then walked to where I'd dropped my pistol. I picked it up, cleared away the mud that had caused the stoppage and worked the action, then stowed it away. I looked back at the house and saw that Addison and Nalda were untying Gabrielle. 'Come on,' I said to Varia.

We trotted over uneven ground towards Gabrielle. There, and already cooling, the dead Alpha stared sightlessly upwards through glazed eyes that would never see again. Was this how it would be? Would we have to kill them all? And what were those red sashes all about? Then I saw the state of Gabrielle and my compassion evaporated. Random knife cuts webbed her exposed arms, and bruises mottled her face. Her olive drab leggings hung from her in torn shreds, and she was sobbing quietly as Nalda gently picked her up. Nalda was over six feet tall and rippling muscles, so she could carry Gabrielle on her own, and that was exactly what I needed.

'Good shooting, Addison,' I said, then turned to Nalda. 'Is Gabrielle alright?' I looked around. 'Did she say anything about what happened here?'

'Gabrielle's fine,' said Nalda. 'But Hudson's missing.'

'Hudson?'

'Gabrielle's partner.'

'Then she's the next one we bring back,' I replied. 'Let's get her inside the bunker.'

'No,' said Addison. 'We're too exposed out here. Gabrielle said they took her and Hudson in an ambush. They're looking for prisoners, and Alex?'

'What?'

'They brought Gabrielle back here for a reason. They know about this place, and they were torturing her because they thought she'd know how to get in.' She paused. 'They were just about to kill her.'

I suddenly felt sick all over again at how close we'd come to losing a Strauss. And two Alphas had had to die to make that happen.

'This is all wrong,' said Addison. 'This is bolder than they've ever been before. We need to get back to the settlement and make plans. And Gabrielle can be the Judas Priests' first...' she wrung her hands as she searched for the word.

'Patient,' I said. 'She can be their first patient. Someone they heal.'

'They'd better do a good job,' growled Nalda. 'Because I won't be patient with them if they don't.'

'How are you, Addison?' I looked at her and we already knew each other better than we realised. Better than *I* realised, anyway.

'What do you mean?' she said. 'It's not like it's my first anymore.'

I looked down at the dead Alpha, stooped, and yanked out the arrow, then gave it back to her. 'Still doesn't make it easy.'

'It never should be.' She wiped a tear from her eye and looked at me, then looked *into* me. 'What are we becoming, Alex?'

'We're doing what we have to if we want to survive,' said Nalda. She carried Gabrielle with a tenderness that contradicted her war-face and weapons. 'If you think I'm wrong, you can ask Hudson about it when we find her. Now let's go.'

Chapter 28

It was a straight march from the bunker back to Purleyont Hames. Once there, we'd drop off the healers, Gabrielle, and the supplies, then do a quick planning session and get back out to find Hudson.

The Judas Priests reverted to type as though a switch had been flicked. Juniper and Sumac fussed over Gabrielle as Nalda gently lowered her to the soft-leaf forest floor. Chive issued quick orders in his softly accented voice, and Beam and Goster fashioned a stretcher within minutes from picked up branches and hastily donated items of clothing. Loaded down with an extra share of plundered supplies, and taking a quarter-share of Gabrielle's stretcher, they kept up the pace and showed a strength that was utterly out of keeping with their appearance.

The route back to Purleyont Hames took us through the crumbling remnants of what was once an industrial complex, but was now sterile and empty. Thorns and ivy burst along the innocuously level ground and climbed over decaying warehouses. Going around it would take time. Going straight through would cut an hour off the trip, by following a narrow, very narrow, path that was maintained by occasional animal footfall. Concrete floor used to cover the whole site, but now it was confined to one barely visible strip, just wide enough to put one foot in front of the other.

Addison had the point and she stopped and crouched just before the first warehouse. The Judas Priests knew enough to stop and get down, while the Outcast security screen fanned outwards and I scurried up to Addison to see what was happening.

A pair of Alphas guarded the path's pinch-point between two metal silos, which were now given up to the encroaching foliage. The Alphas looked bored, like they'd been there a long time and nothing had happened. Hands in pockets, they stared at the ground and shuffled their feet, not even talking to each other, such was their sense of nothing going on.

But why were they even there? Any supplies had long since been sucked up by wandering survivors. The only significance of the place was that it was a thin path through an effective but decaying manmade barricade. It was as though they knew, or were expecting, someone – us? – to try and get through.

Or maybe they were trying to cut off all routes back to Purleyont Hames.

Shit.

We had to get back, and fast. That meant the Alphas were both going to die, and I wasn't even thinking about it. Either one of them could have been part of the same two who'd tortured Gabrielle. Either one of them *would* have done the same. 'Stay here,' I whispered to Addison, then scuttled off to the left and flopped down next to a pair of Outcasts. 'Crystal,' I whispered to one of them. 'With me.'

We snuck back to Addison's position. The Alphas remained in the same place and all three of us watched them. This was going to be an easy ambush, a chance to get the Outcasts more used to killing. Nalda was right: it was just the way it was.

'Addison's going to take the one on the right,' I whispered to Crystal. 'The one on the left is yours. Take him out, straight after Addison's killed the other one.'

Crystal nodded and rubbed her scar, a souvenir from the Alpha attack at the old armoury. She drew her Glock and held it in front of her, getting a bead on the left-hand Alpha. Addison pulled back on her bow and I watched her, willed her to do what her head told her she had to do, regardless of her heart.

A sudden whisper of air and the arrow flew faster than vision. It slammed into the Alpha's chest with a solid thump. He grunted and his legs collapsed beneath him as though his spine had been ripped out. Crystal sighted along the Glock's barrel and fired. I saw the slight dip in the barrel, and I looked back at her. As she fired, she closed her eyes, something about half of the Outcasts did. At the Glock's extreme range, the chest shot turned into a kneecapping. Addison's mark had dropped with barely a sound, but Crystal's hit the deck and screamed all the way up to what was now taken for heaven, his anguished howls reverberating against the empty warehouse walls.

So much for surprise. We didn't want a screaming, wounded Alpha surviving and telling his friends what he'd seen. I rushed forward and tried to aim for his head, but he was writhing around too much to get a clear aim. I put three rounds into his chest and he lay still, a final gust of blood-cloud air leaving his lungs. Looking away and taking a deep breath, I hated myself as tears stung my eyes. None of this was easy.

I turned back the way we'd come and beckoned the Outcasts forward. The signal was passed back, and as the column came on again, we pulled the cooling bodies out of sight and left them in the undergrowth as a ready meal for any passing wildlife.

Chapter 29

A stretch of reclaimed fence, with clear ground in front, came into view. Purleyont Hames to me, but simply the settlement to the rest of the Outcasts. At the treeline's edge, we stopped, knelt, and scanned ahead. The gateway's metal crosspiece looked its normal self, the barbed wire undisturbed and intact, although there seemed more than the usual number of Strauss guarding it. I looked along the length of the fencing as it curved left and disappeared into the forest.

I felt relief washing through me as I looked at the fence, knowing that we could see safety, but there was open ground to cross before we got there. I knelt, then stood, and broke cover first, leading the Outcasts back home.

On the other side of the fence, the guards held their long staves and pikes with easy familiarity. And they were proficient, too. They didn't just gawp at us as we emerged from the treeline like a living mist and walked towards them. Like us, they had eyes everywhere.

Then a bull roar surged over my senses. I looked left and saw what I thought were hundreds, although more likely dozens, of Alphas, boiling out of the trees and running towards us, screaming murder and mutilation.

Had we been tracked from Green Man Common, or was this something to do with Gabrielle?

'Anchor point on the fence,' I shouted. There was no need to emphasise the urgency; we could all see them coming. I chanced a look at them and reined in my galloping fear. It *was* dozens and not hundreds, but some of them had guns, and we were just about to see if they were clean, loaded, and if the Alphas knew how to use them.

Keeping Gabrielle's stretcher party in the centre of our formation, we doubled towards the fence then faced outwards. A thin, very thin, *really* thin line of Outcasts stood still and faced an incoming rush of Alphas. Fear was a silent, deafening scream inside my head. I looked behind me and almost sobbed in despair: they were coming at us from both sides.

'Juno! About face and anchor on the other side.'

Juno looked behind and nodded, then briskly ordered her team. Within seconds, two painfully short and thin lines of Strauss formed a protective shell on either side of the column of Judas Priests, who were now running headlong for the gate, as fast as their double burden of supplies and Gabrielle would let them.

Was this going to work? Shit, I had *no* idea.

'Kneel!' I shouted, and the Outcasts knelt. Glocks pointed outwards. Juno and Addison pulled back their bows, and the Judas Priests filed through the gates.

Now there was more noise, lots more noise, as the Alphas screamed a savage challenge and fired their guns in the air.

'Wait!' I ordered, willing my voice to sound calm, while inside I felt tense and scared and sick and angry all at the same time. 'Wait!'

Less than a hundred metres away now. What was the range of a pistol? Less than a bow. They needed to be closer than that. I pointed my own Glock as the distance rapidly closed.

Fifty metres, and fear crawled over my body like a fever sickness as the Alphas rushed towards us.

'Wait!'

Thirty metres, and I deliberately added another second to my plans, to prove that I was in control.

'Fire!'

Fourteen Glocks and two bows spat lead and death. Bullets and arrows sped outwards and smashed through ragged clothes, puncturing hearts and stopping them, eviscerating major organs and arteries, causing bleed-out and sudden death. Lifeless Alphas dropped to the ground as though they'd been pole-axed. Others skidded along the rough grass and then lay still. The Alphas immediately behind them tripped over the sudden obstacles, and now the firing became constant, a wall of crackling sound that hammered out from our very thin, very short, lines.

The Alphas weren't expecting it, weren't prepared for it, or more likely, weren't trained for it, and their forward movement stopped just short of our hastily knelt positions. On both sides, they recoiled against our bullets and bows. Those that had weapons fired back haphazardly, and thankfully most of their rounds went way overhead, while others whisked the air between us and I blessed their bad aiming.

I heard random orders from the Alphas to fire back, to kneel and take aim, but their momentum had gone. It was seeds of organisation, of co-ordination, but their movement was lost and they inched backwards. Uncertainty gripped some of them, who were now already retreating into the forest. I looked behind me and saw a clear space between my defensive line on the left and Juno's on the right.

'Five paces backwards,' I called out, edging my team towards Juno's. Then I ran across the clear ground between the two teams and did the same with the right-hand line. The Judas Priests had wasted no time getting through the gateway, and now we had to seal the gap to our rear before the Alphas saw what was going on.

I scuttled over to the other line and emptied my Glock, sending bullets hosing towards the Alphas. Their disarray matched the other side, and under cover of their confusion I brought our two lines together, and then, like a shrinking bulge, the Outcasts nearest the gateway edged inside. And while they gave covering fire, this time from inside the fence, the rest of us followed. By now it was slower, more precise shots, but each one took down an Alpha, either killed or wounded. Clouds of blood and screams marked where bullets and arrows found their mark. I reloaded and walked backwards with my Glock in hand, and this time I took deliberate, aimed shots. Two minutes and twenty seconds after the first Alpha charged towards us, Juno and I stood at the gateway, the only Outcasts outside the wire.

The Alphas had been beaten, their cohesion smashed and their broken dead and wounded a violent reminder of the event. Their survivors were gone, swallowed up by the forest, and I felt a buzzing light-headedness. We'd won. We'd won a stand-up fight of their choosing and we'd won.

Over to my left, two Alphas clambered over a carnage wall of their once-living friends. They clearly hadn't got the same memo as the rest of them, and they fixed on me with rabid eyes and screamed defiance. It wasn't a time to talk, and I kept my hands steady as I fired. Whether it was my shots that killed one of them, or the crossbow bolt that thunked into his right eye at the same time, I don't know, but he stopped as though he'd run into an invisible wall, and fell onto the dead-pile at his feet without even a whisper.

With a fluid movement born from proficiency and a fair amount of fear, Juno planted her crossbow at her feet and focussed on a quick reload. The remaining Alpha vaulted the pile of bodies in front of her, screaming a death-curse. Juno's face shot upwards and she pulled desperately on her bowstring. There wasn't time for her to pull her Glock and as she fumbled with her knife I swung my gun arm around, pulled the trigger onto an empty click, and my insides plunged to my boots.

The Alpha sensed our impotence and sped up as he raced to make contact. He lunged forward with filthy hands and chipped nails, his face a feral rictus-snarl, his blazing eyes fixed on Juno who stood firm and held her knife forward.

Addison appeared from nowhere and a single Glock-shot rang out. The Alpha's face disappeared and he dropped at Juno's feet. Addison turned to face her. 'Are you alright?' she asked, holstering her pistol.

'Reload and don't worry about me,' said Juno.

'Both of you get behind the wire,' I snapped. I slammed a fresh mag into the Glock and scanned to my front. The last of the Alphas were doing a death-twitch as their blood soaked into the earth. There was no immediate threat, but another attack could come at any time. Juno and Addison crossed the fence line and I followed them.

The guards started to slide the gate's metal poles across the gap in the fence.

'Wait,' I said. 'Greta, reload and follow me.'

'Where are we going?' she asked.

'Back out there to search the dead,' I said. 'They were firing guns at us, and we're going to get them.'

This was something we'd worked out long before. We'd practiced it over and over again, but now I felt imaginary spiders crawling over my skin as we did it for real. Starting with the nearest corpse, Greta covered me with her Glock. I pulled out any arrows that were lodged in flesh, made sure he was dead, and then searched the body for weapons, food, anything worth using. Checking they were dead was actually pretty easy. Despite what you might think, simply lying still and floppy doesn't make a live person pseudo-dead. A dead person, even a dead Alpha, is cold, pale, and has zero tactile resistance. You simply can't pretend to be like that. The dead are easy to spot, especially when they've had chunks of their vitals shot away from them.

But it's still spooky as hell when you have to move among them and start going through their clothing. I put hands into pockets, finding whatever they were holding and making a snap decision on what to keep, what to leave behind. Morsels of food, blades, and even their firearms and ammunition, all of it was sticky with blood and degraded by poor care or attention. I felt dirty and contaminated just by holding their greasy, sticky, rusty weapons and kit, but we weren't leaving it behind. Whether it worked or not, it wasn't in Alpha hands anymore.

We moved quickly from body to body, picking up a nice collection of blood-stained arrows, a bar of chocolate, and some pistols that might have been 9 millimetre, might have been God knows what. None of them looked hugely functional, but looks must have been deceiving from the sounds we heard as they sprang their ambush.

The first three Alphas were definitely dead. I rolled the fourth one onto his back and checked his pockets. As I did, he flung his arms outwards, roared a wordless challenge and lunged for my throat, his dirt-grimed fingernails reaching for my skin. Greta's pistol shot was sharp and loud in my ears, and an explosion of blood and brain matter spattered the soiled grass as well as my camo. The Alpha flopped back, dead, and I unfastened his belt and pulled the sheath knife.

'Nice one,' I said to Greta. 'Are you okay?'

'Why wouldn't I be?' she replied.

I tried not to think where this brutalisation was leading us. We were living in a world where violence was necessary to maintain our lives, but we still needed bright souls like Addison to remind us of our humanity.

And I needed to get all of this back to Silver.

Chapter 30

'Five Stalkers have disappeared since you left,' said Silver.

Greta and I walked into the meeting hall just minutes after the rest of the Outcasts. Rough wooden benches had been set out, and along with my people, Silver, Collar, and a dozen Stalkers were there. I looked at Silver for a second more than was polite, and it wasn't my imagination. Her skin seemed tighter, more drawn, although her long flowing hair and athletic limbs retained their glossy health. But still, leadership took a toll on you, and I was fast working that out myself. Five missing Stalkers. How would I feel if they were Outcasts? I stamped on my feelings and forced myself to think like a leader, to think the way I thought that Silver would think.

'That's not unusual, is it?' I asked. 'I mean, that's what they do, right? They go out there, look for Alphas, and then come back when they've run out of food.'

'They should have been back by now,' said Collar. 'They *would* have been back by now. Gabrielle and Hudson were sent out last, to look for the others after they were overdue.' There was something different about Collar as well, something I hadn't seen before. Dark shadows under her eyes, the killing stare wasn't there, and for the first time, I thought I saw actual fear. 'Thank you,' she said, quietly.

It wasn't that I wanted to draw attention to her words, it's just that I was so surprised. 'What?' I asked.

'Gabrielle wasn't lost because of you,' said Collar. 'But you brought her back. I've heard enough from the others to know that you didn't have to divert either. But you did, and for that I'm grateful. We all are.'

'Gabrielle says the other Stalkers are still alive,' said Silver.

'Are?' I asked. 'Or were?'

'You're a straight talker,' said Silver. 'And you're right, we don't know. But you and your team did well out there, Alex, really well. You brought those healers in, you *talked* them into coming in, along with some very welcome supplies. Then you rescued Gabrielle and beat back an assault on the fence. If you weren't there, they might have got through.' She looked around the room. 'Someone's organising them, leading them.'

'He's called Sentinel,' I said. 'The Judas Priests spoke about him. He's got control, he's making rules, and he's dangerous. He's got his own group, an army, call them what you want. They're called the Inquisitors, and they rule by fear. He's got a hold on the rest of the Alphas, and to keep them in line he threatens to castrate them or sell them.'

'Sell them?' asked Silver.

'Yes,' I said. 'To some other bunch of bastards that only Sentinel knows about. We're not as lonesome out here as we thought.'

'Can the ones you brought back be trusted?' asked Collar.

'Ask them,' I replied. 'They could have left us anytime they wanted. One of them did, but the others stuck around. They could have stabbed us all in the back at the fence and gone over to the Alphas as heroes, and no one forced them to help Gabrielle.' I turned to Collar. 'A couple of them don't even *like* women. Well, I mean, they don't *want* women.' I fluttered my hands and stood on my toes. 'Oh, shit, you know what I mean, right?'

'They're attracted to other men,' said Silver.

'*That's* what I meant,' I said. 'But the other three aren't, I think. Arc's found a friend already.'

'She would,' said Collar, rolling her eyes.

'Maybe they'll get friendly enough and we can all have a future,' I said. 'Isn't that what you're looking for anyway?'

'You're still trying to find the best in everyone,' said Collar. She shook her head and ran a finger down the scar on her face. 'Could you have talked to the bastards who did this to me? Or what about the ones who held a blade to Gabrielle?'

'Not them,' I said. 'But these ones, the Judas Priests, they seem different. They certainly *dress* differently. Have you seen those cassock things? But there's more than that. They're more nurturing, they're, well, they're more like the Strauss. And maybe that's what's been missing.'

'Maybe,' said Collar. 'But what about our lost Stalkers?'

'We'll find them,' I said.

'You just might,' said Collar. 'I'm putting my faith in you, Alex, and while you're doing that, you need to trust me and the Stalkers to keep the whole settlement safe.'

'Collar's right,' said Silver. 'There have been changes in the wilderness. Some of them we've missed, we haven't anticipated. And maybe we have been too full of our own sense of superiority, but we're suffering for it now. We've never lost so many Stalkers, and it's time to end it. Alex, get some rest, and at dawn tomorrow you go out there, you bring back our Stalkers, and whatever, or whoever, it was that gave them the ability to do this, you'll make sure they never do it again.'

'And Sentinel?' I asked.

'Find out what you can,' said Silver. 'If you can neutralise him, so much the better. But getting the stalkers back is our priority. It's *your* priority. We save our own first.'

*

Nestled at the end of a small close near the hall where the Festivals were held was a large house that was home to Beck's Healing Sisters. The main rooms had been set up like a bigger and more populated version of my med room, with mismatched beds and stretchers set up to treat the sick and wounded. I saw bandaged Stalkers look up in curiosity as Beck and Chive took one look at each other and...I don't know what, but they didn't leave each other's sight after that, and they were constantly talking. What little I overheard was medical talk, some of it I understood, some of it I didn't. Looks, laughs, and eye contact soon followed, and maybe I was thinking a few too many steps ahead, but the question of the next generation might just have been answered.

But that was for another day. Or night. Right now, Gabrielle needed instant attention. She lay on a green canvas bed. The Judas Priests had tied back her long, red hair, spiked her vein, and put up a bag of fluid which hung from a bent clothes hangar that was hitched up to an old wooden coat stand. Juniper and Sumac bustled over her, cleaning her wounds and checking her vitals.

'She's been traumatised and beaten.' Chive's thick accent lilted around Gabrielle's bedside. 'We've started her on fluids and we're keeping a close eye on her.'

'Do you need to know any more?' asked Beck. She might have been talking to me, but she was looking at Chive.

'Can we talk to her?' I asked. Nalda towered over me and glared at Chive, more intimidating than Collar with a hangover.

'She's not up to having visitors.' Chive flapped his small hands and stood in front of her like a living barricade.

'I agree,' said Beck. *Christ,* I thought, *now I've got to get past two of them.*

'It's important,' I said.

'Important for who?' asked Chive and Beck, speaking at the exact same time.

'For her friend, Hudson,' I replied. 'She's still out there and we're going to get her back. Gabrielle's got information and she can help us. So, can we talk to her?'

'Might not be a bad thing,' said Beck, still hovering close to Chive. She pulled back a frayed sleeve and looked purposely at her canvas-strap chronograph watch. 'You've got two minutes,' she said.

'Nice watch.' Almost drooling, I tried and failed utterly to keep my words casual. 'Where did you get it?'

'Stick to the rules while you're inside my empire,' she said, 'and we'll talk. Rule number one is don't tell Silver I've got this and, right now, you're on the clock.' Her eyes looked right into me. 'And *you* know what that means.'

That was something I could get on board with. I knelt down next to Gabrielle. She was awake, and looking up at the damp-patch plaster roof. Her amber eyes blinked rapidly, as though she was still processing the sudden change from captive with no hope to rescued and being cared for by people who should have been the enemy. I knelt down next to her bedside.

'How are you doing?' I asked her. It was a shallow question, and probably not the right thing to say as her lip trembled and her eyes filled up.

Nalda shoved me out of the way and I went sprawling, accompanied by a quiet guffaw from Chive. 'Hey, girl.' Nalda stroked Gabrielle's forehead with a tenderness I'd not seen from her before. 'You'll do anything to get out of hard work, won't you?'

Gabrielle's hand rested over Nalda's and she looked up at her. She didn't say anything, but tears streaked down her hastily cleaned face. 'Hudson,' she whispered.

'Where is she?' asked Nalda.

'They took her,' said Gabrielle. 'I tried to stop them. I tried to fight them.' Her whole body shook as she relived the moment.

'Hey, hey,' soothed Nalda. 'You did everything you could have done, and you survived.'

'Because you found me,' whispered Gabrielle.

'We'll find Hudson as well,' said Nalda. 'And we'll do it with your help. Help us to know, Gabrielle. Where was the ambush? Where did it happen?'

'We set out together,' said Gabrielle, her hand tightly gripping Nalda's. 'Move in pairs, just like we were told. If we can survive the last test alone, ranging together will be easy. That's what they told us, right?'

'There's strength in numbers,' said Nalda. 'And there's sixteen Outcasts with one job: to get her back. Help us do it, Gabrielle. Tell us where you went, tell us where the fight was.'

'We moved out and turned left,' said Gabrielle, talking in short, fast sentences. 'Always turning left, like they taught us. Bigger circles outwards, then stop at the High Ridge. Stop there, search for tracks, and if there's nothing to see, move back. That's what they told us to do, that's what they told us.'

'It's a good plan,' said Nalda.

'Until they found out,' said Gabrielle. 'Until they worked it out.'

'Time's up,' said Beck.

'Is that where they found you?' asked Nalda.

'The Lone Tree,' said Gabrielle. 'We stopped there for a rest. Just for a rest, and then we'd go home.' Her breathing increased. 'We didn't see them, didn't hear them. It was the last time I saw Hudson. I fought them hard, like I'd been told to. I tried, I really tried to stop them.'

'Out,' said Beck, her voice more threatening than Silver and Collar combined. Then she grabbed my shoulder and yanked me to one side. 'We need a word,' she said, and I was hustled into a small storeroom next to the main bedded area.

'If you're bothered about medical cover outside the wire,' I said, looking around at pots of herbs and re-washed bandages. 'Lamp knows her stuff. She'll do a good job.'

'That's not what I'm talking about,' she replied.

'What then?' I asked.

'Quote me and I'll deny it,' she said, 'but if you ever *do* get to Greenwich, I want a chronometer as well.'

'What?'

'And I also know about your stash, so if you've got a long black dress that you don't want, I could do with one.'

It wasn't the conversation I expected, and nor was my instant, unthinking reply. 'I want to sing with the Festival girls,' I said, wondering where the hell *that* had come from.

'You do your part and I'll do mine,' said Beck, nodding slowly.

'Hey,' I said. 'Do you remember?'

'Remember what?' she snapped and looked at me like, like, I don't know what, but not friendly.

'*I* remembered,' I said.

'I know you did,' she whispered. 'Three grey pills, right?'

'You too?'

'Yes,' said Beck. 'Me too. But they didn't want me to.'

'What?'

'I made a mistake at work,' said Beck. 'One mistake, and they were going to fire me. But even if I'd done everything right, I sure as shit wasn't *ever* going to get the pills.' She shrugged. 'Enough of them keeled over and there was no one to stop me. I took mine and then passed the rest around to anyone who wanted them.'

'The Judas Priests?' I said. 'They said their elders knew what to do.'

Beck shook her head slowly, fixing her eyes on mine. 'They're probably a bunch of hermit monks who were so damn isolated they never caught the bug in the first place. Lots of religious orders used to be trained medics, or so I was told.'

'And what were you?' I asked. 'Military?'

'No.' She looked around again and made sure we weren't overheard. 'I was a nurse, that's all. Just a nurse. Just like the bitches who judged me.'

'What did you do that was so wrong, Beck?'

'It doesn't matter,' she said, then flicked straight back into her official role and shoved me into the main room. 'Gabrielle's had enough,' she rapped, solid authority in her voice. She looked back at me with her brown eyes and blinked. 'Thank you for what you did.'

Nalda squeezed Gabrielle's hand, then stood up.

'Nalda.' Gabrielle reached up for her.

'Yes?' she said.

'Bring Hudson back.'

Chapter 31

Getting a night's rest, that's a laugh, but I guess that was the price of being in charge. Most of the Outcasts got more sleep than the one hour I managed, as Juno and I worked out how we were going to achieve Silver's orders, having been given the vaguest parameters.

Still, it was always good to have a challenge.

The operation was a green on, go. The Stalkers would revert to their traditional role, but in maximum strength, ranging out to close fence proximity and hunting down any Alphas who were either brave enough or dumb enough to get that close. If they did, they'd soon learn. Collar and her people were in no mood to be nice.

The Outcasts were for deep penetration. If the captured Stalkers could be rescued, or their bodies recovered, we'd do it. Mission number two was to find and take out Sentinel, the Alphas' mystery leader. How the hell we were even supposed to find them though, I had no idea, so we'd march hard to the bunker, look for clues, replenish, and then head for the Lone Tree that Gabrielle had mentioned. That was where she and Hudson had been ambushed, and maybe there would be some signs to follow. It wasn't much of a plan, but not having much of a plan had kind of become everything in my world from now on.

Pretty soon I'd be multi-tasking.

My phone alarm sent an unsympathetic noise-spear into my cerebral cortex at three o'clock in the morning, and the two Outcast teams coalesced by one of the fence gates just before dawn. Actually, *well* before dawn. We were also joined by Juniper and Sumac.

'Are you sure you want to do this?' I asked them. They still looked really odd in their cassocks, but they both flat out refused to change into camo. 'We'll be travelling hard,' I said. 'And if it comes to a fight, it won't be pretty.'

'You don't expect *us* to fight, do you?' asked Juniper. 'That's why we're still wearing these.' He pulled at his loose-fitting cassock. 'You'll need us to fix your friends if you find them, right? And besides,' he said, 'we owe you.'

'You *owe* us?' I asked.

'Come on, Alex.' Sumac ran a grubby hand through his auburn hair and his green eyes level-stared at me. 'You saw what we are to each other. They'd have grated us within a year. If they hadn't, they'd have sold us on.' He shrugged. 'You've been fair with us, and you haven't judged us. We go where you go.'

I laughed at their faith, and I hoped we could live up to it. 'Alright then,' I said. 'You two might dress funny but you've got enough testosterone in you to make the SAS go blind.'

'What's an SAS?' asked Juniper.

'Imagine an Alpha and a Stalker combined,' I said. 'Then multiply it by a hundred. But just remember that if the wheels fall off the wagon out there, no matter what you're wearing, chances are you'll still be shanked if they catch you.'

'That's our Alex,' grinned Lamp. 'Always giving us reasons to want to go.'

I smiled at Lamp's words, although I was still bleary-eyed and seriously missing my bed. Ahead of me, the shockingly early morning crisped over the landscape, and the lumpy grassland in front of the uneven fencing was still wet with condensation.

I looked at the Outcasts. My team were wearing brown armbands, sometimes barely visible against their camo, while Juno's team wore equally low-vis green ones. 'What do you think?' asked Lamp, proudly lining up her armband, then shyly passing me one with yellow edging. I looked at it, then saw the slight twitch at the corner of her mouth, betraying her nervousness. This small gesture was something I hadn't seen coming, but it seemed to mean a lot to the Outcasts, and I could see that a few paces away, Juno was being given her own yellow-edged armband. The two teams were developing an identity, and Juno and I were being given signs of leadership by our own. I didn't need to read *any* books to know the significance of that.

I had to say something, and I *really* had to say it right.

'We know who we are,' I smiled, pulling my armband on. 'And once we go out there and bring back our own, the Alphas will know it as well. Just so long as we leave one of them alive to tell the tale.' Subdued chuckles filtered back to me. 'The Stalkers are doing their own thing,' I said. 'Keeping the perimeter clear and hosing down any Alphas they find. And heaven help them then, because the Stalkers sure as hell won't.' All of the Outcasts were watching me, and so were some of the Stalkers. 'It's good work,' I said. 'It's really important, and it needs to be done.' I walked to the gate, at the head of the Outcasts, and I turned to face them. 'And we've got a job to do as well,' I told them. 'It doesn't matter what we are, Stalkers, Outcasts or Healers, we're all sisters together.' I paused and thought about where I fitted into that equation.

'All of us,' I said. 'We've got five of our own out there. We're going to find them, and then we're going to find the ones who took them, and we're going to punish them past belief. They'll know who came for them, and they'll know enough to never come looking for us again. Everybody knows the Stalkers can walk the walk, and after today, they'll say the same thing about the Outcasts.'

I nodded at the guard and the gate was pulled open. I faced my people. 'But you don't need to tell me' I said. 'I already know it. I couldn't ask for a better team to have my back, and I couldn't be prouder of you.'

Checking that my Glock was secure, I pulled the shotgun away from my shoulder and held it across my body, then jogged out into the still chilly dawn.

Was this my life now? One mission after another, rapidly put together and hastily planned, against a ruthless enemy where the only price for failure was a pretty nasty death? Being accepted as a woman among women, belonging to a bigger organisation in order to be safer, some of the time, came with its downside, and its price.

We set a fast pace along forest paths that were now very familiar. Three hours later, we neared the rocky slope that the bunker sat within. The morning condensation had been quickly converted to a light mist, followed by a dry heat as the sun rose.

We stopped at the treeline, went flat, and did the usual scan for activity. Grey, squat and malevolently immovable, the bunker had been my home for fifteen years. In the last few weeks, our presence there had probably made us known to any roving Alphas, and once the place was empty, plenty would have wanted to get in. Superficial scratches on the door and minuscule chips in the bomb-proof concrete told me they'd tried.

'Aren't you glad you moved your clothes to the settlement now?' whispered Addison.

'Keep looking for Alphas,' I whispered back at her. 'This isn't a shopping trip.'

'And when we get back,' she persisted, 'you owe me. Once we learned our moves, you'd show us your stash. You promised. You said you'd dress for me.'

'And you need to stop remembering everything I tell you,' I muttered.

'Is that a yes?' she asked.

'It's a let's make sure the house wasn't breached,' I said. 'And then we'll see.'

'Do you know what to do next?' asked Juno.

'*You're* asking *me*?' I hissed.

'It's my team that'll be watching your back,' she chuckled. 'I need to know that we won't have to help you out if you get sloppy out there.'

'Sloppy?' I chuckled. 'Watch this, and try to keep up.'

I raised myself up onto one knee and the rest of my team did the same without a word needing to be said. I stood and they stood up also. In a line abreast we peeled out of the trees and ran straight to the house. We each picked a spot and flattened ourselves against a patch of wall, looking outwards for danger signs. There was nothing, and I saw, or rather didn't see, that Juno's team remained invisible in the woods. I faced the bunker, moved my right arm to the side and pushed against the door.

Nothing. No movement, no noise. The bunker was secure, although close-up, there were even more signs that they'd tried to get in. The thick metal door had splats of dirt and hand prints that told of attempts to smash it down, although the internal deadlock remained untouched. I pulled the key from my camo pocket and opened up, then once again dropped to my knees and looked back towards the trees.

Juno's team were up and running across the cleared ground while my team stayed on overwatch. The Outcasts funnelled inside and I heard footsteps loud on the concrete floors, clearly called out status reports, and no shooting. The place was clear and I didn't need to be told.

But, drills being drills, I waited to be told.

'House clear.'

Varia led my team in, and with a final scan to my front, I followed them inside and closed the door.

I opened the only storeroom with anything left in it and began passing out provisions. This was no time to be holding back. We might be out there for a while.

'How the hell are we going to kill any Alphas with this?' Greta held a tin of bacon grill, then balked as I handed her four more.

'We can always whack them on their heads,' chuckled Lamp, hefting one of the tins.

'Or maybe we can feed them,' said Nalda. 'One mouthful of this crap will send them all to hell.'

'Hell is where they're headed,' I said. 'One way or another.' I carried on passing out the tinned rations. 'But not if we starve before we find them. Food, ammunition, and water for everyone. As much as we can carry.'

'So when do we see your clothes?' Addison shuffled to the front of the queue, smiling as I handed her tins of corned beef and processed cheese.

'When we get back.' I smiled too. She was having that effect on me. 'This is no time to be going glamour girl.'

'Oh?' she said. 'So now you're being a tease?'

'Try wearing this instead.' I handed her a scratched but reliable sports watch. 'Everything else is negotiable. Right, who wants a shotgun?'

Whatever else was going on, I knew how to change the subject.

'Check your kit,' I called. 'Ten minutes and we're ready to go.' I looked at Addison's wrist. 'I want my watch back afterwards,' I said. 'And this doesn't mean we're engaged.'

'Yes, Ma'am.' She grinned. 'What does engaged mean?'

'Never mind.'

Chapter 32

From the bunker, the High Ridge that led to the Lone Tree was a five mile, uphill struggle through densely packed forest, which at ground level was a living barrier of thorn bushes. I wondered what kind of hell Gabrielle had endured when the two Alphas had marched her though it.

Nobody went through the thorn road fast. We stuck to the narrow dog trail, moved in single file, and looked for any disturbance in the double-sided obstacle of spikes and saw-leaves. Anything bigger than a rabbit would have to hack their way through, which would leave tracks that any one of us could have spotted.

As the ground got steeper and higher, the vegetation morphed and the trees emerged, all of them saplings and young growth, while thankfully, the thorns seeped away into eventual nothingness.

We climbed further, and the trees also faded, and then the High Ridge rose above everything, above the trees and as empty as the sky.

We knelt and scanned the grassland that skimmed both sides of the knife-edge ridge. Twenty metres below its summit, all we could see was one side. We scampered up the reverse slope and lay flat along the edge. The far side of the ridge overlooked a gentle descent towards the river, and halfway down was a jumble of decaying farm buildings that were themselves being slowly removed by time and obscured by the emergent trees.

I knew all about the dead farm. As far as I could work out from my map collection, it was near a really weirdly named place called Halfway, and in the early years it had been a good spot to scavenge. And while I almost died of potato overdose poisoning, its legacy made sure my own vegetable patch got off to a good start. As well as that, all manner of farmyard and gardening implements were very easily converted to self-defence items, which until I found my firearms, were quite literally lifesavers.

I'd been back to the farm a few times over the years, but now the crumbling walls were all that was left of what had once been a productive smallholding. It was still a useful landmark, though. Keep the farmhouse on your right and move along the ridge to the Lone Tree.

The ridge was a really long formation. Once, I walked its entire length, and measured it at twenty-one miles. It was one of the last times I slept outdoors, and also when I'd figured out that sleeping in a tree was a damn sight safer than sleeping at ground level.

It wasn't the Lone Tree that I slept in, you understand, what with the Lone Tree being out on its own and attracting attention.

It was, though, a definite navigational asset. Get to the Lone Tree, and you're at the far end of the ridge. Thankfully we'd cut on to the ridge long before its near end, so we didn't have twenty-one miles to walk to get there.

And there really wasn't any mistaking it.

Another reason I never slept in the Lone Tree was because it wasn't actually a tree. It was a tall, one-time electrical pylon. Its burden of wrist-thick power cables had long since fallen away and disappeared, and the pylon itself had weathered green from years of unstopped lichens and airborne spores attaching to it. If humans ever *had* actually made a tree, it would probably have looked something like that, out of place in nature, and gradually being dissolved by it. But while it still stood, it towered over everything else.

Pylons like the Lone Tree showed up regularly enough, and in varying stages of decomposition, depending on their location and what they'd been made of. Over time, I'd walked and ran past a few as they stood over me, a silent, forgotten reminder of the old ways. Sometimes they rose out of decaying towns and cities, sometimes they were surrounded by real trees, and sometimes, like this one, they stood as lonely reminders of the past, exposed and bordered by the sun-warmed grassland along the rest of the ridge.

'What I don't understand,' I said, after we'd gone to ground beneath the Lone Tree's bare-pole shadow, 'is how the hell they got the drop on Gabrielle and Hudson from here.'

'This is a visible spot,' replied Addison.

'Yes,' I replied. 'But we've been scanning and looking around for miles. There's nothing out here.' I stopped briefly to listen, and the birds were still singing. They'd normally up and fly away at the first sign of trouble. 'So what happens now?'

'Hudson and Gabrielle were Stalkers,' said Addison. 'They went after Alphas, chased them down.'

'Tell me something I don't know.'

'I was a Stalker,' said Addison. 'I can look for signs too, and so can Juno.'

'Do you think they made some tracks to lure Hudson and Gabrielle somewhere they wanted them to be?' I asked.

'It's possible,' she said. 'But that still plays our way. We don't want to avoid them, and if they come for us, we'll find them so much quicker.'

'That's why we're here, right?'

'Right,' replied Addison.

'So I guess we've got a plan,' I said. 'Start stalking.'

Juno and Addison holstered their pistols and started circling the tree, looking for slight irregularities in the lay of the grass, any distressed vegetation, even soil disturbance. It all meant something to a Stalker, and when it meant something to a Stalker, they started to work out which direction to move in. It wasn't even a case of being taught what to do, what to look for. You either had it or you didn't. I so didn't, and I was in awe of Juno and Addison for their quite obvious talents.

Not that I was telling *them* that. Juno was getting way too much of an ego without me adding to it, and Addison...well, that was already getting complicated enough. Whether it was said or not, though, they were good, and it didn't take long before they got a hit. They both pored over a nondescript clump of grass, crouched closer, then looked up at the sky. Addison glanced at her watch, they muttered to each other, and then stared at the not so distant forest.

'We've got a direction,' she said. 'This way.'

Addison and Juno had already scampered to the treeline. I motioned the Outcasts to their feet and we followed their trail.

Addison and Juno worked well as a team. While one of them looked for tracks and signs on the immediate ground, the other one looked to the near and middle distance for any signs higher than ground level. If it had been just the two of them, they'd be vulnerable to ambush while they were tracking, but protection was the rest of the Outcasts' job, and we scanned endlessly.

After ten minutes, Juno stood up, brought back her arm and then straightened it in a chopping motion and we followed her point direction. Juno moved first, through the deserted forest, her eyes fixed on the ground, while Addison walked close behind and looked further ahead. On this side of the ridge, the woodland was mainly coniferous and lacking any cover at ground level. Pine needles underfoot were slowly mulching into the acidic soil, and we shadowed Juno and Addison in parallel files, all of us now looking for Alphas.

The slope levelled out and we found ourselves traversing flat land. We reached the end of the ridge and the trail banked to the left, taking us south. My watch hands swung round to mid-day and Juno returned to the main group, shook hands with Caisley, and they swapped places. We were into new territory for everyone. Neither me nor any of the Outcasts had ever come this far before.

Ten minutes later it was the voices that alerted us. We all heard them at the same time and dropped to the floor. Ahead, a hundred metres away and closing, came two Alphas. Both had the same scruffy mix of denim and patched jackets, both were filthy, hair matted and knotted almost like a helmet, and both wore a red sash, as dirty and frayed as the rest of their clothing.

I crawled over to Nalda. 'Come with me,' I whispered. We slinked forward on our bellies toward Addison and Caisley. 'I want one of them dead,' I spoke softly. 'The other one wounded, but talking. Can you do it?' They nodded. Addison readied her bow while still laying prone, and Nalda aimed her Glock. I quickly crept back to the Outcasts. 'As soon as you hear the shot,' I told them, 'get up and run forward as fast as you can. There'll be two Alphas, and one will be dead. I want the one who's still moving and maybe running away, and I want him alive. He's the best chance we've got to find our people. Understand?'

Vigorous nodding signalled understanding. I slung my shotgun and waited for Nalda's shot. Laying down beside a pine tree, I saw the Alphas' heads as they walked along. Then I heard the soft twang of Addison's bow, followed by two shots, so close together they could have been one.

Nalda wasn't taking any chances with her double-tap, and I hoped there was enough of the Alpha left for us to question. I jumped to my feet and sprinted forward. In seconds I was past Juno and Nalda and looking ahead. One Alpha was down and motionless, with an arrow deeply lodged in his chest. Twenty metres ahead and limping badly was the second Alpha. He wasn't looking behind him, he was just getting the hell out of there, and I didn't blame him. If I'd seen my wingman dropped from nowhere then taken a hit myself, I'd be doing the same. He probably knew he was finished, knew he wouldn't get away, but he still tried.

Everybody's got survival instincts when the shit goes down, but it wasn't going to help this guy. I caught level with him, swung the shotgun off my shoulder, pulled back and then rammed the butt hard against the side of his head. For the second time in a minute he dropped to the ground, and this time he was unconscious.

He came to, groaning, with a slow trickle of blood staining the once-blond hair behind his left ear, and a mangled right knee where Nalda's shots had hit him. We'd tied him to a tree trunk and even if he could have walked, he wasn't going anywhere.

'Two shots?' I asked Nalda, who stood beside me and glared at the red-sashed Alpha. Her stare bored into him, she was breathing heavily, and her fists were tightly clenched.

'I wanted both legs,' she hissed. 'I only managed the one.'

'Good enough,' I replied. 'Now let's see what he's got to say.'

I unhooked my water bottle and splashed his face. He shook his head and groaned some more. Slowly his eyes opened, then half-closed.

'Enough of this,' snarled Nalda. She stepped forward and landed a stinging slap across his face. His head shot to one side and his eyes flew open. 'Where are they?' she snapped at him.

The Alpha rotated his jaw, shook his head, and then turned to face us. Despite his obvious captivity, helplessness, and he must have been in pain, he glared defiance.

'Where are who?' he growled. 'And what are you doing asking *me* questions. *I'm* the Inquisitor, or hadn't you noticed?'

'Is that what this is?' I grabbed the sash, then wished I hadn't. It was slick with ingrained dirt and damp with I didn't know what. I quickly released it and wiped my hand on my camo.

'I ask the questions,' he said. 'What are you doing here?' He tried to move and gasped as mangled bone grated against the exit wound. 'We've seen you,' he hissed. 'We'll find you. We'll kill you.'

'Trussed up and helpless?' mocked Nalda. 'And with one leg shot out from under you. You're not killing shit.'

'Nor are you.'

'Tell that to your friend back there,' I said. 'Did you take any of ours?'

'Sure we did,' he scoffed. 'You're nothing. You're…'

Nalda shot out the good kneecap and the Alpha howled.

'Whatever *we* are,' said Nalda, '*you're* not walking. Now talk.'

I'd crossed so many boundaries lately, and this was one more. I steeled myself to what the Alpha had done, what he might have done, *would* have done to any of us if he could. 'Are there many Inquisitors like you?' I asked.

'Loads,' he grunted through gritted teeth. He was tough, I'll give him that. 'More of us than you, and we'll take you all, we'll kill you all, just like we did to your friends. We rule everything. We rule the trees, we rule the meadows, we rule the ruins.'

'Where are they?' I grabbed his jacket and pulled his face towards mine. His body pulled against his lash-tight bonds and he shuddered in pain as his wounds hurt, really hurt.

'Wouldn't you like to know?' He laughed. 'You're too late anyway. There's an affirmation tonight. We've been promised a reward, and you know what that means. You must do.' He broke free from my grip and looked at the rest of the Outcasts with half-closed, hate-filled eyes. 'We dragged one of those bitches back to your base, and you saw what we did to her, right?'

'No,' I hissed. 'We saved her and we killed your friends. Two more losers with red sashes, just like you.'

'You're lying.'

'Really?' Varia stepped forward and flicked her butterfly knife. She skimmed the blade millimetres from his grime-crusted face. 'Recognise this?' she said. 'Which dead Alpha do you think I got it from?'

'Enough,' I said. 'Let's move. Juno and Addison, follow their tracks backwards. We've got what's left of daylight to find them.'

'What about him?' asked Nalda.

'Leave him.' I looked at the Alpha, bound to the tree-trunk, both legs shot away and still bleeding. It was a coin-flip whether the dogs would find him before or after he lost consciousness. One thing was for sure though, whatever the affirmation meant, he wouldn't be going.

But we would.

Chapter 33

At the point we'd ambushed them, the two Alphas had been practically ambling through the gloom-lit pine woods in such a non-tactical way that even I could have followed their tracks. Our weaponry was now augmented by two savage looking, long bladed knives which I gave over to Juniper and Sumac. The clock was now really ticking for our lost Stalkers and we had no idea when the affirmation was supposed to start.

It suddenly dawned on me where we were headed. Hell Corner. I didn't know anything about it apart from what I'd seen on the map, but even the name made me nervous. If it was called something like that, it couldn't have had a good history. We were moving west on a slight downhill slope. The roads and buildings from the map had long since gone, but no one knew contours like me.

Rescue was headed to Hell Corner.

And then we saw the signs. The disturbed vegetation gave way to cleared woodland, with branches hacked away for building or firewood. The remaining trees were all black pine, with their night-time needles giving the place a scary, god-forgotten feel. Piles of literal shit were haphazardly strewn everywhere, the stench of which hit us long before we saw it. Everyone's awareness rose, and even though my eyes felt like they were bugged out on stalks as I looked everywhere for roaming Alphas, I saw none.

The forest sloped gently downhill into a natural basin that had been partially scoured of vegetation, which, much like the intermittent fence line at Purleyont Hames, then gave way to buildings. Here though, they were more rudimentary, rougher, and altogether more haphazard. Branches were used as basic poles, with occasional ferns and salvaged, tattered tarpaulins that had survived the years being repurposed as walls and roof coverings.

Maybe they felt secure by the remoteness of their camp, or maybe the threat of them being Inquisitors gave them a sense of collective safety, but no one challenged us, and we crept forward unseen, stopping just short of the first forest shack.

The spice-like smell of burning pine drifted around the area, and right at the centre of the shelters, two Alphas tended a small fire of damp wood that constantly smoked. We lay flat beneath what sparse undergrowth remained and eyeballed the camp. Seconds later, three Alphas emerged from one of the lean-tos, carrying a tall stake between them. In between bickering and arguing, they managed to plant it into the dry, sandy ground near the fire. Then they shuffled towards another decaying hut and came back with a second stake, and then a third until there were five de-barked wooden poles pointing skyward. It didn't take the brains of a mathematics game host to work out that they were intended for our five missing Stalkers.

All we had to do was rescue them.

'Right then,' I said to Juno. 'This is what we're going to do.'

Chapter 34

The sun sank low, the shadows lengthened, and Plan Alex kicked in. Nalda and Arc scuttled around to the camp's far side, and then the Alphas came out in ones and twos, all of them wearing the same kind of patched, distressed clothing, all of them filthy, and all of them with the same red sashes we'd seen earlier. It looked like a whole camp of Inquisitors, and from our perspective, they were the worst of the worst Alphas. They'd already traumatised Gabrielle and had who knew what planned for the other five. But if this group were exclusively Inquisitors, were they a just small part of a bigger whole? How many other camps like this were out there? And if there were others, where were they?

With each event, each incident, there were some answers, but always more questions.

The Alphas gathered around the fire, and that was expected. The show, the spectacle, that was expected. The low hum of voices gradually picked up in volume, a building sense of anticipation among the Alphas. It was all expected. Then, with the setting sun, we watched them drag their struggling captives out into the open.

Still resisting, their clothes now ragged and bloodstained, the condemned Stalkers fought back, refusing to give up. It was absolute bravery and defiance, but useless against the numbers they faced. They were tied to the stakes and then the Alphas faced the campfire, standing in front of the prisoners, and ignoring them in their helplessness. How many Alphas could I see within the drifting smoke? Twenty? Fifty? A fraction of the Purleyont Hames population, but still way more enemies in one place, in one group. In front of them, the wet-wood fire had now been built up and the flames and smoke took on a greater focus. All of the Alphas now stood on one side of the fire, leaving the far side clear.

'Sentinel,' they chanted, low voiced, slowly and rhythmically. 'Sentinel.' As one, they knelt and continued chanting the name.

Sentinel! This was their leader, the name we'd heard mentioned from Chive and the rest of the Judas Priests. The secondary mission was about to appear right in front of us.

'Sentinel.'

Sentinel. He used terror to rule and now I was about to see him. What would he look like? I imagined a small, round, pock-marked ugly bastard, his body consumed by spite and hate to make up for his inadequacies. Utterly evil, utterly despicable.

'Sentinel.'

It was always easier to see your enemies with no positives at all.

And then he appeared from a hut on the far side of the fire.

Except he wasn't a he.

Sentinel was a woman!

What?

No way.

But it was true. There were no Alphas dragging her out. She wasn't resisting, and the Alphas all turned towards her, still kneeling. What the hell, a woman in charge of a group of Alphas, and a particularly nasty bunch of Alphas who now had five Strauss prisoners.

Sentinel was a woman!

Here was someone who had the best of whatever resources these Alphas had. Her blonde hair was sleek and combed back, she was clean and fresh, and dressed in black leggings and a long beige coat that was fastened at her waist, none of which was dirty or patched. Washed and wearing clean clothes put her a whole world apart from the rest of the Alphas, and even us at that point. It also marked her out as high value, high status.

I suddenly remembered what I'd said to Silver only a few short weeks ago. *Maybe she managed to find a band of followers out there who were less choosy than you are.* And so, it seemed, she had, but it absolutely didn't answer the one burning question, which was why?

'Slight change of plan,' I whispered to Juno. 'We get our girls back, but that bitch stays alive. No one kills her. She needs to answer a whole load of questions before she dies.'

'Way ahead of you on that one,' replied Juno. 'How do we play it?'

'Same as we've said,' I told her. 'We get our people cut free and away from the Alphas, and then you and I will go straight for her.'

'Any other details?' she asked. 'I mean, even for us, that's a bit thin.'

'Let's work it as it happens,' I said. 'Christ, what the hell is she doing in charge of this lot?'

The woman chief raised her hands and the wordless chanting stopped. The Alphas were all looking at her and I couldn't understand it. They could have easily overpowered her, and as confused as I was about the whole thing, I hadn't missed her long limbs and shapely curves, accentuated by her coat's tightly fastened belt. Despite what we were there for, despite the immediate need to rescue our own, I was still drawn to her. I found her fascinating and terrible, unattainable and irresistible, as well as seriously attractive, all at the same time.

The Alphas must have felt it too.

'Inquisitors,' she said. Her voice was deep for a woman, strong, and her words carried right around the camp. 'Ever since I came to you and taught you my ways,' she continued, 'you've sown fear among our friends and enemies alike. It makes us strong. It makes *you* strong. And it makes them weak. Only by working together, by following me, by adhering to our code, will that remain. You know it's so and you reap the rewards. Your red sash tells our enemies that we will catch them, and we will know what they know, learn what they have learned. Whether they want to tell us or not.' She flashed a smile, showing white, even teeth. 'And as for our friends, they fear us more. They fear *you* more. And so they should. Their fear gives us obedience. That fear lets us shape them, control them, and bring glory to us all. You have learned what I taught you and it has made you strong. What's our motto?'

'No time for traitors!' The prostrate Alphas thundered back their reply. 'The weak will talk.'

Holy shit, but this was team building in a brutal, horrific, and yet probably successful way. And if she was telling the truth about just half of what she'd been saying, then the Strauss had some real problems coming towards them.

'And we've got five weaklings right here.' Her voice rose, getting louder and commanding attention. 'They will learn what it means to be weak. We will teach them. *You* will teach them, and then you will enjoy them, before taking them to eternity.'

I looked beyond Sentinel for a sign from Arc and Nalda. If they didn't start soon, we'd have to rush in, all guns firing.

Then I saw what I was looking for, a solidly burning branch tumbling through the air beneath the pine branches and landing right on target atop a flimsy Alpha shelter.

The hut woofed into flame as the thrown torch landed and spread the pyromaniac love. Even though it was expected, I watched it and felt my guts slide. Fear of fire does that to everyone. On either side of the now burning shack, flames sprouted, took life and spread. The timing was immense, perfect, and to the second. Any later, and the Alphas' attention would have been fixed on their captives, but now it was focussed on the sudden fire, and the problem with fires was that with the correct application of friction to material, they remained relatively easy to start, but they were also really hard to stop, especially in a desiccated pine forest in the middle of a post-apocalyptic summer. And this wasn't just trees going up in flames, it was their homes, such as they were, and everything of value that was inside them.

To say nothing of themselves.

The flickering sound of flames consuming mixed pine leaf, the smell of burning wood, and the instant fear on the Alphas' faces told us they knew. Sentinel knew it too; she registered the new focus of her troops, and her attention went straight into survival mode as she swung around to face the new threat.

'Kill that fire!' she screamed. 'Kill it!'

Sentinel leapt onto the roof of her hut, swept her arms towards the fire, and started yelling orders to individual Alphas, telling one to beat out the flames, another to empty the huts and move combustibles. It was an instant and collective mobilisation that made them both impressive and dangerous at the same time.

I led the Outcasts forward, and we emerged through the drifting smoke like avenging hell-bitches from the underworld. I reversed my shotgun and rammed the butt into an Alpha skull. He dropped like a badly dressed sack of dogshit and then we were around the five Strauss. Boots kicked into Alpha balls, nails gouged at eyes, and fists crunched into faces with zero mercy. The remaining Alpha guards were dropped, punched, kicked, or stabbed into senselessness, and within seconds Crystal and four others had sliced through haphazardly knotted bindings and pulled the rescues back towards the treeline.

All around me, I saw Lamp throwing kicks and blows into Alpha nether regions, while Greta stamped on insteps, elbowed throats and planted her clenched fist anywhere it would land and deliver pain. The first wave of Alphas we met dissolved like snow on a summer day.

And Sentinel, damn her, seemed to have real sense for it. While she should have been focussing all her attention on putting out the fire, which really was getting out of hand – tree trunks were now blazing and no way was anything on two or four legs stopping it now – something, I don't know what, made her turn around at exactly the wrong moment.

The fear in her eyes turned to anger, turned to triumph. Her lips curled upwards, revealing perfect teeth and the most evil smile I'd seen since way before my puke-soaked wake-up, fifteen years earlier. It felt like she looked straight at me, and even at a distance I saw the rage in her scowling half-shut eyes. I could practically hear her snow-white teeth grinding in frustrated anger.

'Alarm!' she screamed, her voice sending an ice-spear down my spine. 'We've been breached. Lines five and six, kill those fuck-bitches and bring me their leader alive.'

Whoever the hell lines five and six were, they hadn't reached us yet, but I knew that wouldn't last and we weren't sticking around to meet them. We'd got our Stalkers back, but Sentinel was close. Tantalisingly, teasingly, and dangerously close. The rescue was our priority, but could we really leave Sentinel out here without at least *trying* to take her?

No.

Juno and I rushed forward and Sentinel screeched laughter, leapt down from the roof of her hut, and strode towards us.

'Have you come for a quick death?' she snarled. 'Or glory? You'll get neither from me.' She strode into the small clearing where once the Strauss sacrifice was going to happen, and gauged us both as we ran forwards. I felt a slight faltering in my steps. This was Sentinel, the Inquisitors' leader, this was Sentinel, whose name was on every Alpha's lips, even the ones who hadn't seen her. This was Sentinel, who'd moulded her own army out of what should have been her enemies.

This wasn't going to be easy.

We were all three of us now at immediate risk of burning to death, but honour, pride, whatever the hell it was, stopped us from running to safety and drew us into a fight that all three of us simply had to win. Juno was a step ahead of me, her fist blurring forward, propelled by her sprinting legs and growling anger. One second more and Sentinel would be floored out and dragged away from her followers.

Except she wasn't. She blocked Juno's fist with a minimal hand-swipe and followed up with a lightning-fast counterpunch into Juno's abs. Juno didn't see it, but her body sensed it, and although she tensed her muscles in automatic anticipation of the blow, she couldn't avoid it. I heard her grunt in pain, but it gave me the micro-second of distraction I needed. I put my head down and ran towards her in a parody of a rugby tackle.

Sentinel thought otherwise. She swung around and brought her knee into my face. My vision exploded and I dropped like a pole-axed grizzly bear.

Seconds or minutes later, I wasn't sure, but I drifted back to awareness. I heard crackling flames, loud voices, scared voices, all calling out incoherently. I tasted blood trickling down my throat as I sprawled on the pine-pin forest floor.

Then Juno gripped the front of my camo smock and screamed at me. 'Get up and help me carry this bitch out of here!' She slapped me once around the face. I shook my head and forced myself to my knees, then got to my feet. 'I never thought you'd be sleeping on the job,' she snapped, 'even at your age.' Juno's eye was half closed and swollen from a recently landed punch, but her face showed fierce achievement, and she had one foot planted on a prone Sentinel's back, who was stirring like a drunk and had blood seeping from the corner of her mouth. Juno knelt and quickly bound her wrists.

'Don't tell Addison,' I slurred. 'It's been a long day.'

'So let's make the most of it.' As Juno spoke, gunshots crackled and deep-pitch screams reverberated around the Alphas' camp. Arc and Nalda appeared through the burning trees.

'Pack this bitch up,' said Juno. 'We're out of here.'

Still dizzy from the fighting and Juno's wake-up methods, I wasn't as fast as I should have been. A line of Alphas had seen us taking Sentinel, and they wanted her back. Out of the firesmoke, I saw a nightmare view of vengeance-seeking enemies running straight towards us.

They had speed and numbers, and they were close, really close. I took a step towards them and pulled up my shotgun. I couldn't even remember if I'd pumped a cartridge into the chamber. It would be my last move as an Outcast if I hadn't. I saw the Alphas, and they were practically touching the gun barrel. I closed my eyes and pulled the trigger.

The gunshot landed like a hammer-blow against my eardrums and I felt the folding metal gun-butt slam into my shoulder. I fired off another two rapid shots without even realising it, then the gunsmoke cleared and I saw a writhing mass of Alphas on the ground. Some were still, some were moving, but only just. Man-blood spattered the forest floor.

Nalda swung Sentinel over her shoulder as though she were little more than a bag of newly picked potatoes. It was time to move, and all four of us scuttled after the others. Smoke clouds chased us and we started to cough as we ran.

At the treeline we regrouped. Random tendrils of smoke clouded around us and I knew we couldn't stay long. Wildfires spread fast in this world and we had to get away. I counted off the soot and grime streaked Outcasts. We are all there, and then I looked at our rescued Strauss. They'd been hastily dressed in new leggings and camo over their ragged clothes, and Sumac and Juniper were twittering over them like stray butterflies, cleaning their cuts and applying ointments to bruises. The relief on all of their faces shone through the accumulated dirt and matted hair.

'Is Hudson here?' I asked.

'I'm Hudson.' One of the rescued Strauss turned around. She was tall, willowy, with wavy blonde hair. Rope marks seared her wrists and a superficial gash smeared her lower lip. 'Where's Gabrielle?' she asked.

'She's safe,' I replied. 'She's back at the settlement.'

'They said she'd die,' said Hudson. 'They said they'd kill her.'

'They didn't,' I replied. 'We got there first.'

'She's telling the truth,' said Juniper.

'*She?*' Hudson looked at me again.

'This girl's got real bass tones,' said Sumac. 'You should hear her sing.'

Chapter 35

You can say what you want about the Alphas, but they were damn good at fighting fires, even ones that we'd lit right under their arses. However, while they were doing that, they were also pretty shit at stopping us from getting the hell out of there. To be fair, though, putting out a fire in the middle of a forest *was* kind of a big deal, and to be even more fair to them, they actually managed it.

While they were doing that, we were hauling arse eastwards and putting some serious distance between us and them at our fastest pace, because even the most optimistic among us knew that the fire would either eventually go out, or be put out. And when that happened, the Alphas would be weaving between the pines and coming after us and Sentinel.

We made good speed and within minutes, the Alpha camp was out of sight. A dark pall of smoke hovered high above the trees, but there was no sign of pursuit. The rescued Stalkers were shocked, scared, and their exposed skin was spider-webbed with cuts and bruises. Sentinel walked along at the group's centre, head aloof and staring scornfully at us, even though she was wrist bound and pulled along by a rope leash loosely fixed to the choker she was already wearing.

And all of that would have been fine, except that she just wouldn't shut the fuck up. Even Varia, who loved to talk, had had enough of it. And it wasn't so much that she was talking, it was what she was saying.

'You'll never get away with this,' she said.

'We seem to be doing that exact thing,' I replied.

'And just who the hell are you?' she sneered.

'Who the hell are *you?*' I shot back at her. 'Bringing this kind of misery to the future? Haven't enough people died already?'

'Oh, spare me,' said Sentinel. 'Another bloody peace loving sheep. You're just like all the others. You and your kind haven't changed since all of this happened, since *before* all of this happened.'

'You remember?' I shot back the question.

'Sure, I do' she said. 'I was given the tablets, and if you're asking me that question, you were as well.'

'Christ,' I said. 'What the hell kind of job did *you* do in the past?'

'Infantry,' she replied. I didn't need to look at her face to know that the pride she'd been trained to believe in still remained, although it was now twisted beyond recognition. 'There weren't many women who made *that* job their own,' she said. 'You had to prove yourself more than the men ever had to.'

'I bet you managed,' I muttered, looking around and behind us for any sounds of pursuit.

'Believe it,' she said. 'The first chance I had. No one killed better than me. No one.'

'That's not why we served,' I said.

'*You?*' she snorted. '*You* took the oath?'

'Why not?' I asked her as we walked among the seemingly endless pines. 'You did.'

'That's because women have always had a hard streak,' she said. 'Women have always fought, and that's exactly what I taught my Inquisitors.'

'Sure you did,' I replied. 'But we've sent a few of yours on their way lately, and as for the rest of them back there, they were too busy saving their own arses to worry about yours.'

'When they catch up with you,' said Sentinel, 'you can tell them that yourself.'

'They won't get within a mile of us,' said Addison. 'And what the hell is this Sentinel shit?'

'It's my name,' she replied, still managing to sound utterly regal, despite being a bound captive.

'And I thought you were called Logan,' said Addison.

'That's not—'

'It's what you were called seven years ago when you beat our best Stalker in a fair fight.'

Sentinel looked at Addison as we speed-marched between the trees, and suddenly it dawned on me just how much of a secret Logan's disappearance had been. No one else had even mentioned her name back at Purleyont Hames. Bloody hell, the Alphas were being led by a Strauss runaway who wanted to tear the whole damn thing down. Suddenly, it didn't matter whether she was called Logan or not.

'Why?' I asked her. 'Why did you do it?'

'Oh,' said Sentinel. 'You think it's all girls together? You think you're all wonderful and the men are all bad? Shiiiiit,' she drawled. 'You losers won't last another ten years if you don't start getting over yourselves and letting us in. And you've only got yourselves to blame. At least I reached out to them, and you know what, they appreciated me for it?'

'They weren't doing *me* any favours,' Hudson chipped in from the left flank. 'Didn't you give *that* any thought?'

'You're asking *me*?' she replied. 'You, who spend all your time seeking out your victims and killing them? My boys are mine, all mine. I found them one at a time out here, and I brought them together one at a time. I beat them into it if I had to, and they learned that they couldn't beat me. I showed them the power of fear, of control, and it worked. I've got enough followers now to unite all the nomads. I'll take them one by one, but I'll take them or I'll kill them. It's as simple as that, and with my loyal Inquisitors to back me, I'll never lose.'

'But you're a woman,' I said. 'You know what they do to us.'

'*Us*?' she retorted. 'You can forget about this "us" shit, and realise that men are men, good or bad, like them or not, and we're all of us here to stay. You, you're nothing, just like the rest of these nothings all around you. And when my people, *real* people, catch up with you, nothing is what you'll wish you could be.'

'Enough talk,' I said. 'Keep moving.'

Which was good advice, because whatever Sentinel, or Logan, said, her words weren't designed to build our morale, and we had to focus on getting past, or better still, staying ahead of, the Inquisitors. Everyone was alert to danger, and whether we could see it or not, it was there. We didn't even know how many Alphas were in the area, or if they'd had contact with any others.

We cleared the pines and approached the ridge, climbing ever higher as the sun dipped lower. The Lone Tree was our first landmark. Just short of it, we stopped and lay flat, feet overlapping, and none of us needed to be told to scan in front, behind, inside, and out.

Nothing. No birds, no rustling vegetation, not even a sense of unseen animal eyes watching us, seeing us.

And that was weird.

'It's too quiet,' whispered Juno. 'No birds means no friends. Isn't that what you said?'

I looked for something, *anything* to tell me they were out there. A footprint, disturbed vegetation, even a discarded piece of equipment. There was nothing except the silence and our own screaming senses.

'We're not going to just sit here and wait for the birds to start singing.' I replied.

'So what do we do?' asked Juno. 'It'll be dark soon, and they won't be far behind us.'

'You're right.' I looked into her pale blue eyes. 'What do we know about being exposed on a hillside?'

'It's a dumb place to hole up,' she said. 'You can't defend it.'

'Right again,' I said. 'So we head for the dead farm, button up for the night, and strike out for home at dawn. You take the treeline. My team,' I called. 'With me.'

With Juno's Outcasts keeping hold of Sentinel, I led my team up the slope towards the Lone Tree. My senses were alive and flickering around my body like a bolt of renewable electricity. We followed the playbook, we had a route to traverse and, crucially, we had an objective, but it still felt wrong, as though we were being watched all the way there. I felt that whatever we were doing, someone knew our moves and was just waiting for us to do exactly what they wanted us to do.

All that from the birds not singing.

But there was nothing else we *could* do. It really would be dark soon and we absolutely needed to find a defensible position. We sped along the bare hillside and kept moving east, fast. Juno did the same with her team, which included Sentinel, Sumac, Juniper, and the rescues.

The dead farm emerged out of the lengthening shadows, and I felt the ghosts of its former inhabitants all around us as we filed past its crumbling outer walls.

'Not much left of the place,' said Addison. The outbuildings had fallen in on themselves, now nothing more than drystone piles, while the deserted farmhouse silently watched the decaying stead that was being disappeared by the encroaching forest. The doorway and windows yawned empty and the half-missing roof offered a mute, open welcome to the weather.

'There won't be much of you left, either,' hissed Sentinel, 'not once my boys track you down.'

'Has she been like this all the way here?' I asked.

'Pretty much,' said Juno. 'I hope you don't want my team guarding her all night. I've really had enough of her shit.'

'Don't worry,' I replied. 'I've got it all figured out.'

Chapter 36

I put the last Outcast into position just as dusk settled over us. Shelter in the ruined farmhouse was patchy, and I wondered if any rainfall that night would help us or the Alphas more. The immediate perimeter had been partially cleared, barricades had been set up, but nothing like the fence and guard system around parts of Purleyont Hames.

'They're coming to get you,' crowed Sentinel. 'They'll never abandon me, and why would they when you're miles from home, miles from help, and they know I'll let them have you.' She was kept in what was once probably the farmhouse scullery, a room with no outside walls, and our unspoken place to retreat to if we had to make a last stand.

'Keep her quiet, but alive,' I said. 'I need her ready to walk at dawn.'

Hudson unlaced her running shoe and stuffed a damp sock into Sentinel's mouth. Her nose wrinkled and she glared pure hate at Hudson, who then secured the sock in place with a kit strap. Quiet descended on our small outpost, and we settled down for what we hoped would be an uneventful night.

And to begin with, it was. Along with Juniper and Sumac, the rescued stalkers kept a watch over the muffled and tied up Sentinel, while four Outcasts took a break and tried to sleep. The rest rotated through and took up stations at the open doorway and windows.

Part of me thought the Alphas were welcome to have Sentinel back, but I knew that wouldn't work. She was way too dangerous to have as an enemy leader, and we absolutely had to know what she knew. I smiled to myself as I wondered at what point 'we' had come to include 'me.'

The night wore on and the weather cooled noticeably. Gone were the stifling summer nights now that the carbon was slowly being assimilated by the growing numbers of trees. I pulled my camo smock tightly around me and shivered slightly. The crickets gave some sense of normality to the darkness, but that night, the usual lullabies from corncrake and nightjar were absent.

And that lack of birdsong told us all we needed to know about not being the only ones out there. We couldn't see them, we couldn't hear them, and for once we couldn't even *smell* them, but they were there.

An hour passed slowly, then two, and the first watch changed. I told myself I'd be staying on point through the night. Then the rustle of foliage and tramping footsteps announced the Alphas' approach. There was even the odd curse as they stumbled into Canary Island stone piles that we'd placed along likely approaches.

'Wake up the others,' I whispered to Lamp.

I pulled the shotgun off my shoulder and sighted into the darkness. Not that I could see a damn thing. With no moon and a light cloud cover, visibility was seriously zero.

'Heeeeeeeeeave!' An unseen roar ghosted through the darkness, and a burning mass of tightly bound kindling flew into the air and then fell straight towards us. Fear of fire was natural, fundamental, a part of all living things, and the sight of it coming at us unexpectedly from the night sky pulled my nerves tighter than Addison's bowstring at full stretch. I started to think about what we'd put the Alphas through when we set fire to their homes, and then I pushed my emotions away.

This wasn't the time to start feeling sorry for them.

Even as I watched it, I registered that they'd kept the light hidden from us until they'd launched their weapon. Sentinel had taught them well.

'Juno's team,' I called out. 'Watch that flame and stamp it out when it lands.'

'They're here, you losers,' screeched Sentinel, a soggy, spat out sock congealed at her feet and the kit strap hung loose around her neck. 'Come on, my boys,' she shrilled. 'Show these bitches what a real man can do.'

Stone chinked in front of me but my night vision had been seared by the flame-ball streaking into the air. I levelled the shotgun and fired. After the night quiet the sound slammed into my ears, and out in the darkness I heard what I thought was a body hitting the ground with a gratifyingly solid thump. Wounded or killed, one of them was out of the game, and unless they had firearms as well, we had the edge.

Even if we couldn't see them.

After I fired, the other shotguns joined in. Solid, sharp *crumps* of noise and uncertain screams now surrounded our tiny all-girl Alamo in the woods. The flame-ball landed behind me. 'There it is…Get it, quick…Keep it away from the joists…Keep stamping…Harder!' The urgency and edge to the voices told its own story. The Alphas' tactic was scary and distracting at the same time, and every Outcast that was stamping out a flame-ball wasn't looking for Alphas to shoot. I strained my eyes outwards. I thought I could see three Alphas on the floor, one moving slightly and the other two still. I fired the shotgun again, then shouldered it and drew my Glock.

'Heeeeeeeeeave!'

Another flame-ball shot upwards and I heard more than one despairing sob behind me, even though we'd dealt with the first attack. 'Two Outcasts take care of the fires,' I called. 'We put the first one out, we can do the same again. Everyone else, face front.'

But would we? Could we still fight when flames came down on us from the sky? A detached part of me recognised the effectiveness of their moves, while a much bigger part of me feared that it would work, that it would be our undoing. I stared into the night and looked for the terrifying sight of approaching Alphas, while inside our perimeter, the fear built.

Behind me, the flame-ball landed, I heard frantic stamps on stone, Juno's hurried orders, and then sensed extra Strauss at the gaps in the farmhouse. This round had gone to us, but what about the next? I glanced at my watch. It had just passed midnight and there were four hours of darkness left. That was a long time when you couldn't see your enemy, when they knew where you were, and had some sort of unseen way to chuck home-made fireballs into the air. I had in my mind images of some sort of handheld metal-mesh sling, or maybe a collapsible apparatus that fitted together and relied on joint muscle power to throw projectiles.

Whatever they had, it was working, and it didn't help when their captured leader was screaming encouragement to her troops.

I'm not going to lie, fireballs raining down on you was bloody scary, but thankfully there was very little left inside the crumbling farmhouse that could go up in flames, apart from us, and so as long as we avoided them as they landed, stayed put and kept the Alphas outside, we were safe, and alive. But for how long?

'Fire and move,' I called out. 'Don't give them a bead on you, and watch for flame-balls. If any more come our way I want them stamped out the second they land.'

A third fireball leapt into the air. I thought to myself that if they had the ability to send more than one at a time at us, we'd be really screwed. Even as it was, what was already happening was stretching us, scaring us, scaring *me*. It wasn't that they were actually harming us, but the threat of that harm, of a fire starting and getting out of control when we were already surrounded by unseen Alphas, it wasn't a good thought to be dwelling on.

And there was nothing we could do about it.

Or was there? I followed the flame's path upwards and as it started to drop, I tracked it with the shotgun and then squeezed off a round. Had I even hit the thing? I didn't know. Nothing seemed to change as it started to fall groundward, but it quickly became clear that its path had been altered.

The ball hit the tiled remains of what was left of the roof. It stayed where it was for a second, then gravity took hold and it rolled over the tiles, then out into the air, landing into the semi-cleared ground just in front of a yawning, empty window frame.

And then, nothing. The flaming collection of what looked like rags and twigs just sat there. I thought it might gutter into embers, but as I watched it, the low bushes and dried grass caught and the flames spread. Shit! I'd just turned one problem into another. The Alphas cheered at the fire they'd made, and I saw them as the flames banished the dark and made targets. Glocks fired as we made the most of the opportunity, their noises adding to the crackling flames. I saw movement in the illuminated scrub and fired two shots. There was a pink explosion of blood, a short scream, and I heard the thud of an Alpha's body hitting the floor. Receding footsteps told of a retreat back to the treeline, the flames slowly sputtered down to nothing and a tense stalemate ensued.

Maybe they just wanted us to feel the same fear of fire that we'd inflicted on them. If that was their aim, they'd done it, but out here, flames weren't easy to control. Three more flame-balls arced up into the darkness, each one pushing our nerves to the limit, even after we tracked them and dealt with them one at a time. Physically, it was a threat contained, but it sawed away at everybody, hearing the disembodied Alpha chant, and then seeing a ball of living fire come arcing towards us. We watched them drop towards us, wondering where they'd land, and then having to jump out of the way, thinking about what would happen if we didn't.

'You think we should make a break for it?' Addison materialised next to me. In the darkness she was a vague shadow, but I recognised her voice, even when she whispered.

'They'd be on us every step of the way.' I replied. 'We wouldn't see them coming, they'd bleed us dry, and that bitch leader of theirs would be shouting them on.'

'What if we left her behind?' asked Addison.

'Christ,' I said. 'Even if I thought so, you'd never get Hudson and the other rescues to agree.'

'Who said anything about leaving her behind alive?'

'Bloody hell, Addison. When did you turn into Collar?'

'Alright then,' she said. 'But seriously, what do we do?'

'Seriously, we stay put. We wait until daylight, find out how many of them are out there, and make a plan.'

'And they're going to just *let* us?' asked Addison.

'Right now, they've got no choice,' I said. 'They tried those fire things and it didn't work. They tried to force their way in and we shot them. If they had any guns, they'd have used them by now. They can't get in, but until it gets light, we can't get out.'

'Bitches!' A deep voice growled out of the darkness.

The Alphas were negotiating?

'What do you want?' I called back.

'Fucking hell, are you a woman?' the questioning voice called out.

'Come over here,' I replied. 'I'll turn *you* into one.'

Confident, disembodied laughter didn't sound like they'd had at least three killed.

'Here's what's going to happen,' shouted the Alpha. 'We've got you bottled up, and at first light we're calling in all the Inquisitors. Then it won't matter how many of you are in there, or how many guns you've got. We'll roll right over you, and we'll take every single one of you alive. Alive for a while, that is.'

'So why are we talking?' I replied. 'Go get your friends right now and we'll gut the lot of you. Don't keep us waiting, though, we get grumpy when we're tired.'

'You can always leave right now.'

'You think we're stupid?' I shouted back.

'No, we think you're a bunch of thieving skanks and we can't wait to see the back of you. Give us Sentinel and we'll let you go.'

'You think it'll be that easy?' I asked.

'It could be,' said the Alpha. 'If you wanted it to be.'

'And we're supposed to believe you?' I replied. 'A few hours ago you were all set to kill five of us for fun.'

'And now you've got our leader,' said the faceless Alpha. 'You've got something to bargain with.'

'She stays with us,' I said. 'And we're leaving when we say we leave.'

'Are you so stupid that you want to die out here?'

'You'll be the ones doing the dying,' I shouted. 'Walk away while you can and leave us alone.'

Loud, guttural laughter rang around the treeline. 'Dream on,' growled the Alpha. 'But if you're still here come daylight, don't say you weren't warned.'

'That's it,' laughed Sentinel. 'That is so it. This is your last day on earth, for all of you.'

'Somebody keep her quiet without killing her,' I said. 'And make sure the next gag stays there.'

Indignant muffles followed a sudden stop in Sentinel's rants. The Alphas stopped needling us, but nobody slept. The rescues watched Sentinel, and everyone else stood guard at the farmhouse walls. Time slowly ticked by. Everyone had heard what the Alphas said.

'Do you think they'll let us go if we release her?' asked Lamp.

'Do *you* think they will?' I replied.

'No chance,' she said.

The wounded Alphas stopped moaning, the live ones kept their distance, and in the reclaimed darkness, new sounds took over. Stealthy footsteps through the undergrowth, rapid panting, loud, bronchial sniffing, then growls that turned into barks. My insides chilled as the dogs flowed around the no man's land between us and the Alphas, gorging themselves on the dead. Barking and wet snuffling noises mixed with the sound of human insides being pulled into the open by fangs that once upon a time were fed with tinned food. The metallic smell of fresh-spilled blood mixed with the stench of ripped-open intestines, as multiple canines feasted on their target food: humans.

Directly contradicting the anonymous horror on the ground, in the trees all around us, sedge warblers began a nervous twittering, safe from the predators. I walked the small perimeter, talking with everyone in hushed whispers, while Sentinel glared murder-hate at me and mummppf-ed some form of death curse from behind her gag.

Time sludged past, and there was nothing to do except stare out into the darkness, listen for any surprise assault, and keep a lid on our thoughts. It was nuts to think we weren't scared, only a screaming idiot wouldn't be, but if it took a hold on any of us, we'd be more finished than the internet.

And that wasn't going to happen, not on my watch. I thought about our options when the dawn came. We'd have to do something before their reinforcements arrived, and I worked out a plan.

Chapter 37

The pre-dawn was chilly, but inside the remains of the farmhouse, the stone walls retained some of the heat from the previous day like some long-abandoned storage heater. For us, the night had been dark, humid, sweaty, and scary.

Nobody slept, even if they'd wanted to, and as dawn slithered over us, I crept from one Outcast to the next, making sure that everyone was ready to go.

Technically, it *was* a plan, it just wasn't much of one. I was finding out, though, that not much of a plan was better than none, and when the unexpected kept happening, it was usually all there was.

'Are you ready?' I asked Juno. She crouched in what was once the kitchen leading to the outhouse, but was now little more than a half-height wall and a decaying doorframe. Crammed behind her were all of her Outcasts, the rescues, and Sentinel. Wrists bound and still gagged, the Inquisitors' one-time leader wriggled and shook her head.

'I don't like it,' said Addison.

I looked at her in the darkness, somehow knowing exactly where she'd be. 'Nor do I,' I said, 'but we've got no choice.'

'What if I stayed?'

'No,' I interrupted her. 'Juno's leading her team, and I need a level head to watch over the rest of mine, and that means you. Besides, the two of you work well together, it's like you're related somehow.'

'We all are,' said Addison.

'Then we all work together and we'll get through this, together, according to the plan.'

Which, if I was being honest with myself, wasn't a very good one. 'Juno,' I said. 'What's the signal?'

'Two whistle blasts,' she replied. 'And then we go.'

'Don't stop for at least an hour,' I said. 'We'll be right behind you.'

'You promise?' asked Addison. It was light enough to see her face, the tension lines around her mouth, and the direct stare from those deep brown eyes that always unsettled me. 'This isn't the time for any of us to be heroes, Alex.'

'It's a promise,' I whispered. 'I'll be there.'

'You'd better be, Princess.' My insides flipped. Christ, what was *wrong* with me when she said stuff like that?

'There's only fifty unseen Alphas out there,' I said, lightly. 'They'll be history before breakfast.'

'Just be careful,' she said.

I forced a smile. 'It's my middle name,' I replied.

I crept to the front of the house and crouched next to Varia and Nalda. Everyone else was with Juno. Now that it was go time, I was thinking that my idea was really stupid.

'Are you sure about this?' asked Nalda. 'I used to think you were clever.'

'It'll work like a dream,' I said.

'In *your* dreams,' she muttered.

The Alphas had already told us they were going for reinforcements, and even if they hadn't, we'd have worked it out. However many had gone off for help, it was those left behind that we had to fight. We had until the extras turned up to make the most of it.

All three of us had shotguns. I stepped out of the doorway first and fired a shot into the treeline. To hit or not to hit, that wasn't the question. Nalda ran past me, crouched, and fired. Branches quivered as lead shot peppered the vegetation and then Varia joined the party, moved to my left, and fired.

A gaggle of shouts and hurried, unseen movement met our shots. We moved forward slowly, step by step, keeping to the cleared ground and making sure the farmhouse was at our backs. On the scorched grass I saw two Alpha bodies from last night. Gaping wounds in their chests, ruined faces, and blood slicked in matted hair told of their violent deaths. After we'd killed them, the dogs had eviscerated them in the night, shreds of chewed-up intestines leaving their own grisly evidence. An arm had been savaged clear of one body. Flies already swarmed over the exposed wounds and I knew that once the morning sun rose, along with the stink, the dogs would return. Another reason to be out of there real soon.

'Prepare to move!' I shouted out to no one in particular, but the Alphas didn't know that. We each took another step forward and sent a synchronised trio of shots into the trees. 'We're clear this way,' I shouted out, then blew two loud whistle blasts. 'Let's go!'

This was the dangerous part. Well, the *more* dangerous part. I shouldered the shotgun, pulled out my Glock, and rushed forward. Nalda and Varia formed a loose file behind me, a Strauss lifeline back to the farmhouse. An Alpha head peered cautiously out from behind a tree trunk and I squeezed off a double tap. A dirt-red cloud of blood-drops misted the undergrowth and I heard a surprised grunt, and then a solid thump as a body flat-dropped to the ground. My head shifted in all directions like a sentry pigeon. I couldn't see any more Alphas, but I wanted them to see us and hear us. 'We're all clear,' I shouted. 'We've scared the bastards away. Everybody, follow me, now!'

We crouched down and waited for the rush of Alphas. This was the plan, the only plan I could think of. A small but noisy distraction to bring the Alphas to the front of the farmhouse, while everyone else buggered off out the back. Varia, Nalda and I would then catch up with them at our best speed.

Except that no one was coming to block our bogus escape.

Maybe they'd all gone back for reinforcements.

Maybe not.

Insides tingling, my stomach butterflied and I looked around the forest. There was nothing moving, just the terminal twitches from a single Alpha who was now feeding the forest critters. This didn't feel right. Nalda's expression matched my feelings: wide-eyed and tight-lipped, her readied Glock poised for targets that weren't there. I jerked my head towards the clearing and we slowly stepped back, over the grass, and then to the farmhouse.

'Stick to the plan,' I said, as soon as we were back inside. We scrambled from the front to the back of the farmhouse, then sprinted out in a direct line to the forest, taking an oblique path uphill. If we could reach the ridge safely, we'd see any approach and keep them at bay with our firepower.

Hopefully.

Up ahead I heard shouts, male and female, and then the unmistakable crackle-pop of pistol shots. Not that I needed the sounds to get a fix. In the forest dawn, the Outcasts had left a pathway through the trees that a blind woman could have followed.

I suddenly saw a group of four Alphas, lying behind cover and with their backs to us, looking to their front, which screamed out to me that my plan hadn't worked. We stopped and I knew that however it had happened, they'd figured out our moves and they'd been waiting for Juno, who'd unknowingly led everyone straight into their ambush. The shooting up ahead was what might well turn out to be a last stand, and the four Alphas to our front were there to make sure no one escaped this way to tell anyone about it. I looked left and right at Nalda and Varia, pointed to the four Alphas and then gave them a thumbs down. We knelt as one and each of us fired two shots into them.

Through the dissipating gun smoke I saw four motionless Alphas, their blood mingled with the red sashes that marked them out as Inquisitors. Even Arc wouldn't have found friends with this lot, and we ran past their lifeless, broken remains and focussed on reaching the rest of the besieged Outcasts.

The Alphas had learned well. The pathway was blocked with tree trunks that had been manhandled into position, and dense growths of thorns and bushes herded everyone into a wooded dead end. Stones and roughly fashioned spears fell on the Strauss and the two healers. Firing left and right into dense undergrowth, Nalda, Varia, and I ran to the sound. I couldn't see anything in the dense greenery except a rain of missiles hammering down on my small force. The Outcasts had taken cover behind trees and the occasional dead Alpha, and they looked wildly about them, but the attacks came from all sides. I did a lightning appraisal of the ground, registered, and at the same time didn't register, the situation as hopeless.

'Varia,' I shouted. 'Move left. Nalda, go right. Both of you kneel and shoot.' Neither of them needed to be told to, but I hoped that calm orders would give the rest of us something to cling to.

Some hope.

We were surrounded, we had no escape route, we couldn't see the enemy, and the slight dip we'd been corralled into meant they had the high ground. None of it was looking good.

Already, the casualties were piling up. I looked around our dwindling circle of resistance and saw people, my people, lying on the ground, and still the hits kept coming.

While those still standing kept on fighting.

Lamp was unrecognisable as the Outcast medic I was training her to be. Her eyes scanned the undergrowth for targets and her Glock followed the movements. Her shots were spaced and deliberate, and she shifted with each shot, tying not to become a target herself. It wouldn't last, couldn't last. Two Alphas broke cover and ran towards her. A single, terminal shot cracked out and one Alpha dropped, his legs flying out in front of him and his head disappearing in a cloud of blood-smoke. Lamp swung around to the second Alpha and her pistol clicked empty. They were too close for the shotgun and in my panicked response I wasted three pistol shots into his chest when one would have done.

And all for nothing. In response to my three bullets, three spherical rocks sailed through the air and balled into Lamp, hitting her at thigh, chest and head. She fell into the knee-high ferns and disappeared as though she had never been there.

But even though it seemed to be a battle lost, the Alphas were having the memory of this fight burned into their genetics. Every time they rushed forward, Glocks snapped defiance and they were snatched backwards. Screams where they fell told of slow dying.

How many of them were there? Where had they come from? I'd never know. I'd read somewhere that quality had a quantity all of its own. I could never quite understand it, and thought that maybe it was the other way around. It definitely was with the Alphas, because soon we'd run out of ammunition in a glut of killing, and still there would be more of them, coming howling and screaming towards us.

I tried to make sense of our crumbling defence lines. Sentinel had gone, no longer at the centre of a Strauss guard, who were themselves far too busy trying to stay alive, dodging thrown rocks and snarling defiance in between paced pistol shots. I heard the deeper, authoritative shotgun barks. We were still fighting, but for how long, and for what?

My attention moved and shifted, and I suddenly heard Sentinel's high pitched shrieks from behind the Alphas' positions.

'Kill them,' she screamed. 'Take them, my boys. Beat them. There can't be more than ten of them by now, and they're all yours when you get them.'

I looked right and saw Hudson standing at bay with her back to a tree, rescued, saved, and now in the despair of being taken by the Alphas once again. Tears of defeat ran down her face as she picked up an Alpha's fallen club and faced front. An Alpha weaved through the trees towards her. 'Remember me, bitch?' A scar covered one of his eyes. 'You were promised to me last night, but I'll take you now.'

His cycloptic gaze was focussed on Hudson and his tunnel vision obscured the swirling undergrowth at his knees. Out of the greenscape, Juniper and Sumac launched themselves at him from opposite sides like a pair of demented Chucky dolls, slashing with their knives, their hands nothing but blurs as they shanked him again and again. The Alpha's contorted snarl turned into an agonised grimace. Then, with Juniper and Sumac looking like they'd had a bath in a slaughterhouse, the Alpha bled out from multiple stab wounds, his blood pressure collapsed, and he vanished, lifeless, into the undergrowth. Juniper's and Sumac's arms stopped moving as they knelt over their dead attacker.

'You don't touch our patient,' hissed Juniper, although the Alpha was beyond hearing. Both of them stepped backwards, scowling at the now unseen Alphas to their front, and formed a cassock-clad barrier between Hudson and the enemy. By that point, though, three defenders was a large number, and they attracted an increasingly thick blizzard of incoming missiles. And despite the impending tragedy of closeness in numbers, I felt a desperate need for company.

Juno's crossbow was slung over her back, no time for a reload and too many to face if there were. She knelt behind a fallen, long-dead tree trunk and calmly searched for targets, taking aim with the Glock, firing and then ducking into cover, only to reappear somewhere else. I fired my shotgun into the trees above her head and edged towards her. The tree trunk gave solid protection, and seemed as good a place as any to delay our fate. I pulled the trigger and reloaded in fluid, unthinking movements. A red sashed Alpha exploded from the undergrowth to my front, almost touching my gun barrel, and I fired. Pink spatters of blood and brain matter peppered my face and camo and I smelled his stale, dead animal breath. I pushed the last three cartridges into my shotgun. Soon it would be knives and bare hands.

And then?

'They knew what we planned,' gasped Juno as I knelt next to her.

'They must have worked it out,' I replied. 'They're not as dumb as they look.'

'Still making jokes?' Addison threw herself down next to me. I peered over the tree trunk. I couldn't hear many noises behind me. Were we the only ones still fighting? Addison had one arrow left. She stood up, shot, then quickly ducked down again. Ambushed and in real trouble, I still admired her smooth actions, even though her last arrow was answered by more rocks being thrown her way. 'This is hopeless,' she said.

She was right, and I hadn't realised it until she said it. We'd been funnelled into a trap and, one by one, we were now being stoned into unconsciousness or worse. Pretty soon they'd walk in over our limp bodies, and that would be that. Unless they caught us alive, in which case we wouldn't be limp and dead for a long, long time.

Juno's Glock traversed left and right, still firing slow deliberate shots. As she clicked empty, a large stone whistled incoming and glanced against her temple, dropping her to the floor.

'Juno!' screamed Addison. She barged past me, shook Juno and got no response, then she turned and quick-fired her Glock at the Alphas. Seconds later, I knelt next to Addison and looked anxiously at Juno. Her face was pale beneath the smoke-grime and blood matting her skin. Her eyelids fluttered, signifying life, but for how long? How long was left for any of us? It was now all so pointless, surrounded and miles from any help, and even further from home. All formation was gone; we were seconds away from being overwhelmed.

'I'm sorry,' I said, not really knowing who I was speaking to. Juno, Addison, the Outcasts, the rescues, Sumac and Juniper. All of them sacrificed because we'd failed, because *I'd* failed to out-think and out-plan the Alphas. Tears stung my eyes as the rocks and pointed sticks landed all around me. Was this where it ended?

Addison squeezed my arm and, behind me, I heard a rock thunking into someone. 'Sorry for what?' she said. 'We came out here together, we fought together, and if we have to, we'll die together.'

'I wish we'd been together for real,' I replied, finally showing the nerve to look into her eyes and say what I thought. 'But I've got no idea how that would have worked.'

'If not in this world, Princess, then definitely the next.' She looked at me and I saw a tear catch her eyelashes.

A solid-thrown rock slammed into Addison's chest and I heard a deep cheer from close by. Addison stared blankly at me, her eyes wide open and all air forced from her lungs. She slowly sat back and her grip on the Glock relaxed as she fought for breath.

I stepped forward and stood in front of them both, my last act of defiance, of protection, and I knew that now it was all just symbolic, all just a gesture.

Rocks thudded around us like an old-world artillery barrage. I pointed the Glock, and as I pulled the trigger, a stone hit my forearm, numbing my fingers. The pistol fell from my hand and I heard another disembodied bull cheer from the surrounding woodland. I unslung the shotgun. Everything was now instinct. I wasn't thinking, wasn't feeling. I knew that if I stopped it would be over, even though part of me accepted that it already was. A cold detachment over the future blanketed my senses and I moved automatically. I brought the shotgun to my shoulder, looking out now through a virtual rain of incoming missiles. I couldn't feel my left arm and I don't know how I held the weapon straight. As long as I just got one more shot off, I said to myself, just one more shot, hurt them just one more time.

Whether I took the shot or not, I'll never know. I felt a sudden smack into my forehead, my vision starred brighter than the sun, and then nothing.

Chapter 38

'She's not moving.'
'She's breathing.'
'ALEX! ALEX!'
'Fuck it, just slap her.'
'Screw that, this'll work better.'

With a Baltic splash, water scooshed all over me, and Christ it was cold! My whole body tensed and a shot of pain bolted through me. My left arm was on fire and my head felt like it was exploding. I opened my eyes and a flashbomb of sunlight smashed through my optic orbital and made my headache near-terminal.

'Jesus,' I gasped.
'Who's Jesus?' someone north of my eyesight asked.
'Never mind that, just stand her up.'

Hands grabbed my shoulders and suddenly I was yanked upright long before I realised I still had legs, and way before I knew if I could use them. My whole body felt like jelly and if I wasn't being held up I'd have dropped to the ground like a sack of liquefied horseshit.

I shook my head, but once, twice, and even three times wasn't enough. I kept on doing it and eventually my vision returned. Returned blurred. But how, why the hell was I even still seeing again? I was supposed to be dead, wasn't I? And if I wasn't, that meant I was now an Alpha capture.

But none of the voices I heard were male.

Slim figures in dark leggings, soft hands holding me up. Hair, long hair and ponytails, and a hidden, unsaid, but somehow detectable sense of order, organisation.

These people were Strauss!

I shook my head again, and chucked in a few body shakes as well. 'Strauss,' I slurred. 'You're Strauss.'

A hand gripped the back of my neck, forced my face upwards. My vision slowly cleared and I looked at a woman with a scarred face.

It was Collar, and I was glad to see her. I was actually glad to see her.

I smiled and sobbed at the same time. I felt my legs shaking but I struggled free of the hands holding me upright and gripped Collar in an embrace I never thought I'd make.

It was Collar, and by the grace of I didn't know what, I was alive because of her.

'What the hell happened?' I asked.

'After you got herded into a trap, you mean?' She was asking it but she was smiling as she said it. Collar was smiling? Really? Collar was *smiling*?

Maybe I *had* died and gone to heaven.

'You hit them hard?' I asked.

'Harder than your lot did,' she chuckled.

'The Outcasts?' I said. 'Are they…?'

'Lots of broken bones and concussions,' said Collar. 'I guess you could say that we got here just in time. We should never have come out this far, but yesterday, that smoke cloud in the distance couldn't be ignored, any more than all that shooting last night could have been. We had eyes on you from dawn, and as soon as we got sunlight, we knew what to do. It was pretty stupid to do what you did,' she said. 'But you know what, I don't think you had any choice, and between you, me, and the nearest thornbush, I'd have done the same thing with my Stalkers. All said and done, you did really well.'

I looked around at the post-battle carnage. In among the undergrowth, dead Alphas were strewn where they fought and fell, little of value to ever mark their passing, even their bravery earning them nothing. Wounded Outcasts were slowly being helped up, limping between Stalkers and making their way to the ridge, where a long line of Strauss were headed east, back to Purelyont Hames, back to safety.

Numbers, scenarios, possibilities and questions, they all flashed through my mind.

'Is Addison...?'

'That's the first thing she said about you as well,' chuckled Collar. 'You know, if you two were Stalkers, you'd have both been sent to different parts of the fence and kept long way from each other, but I guess you Outcasts do things differently.'

'What about Juno?'

'Up and walking an hour ago,' said Collar. 'They both wanted to stay with you but I wasn't having it.' Collar quickly held up her hand. 'It's nothing personal, Alex, and this mission is clear. Get everyone back, which doesn't mean staying out here, making yourself into a target when you're good and ready to leave.' She fixed me with her intense stare. 'Do you disagree?'

'No,' I replied. 'It sounds good to me.'

'Just as well,' said Collar. What the hell? Collar was bigging up the Outcasts? I had to be dead, because that kind of endorsement could *only* happen in heaven. 'You stuck together,' she said. 'It gave us a fix, and we just rolled right over those stupid Alpha bastards. All they had eyes for was you and your dropping numbers.' Collar then actually preened and flicked her hair. 'They didn't even see us 'til it was too late. Too late for them that is.'

'Did any of them get away?' I asked.

'A few,' replied Collar. 'But not enough to give us any problems. And thank you for taking care of our own. Hudson and the others owe you. *I* owe you.'

'Anytime,' I stepped back as I felt my legs slowly stop shaking. 'Every one of us for everyone else, right?'

'Right,' smiled Collar. 'And those two quacks you brought along as well, they were standing their ground right next to Hudson and the others. They both look like a pair of butchers with their own knives and none of us, including me, has got the juice to take their blades away.'

I laughed, and it felt good to still be alive. Alive, and not an Alpha captive.

Captive?

'What about their leader?' I asked. 'Sentinel?'

Collar's scar shone and her eyes froze over. 'You mean Logan?'

'It's really her?' I asked.

'Addison was right,' said Collar. Then she looked hard at me again. 'She was right about a few things.'

'So what happens to Logan?'

'Oh, she's ours,' said Collar. 'We've already got her walking back under escort. She won't see the outside of our fences ever again.'

'Again?'

'You've spent your whole life trying to get in,' said Collar. 'She's the exact opposite. She couldn't wait to get out, and when she did, she left a whole trail of lies and two dead Stalkers behind her. She's on a life sentence.'

'Not a death sentence?'

'Too valuable,' said Collar. 'Think what she knows about living out here, think what she knows about the Alphas. And think about what she's told them about us, things we'll need to change to make that intel worthless. We need to take a long, hard look at ourselves to counter *this* threat.'

'Will she talk?'

'We've got all the time in the world,' said Collar.

'Then what?'

'Then she lives out her days with us. Never alone, and never trusted.' Collar looked at me and smiled once more. 'But are we going to stand here all day? There's miles to do and a hot meal at the end, so lace up your stuff and let's go. Silver's already got your next job planned. And you might want to think about changing your name.' She looked at me and her smile returned. 'You're not outcasts anymore, Sister. None of you are.'

The End

Cold Steel on the Rocks

Rick Brindle

When the pirate Blackbeard buried his treasure, he could never have imagined that it would fall to the heavy metal band, Cold Steel, to come looking for it.

Cold Steel, high-octane British rockers who came close to legendary status, until the release of their fourth album, when their excesses send them spiralling into terminal decline.

Struggling small-time band manager Johnny Faslane, in the right place at the right time, lands the dream job of managing Cold Steel, and then has the seemingly impossible mission of turning the band around.

Cold Steel's singer, Maxwell Diabolo, claims to have a treasure map that he thinks will lead him to Blackbeard's lost riches.

With the band bent on a terrifying path of self-destruction, Johnny wonders if they will even complete the tour, much less get to the Caribbean to embark on a treasure hunt.

Against all expectations, the tour ends on a high and they sail halfway around the world chasing a long-dead pirate's map. Once there, it seems as though they were safer on a decaying tour, as they face their biggest challenge.

Only the combined talents of Cold Steel and Johnny Faslane can stop a war, and save their own skins.

'A heavy metal/pirate crossover, with a smart and sarcastic romance, an awesome rockstar vibe and a feel good ending.'
Goodreads

We Are Cold Steel

Rick Brindle

A day after their historic concert on the Caribbean island of St Clements, heavy metal band Cold Steel are heroes. Now, all they have to do is stay out of trouble and enjoy a well-earned holiday until they start work on their next album.

Except that the owner of the recording studio hates all things Cold Steel.

Except that Cold Steel's record company has blackmailed the studio into accepting them.

Except that not all reporters are as friendly as band manager Johnny Faslane's girlfriend, Rachel Shaw.

With a tight deadline, Cold Steel have to get the next album out before their tour starts. They can't afford any delays, and Johnny has his work cut out keeping the band in line.

Feral former soldiers, reporters with an agenda, cake-obsessed studio execs and international criminals all work their way into the mix as the band hurtle from one improbable incident into another. They just want to meet their deadlines, but it seems that everyone else is out to stop it happening.

Can the band get the album recorded on time? Will it ever get released? And what will happen as their upcoming tour approaches? With friends and enemies in the most unlikely places, events unfold in a way that could only ever happen to Cold Steel.

We Are Cold Steel is the explosive sequel to Rick Brindle's acclaimed novel, Cold Steel on the Rocks.

'The author likes his characters a lot and knows how to make the reader join in the fun.'
Amazon

Cold Steel and the Underground Boneyard

Rick Brindle

Cold Steel are back!

Their new album has just been released. Their previously cancelled Spanish tour dates have been rearranged, with the female trio and Spain's biggest metal band, Damas Infernales, supporting.

Cold Steel's biggest asset though, is Johnny Faslane, their brutally talented manager. But even Johnny can't fully eliminate Cold Steel's innate ability to spectacularly destroy their prospects, and even before their second concert ends, the tour is scrapped after an ill-advised trip back to the eighties, and the band are put into creative deep freeze by their record company. Only an unprecedented event and a lot of money can possibly turn their fortunes around.

Like a five hundred year old treasure hoard that a long dead pirate once offered in return for his life, treasure that has never been found.

Cold Steel find a vital clue that gives them a head start in the search for the missing treasure and they seize on their one chance to prove that even spoilt rock stars can actually do something for themselves. At least, that's their plan, and it puts Johnny Faslane in a race against time to find Cold Steel before they engineer the mother of all musical disasters.

And it's not just the clock that Johnny has to fight. There are also two vengeful bands out for piece of Cold Steel, enraged mob family members and a reporter with a grudge.

It was never going to be easy, but now, is it even possible?

> *'Great characters brought to life as always in such a fun imaginative way.'*
> *Amazon*

It's Not For Everyone

Rick Brindle

What do you do when your dream job turns into a nightmare?

Rick Brindle was a third generation military child. His father and grandfather served their whole lives in the Army, and all he wanted to do was be a soldier.

In 1989 he joined the RAF Regiment.

But life in the Regiment was a world away from what he thought it would be, and it quickly became toxic. Facing a culture of bullying, beatings, verbal abuse and sexual harassment, the community he wanted to be a part of became more like a prison. Most people around him went along with the abuse. Some agreed with it, some joined in, while the chain of command routinely looked the other way.

Set over thirty years ago, this is a story of surviving abuse that still resonates today. It's Not For Everyone is essential reading for anyone considering a military career. Sometimes funny, sometimes shocking, and sometimes sickening, it's one person's unprecedented true story of life in the RAF Regiment.

'Brutally honest depiction of the underbelly of the UK military.'
Goodreads

Printed in Great Britain
by Amazon